POST-TRAUMATIC
New South African Short Stories
Edited by Chris van Wyk
and Vagn Plenge

BOTSOTSO PUBLISHING

Published by Botsotso Publishing 2003

BOTSOTSO PUBLISHING

PO Box 23910, Joubert Park, 2044
botsotso@artslink.co.za

Originally published under the title *Opbrud* in Denmark by AKS/Hjulet 2000

Set in 11pt Book Antiqua

ISBN 0-620-30500-2

Cover design and layout by Michael Vines
michaelrvines@yahoo.com

This book was funded in part by the

NATIONAL ARTS COUNCIL
OF SOUTH AFRICA

CONTENTS

Other titles by **BOTSOTSO PUBLISHING**

Botsotso, an annual literary magazine

POETRY

We Jive Like This
Botsotso Jesters
(Siphiwe ka Ngwenya, Isabella Motadinyane,
Allan Kolski Horwitz, Ike Mboneni Muila, Anna Varney)

No Free Sleeping
Donald Parenzee, Vonani Bila, Alan Finlay

Dirty Washing
Botsotso Jesters

5
Clinton Du Plessis, Kobus Moolman, Gillian Schutte,
Bofelo wa Mphutlane, Lionel Murcott

Purple Light Mirror in the Mud (compact disc)
Botsotso Jesters and Lionel Murcott
(a joint production with 111)

SHORT FICTION

Unity in Flight
Maropodi Mapalakanye, Peter Rule, Zachariah Rapola,
Michael Vines, Phaswane Mpe, Allan Kolski Horwitz

Un/common Ground
Allan Kolski Horwitz

ART

Manuscript Exhibition 2000

Manuscript Exhibition 2002

INTRODUCTION
Chris van Wyk

THIS ANTHOLOGY IS UNIQUE in that it was originally published in Denmark, in Danish of course, and is now being published in South Africa. The Danish edition was conceived and sponsored by the Danish organisation South Africa Contact (SAC), formerly an anti-Apartheid movement. This English edition is sponsored by the South African National Arts Council and Botsotso Publishing, a non-profit writers' collective dedicated to exposing contemporary South African literature.

SAC's very generous sponsorship of this anthology went beyond a desire to help give exposure to South African writers. On a visit to Denmark in 1998 the organisation — involved for many years in South African politics and culture — intimated a burning curiosity at what South Africans were writing about now, six years after the historic first democratic elections and at the dawn of a new century — a question which in recent years has provoked much vigorous debate inside the country too.

So the brief which I sent out to over fifty South African writers was to submit a story on any theme as long as it was written after 1994. And the twenty-two most positive responses in my opinion and that of the Danish publisher, Vagn Plenge — are what are contained in this anthology.

The contributors make up a wide spectrum of South Africans: black, white, men and women, established and budding who write in either English or Afrikaans. Among these are writers who began their careers in the fifties (George Weideman), to those who were active in the black consciousness period of the seventies (Achmat Dangor, Chris van Wyk, Maropodi Mapalakanye) through to writers who first appeared in print in the eighties and nineties (Rayda Jacobs, Finuala Dowling, Zachariah Raphola, Roshila Nair, Roy Blumenthal, Allan Kolski Horwitz.).

While many of the writers in this anthology have established themselves as poets, novelists, dramatists and oral storytellers, they all choose the short story as another means of expressing a diverse South Africa of rural and urban life, white suburbia, black township, childhood, love, hate, reconciliation, the grim as well as the funny that make up the tapestry of a country as it used to be and as it is today.

While apartheid did end in 1994, its effects will be felt for many years to come, and the memory of it will not easily disappear from the country's consciousness — and, I hope, it never does.

Many of the black writers represented here began by using their writing as a means to an end; as part of the fight to win freedom, aligning themselves to a specific political ideology. In the seventies this ideology was the black consciousness movement, and later, in the eighties, the United Democratic Front/African National Congress. These allegiances are no longer prevalent in the writing as the writers increasingly express themselves as individuals, turning their attention to issues outside overt political confrontation towards those ordinary relationships between friends, relatives, spouses, lovers, neighbours and strangers that in the past were largely ignored as mere indulgences and concerns which were not at the top of an agenda during the struggle against oppression.

South Africa has never been short of catchphrases to describe its changing moods and passions. "Swart gevaar", "total onslaught" and "liberation now, education later" of the turbulent seventies and eighties have been replaced by "African renaissance" and its odd twin "Afro pessimism".

Mapalakanye's "Dance Cycles" and Moira Lovell's "There is Too Much Sky" acquaint us with people whose first experiences of the new South Africa have not been pleasant. Mapalakanye's character makes his way across Joburg city bearing in his heart the heavy burden of the past which the new democracy has not relieved him of. He begins a dance of freedom, drawing crowds and provoking ridicule but never stops his routine, spending his days in an insane gyration. Lovell's frail character becomes the victim of muggers and burglars and creeps into a shell of paranoid terror, away from the real new world from which white privilege can no longer protect her.

Dangor's characters gather at a party to celebrate an aspect of the new country when issues from the old times creep up on them to turn their lives into an uncomfortable analysis of the recent apartheid past. In Karodia's "A Chance Encounter" a man, well-intentioned but naïve, insists on living in his own recent past when a chance meeting with someone from that past forces him to grapple with issues which need his attention in the present.

Ivan Vladislavic ("The New Ford Kafka"), Zachariah Raphola ("Lesiba the Calligrapher") and Ken Barris ("Cat Got your Tongue") take the reader on journeys into dreamworlds where the paths twist and turn in unexpected directions and where quirky people inhabit locales not often visited in South African fiction.

Maureen Isaacson's narrator is a journalist in the real, present South Africa who has a nightmarish encounter with one of apartheid's ruthless killers now seeking amnesty at the Truth and Reconciliation Commission. A white family in Barrie Hough's "Changes" optimistically prepare for the inevitable transformations which the democratic elections will bring. But an unexpected, tragic death, on election day, brings these changes quicker than they had anticipated.

Graeme Friedman, on the other hand, indulges in the genre of science fiction to make a point about communication and passion in the world of fiction and modern technology.

Roy Blumenthal's mini novel, "A Mother, her Daughter and a Lover", Horwitz's "Gemors", and Arja Salafranca's "Couple on the Beach" deal with the age-old aches of love: unrequited, elusive and destroyed. Finuala Dowling's "Julie and the Axeman" uses subtlety and humour to help us look deep into a modern marriage and marvel at how the small, innocuous problems are the hardest to resolve.

The new South Africa is well on its way, but we all carry into the future the products of the old — as lingering memory, anger, shame or contrition — whose sell-by date has not yet expired. Seven writers — Rachelle Greeff, Rayda Jacobs, Chris van Wyk, Johnny Masilela, Roshila Nair, Gcina Mhlophe and George Weideman — have chosen childhood, adolescence and youth, to bear witness to incest, rape, alcoholism, family breakdowns, poverty, and madness — as well as happy memories. Many of these stories could and should have been told in the old South Africa but their authors were tethered to ideologies and had preoccupations that had the label of apartheid and political struggle attached to them. These searches into the past are not a refusal to move on, rather I see them as a need to dredge up and scrutinise the personal histories of people whose world was cordoned off by politics.

The years under apartheid saw the stifling of our culture and history through censorship, bannings, exile, jailing and even death. Now, in the new South Africa, not only has this repression been halted, but a positive reversal has begun. Chaired by Archbishop Desmond Tutu, thousands of South Africans have come forward to tell their stories, victim and torturer, black and white, orphaned children, mothers whose sons and daughters had been tortured, maimed, scarred — in harrowing and heart-rending tales none of which would have been allowed into the public domain of the old South Africa.

This anthology is as representative of new South African writing as can be offered within certain unavoidable limitations. Some of the writers approached did not have new work to offer at the time while others submitted stories which did not fall within the ambit of our criterion. But here then are twenty-two new South African stories chosen to showcase the new as well as for their entertainment value — which after all is one of the primary reasons why people all over the world write and read.

SOUTH AFRICAN SHORT STORIES TODAY
Michael Gardiner

The richness, diversity and tenacity of short story writing in South Africa tends to persuade one that short stories are probably the brightest and liveliest star in this country's literary sky. That needs to be said, despite the presence of a really powerful tradition of poetry that persists to the extent that today, in Johannesburg, for example, it is possible to attend a poetry reading every night of the week at a different venue.

Some would have us believe that we are unique in the unusually varied contexts in which stories are told. That is patently absurd. Storytelling in all and every human situation goes on all the time.

Perhaps it is possible to say that the stories that are written in South Africa are not written for books, but for people, and that the stories usually show an interest in and a care for listeners and readers and are not there for their own selves or sake. In other words, the local stories believe that they are speaking about real concerns to real people. This is true of even the most absurd and most seemingly far-fetched of the stories, of which, happily, we have numerous examples.

Because the writing of stories is accounted a worthy, long-standing and respectable occupation in this country, there is a sense for writers that they belong to a well-established literary environment that now has the configuration of a tradition.

This being so, short stories need no longer strive for unnecessary inclusiveness, nor need they contain the excessive detail that was supposed to give South African short stories their peculiar and particular qualities. Today's stories can comfortably and disconcertingly resonate with the echoes of experience and achievement that is both local and global, while pursuing their own, specific ends.

In addition to this, there is the more active quality in current stories, as Liz Gunner puts it, of a "country being remapped through the disparate stories of its writers... alongside the liberating absence of an overall organising narrative" ('Writing for the City: Four Post-Apartheid Texts', February 2003).

The absence of an overall, organising narrative in this country and for this country at the moment is itself significant. Yes, the political and social imperatives seem less overtly there, less stridently presented and present, and there does seem to be, perhaps therefore, greater diversity of theme and topic and concern in today's stories. But that diversity is also unmapping, not only remapping. Also, we must not forget that the part or the fragment often can be more evocative and more accessible than the whole or the entirely configured.

The story that has been told most widely and most globally is what is known in Europe and in English as Cinderella. This is that story of the young girl who is abused by a step-mother and her daughters, and who is able to attend the royal ball because of the intervention of her fairy godmother, but who has to flee from the handsome prince on the stroke of midnight, when she is changed back into the clothes of a servant-girl. But she is rediscovered when her foot, and her foot alone, fits the glass slipper or shoe that she dropped in her haste as she ran from the palace. Over two hundred variations of this story exist across the world.

Now, the weak versions of this story, which moralise and seek ways through awful things like 'lessons' to oppress young people (and therefore all people), make the character Cinderella a whining, self-pitying individual who is rescued from degradation because she is lucky enough to have a small foot - much like having a winning Lotto ticket.

But, as Elizabeth Cook points out in her study of myths, legends and fairy tales, Cinderella in fact undergoes trial by humiliation and abuse, having been dispossessed of what is rightfully hers, and that eventually her true worth (which includes the capacity to endure suffering) is recognised, and those who usurped her rightful place are exposed and punished.

Now that is a good story, for it touches the real concerns of people.

Short stories in South Africa are the providers of the myths, legends and fairy tales that every society needs and creates. And these accounts, in their brevity, in their intense focus, in their diversity and through their careful structures, tell South Africans and other people about themselves.

It is true that these stories rarely deal with heroes or with heroic deeds, and that there is not usually space in them for gods and elemental forces. The stories do seem to deal, in the main, with the ordinary rather than with the fabulous.

But that is the point. Life as writers see it today is not lived by super heroes, while everyone else is a spectator. These stories constantly stress how we are the living centres of our own lives. Is the South African achievement of a true democracy, without violent conflict, a topic of myth, legend or fairy tale? All are mighty powerful forms of story and story telling.

Another feature of contemporary South African stories is the consequence of the many processes of individual and collective truthtelling that began after the election of April 1994 and which continue today. There is no doubt whatsoever that it is possible to think about and express things today in this country that were impossible before. And this is not attributable only to the elimination of censorship or political fear, nor is it owing solely to the official Truth and Reconciliation process, though that did emerge from a broad impulse towards particular forms of conflict resolution. Huge dimensions of the human and the personal and the social and the imaginative and hence the creative were suppressed and made incapable of access while South Africans lived under apartheid. And this is probably as true of exiles as it certainly was for those who remained here during those times. This is a large assertion that risks being too vague to be useful. But poets, painters, academics, family members, teachers and many others have quietly testified of late to the experience of becoming able to recognise, acknowledge and give shape as well as expression to dimensions of their lives and to experience generally that was impossible to do before. In this respect, the writers of short stories are no different from others. They are telling tales that can be told only now.

As these remarks have suggested, stories are not only written. Those published in collections such as this one represent but one aspect of the story telling of a community and a nation. Our courts, schools, families, places of business, factories, farms and offices are in a constant buzz of stories. And it is not only the written stories that are crafted and honed, polished and shaped. The deep oral traditions of Africa and South Africa teach how to shape stories so that they become bearers of the history, the wisdom, the insights and the ironies of people.

It would be a mistake to limit South African short stories to the local and the familiar. This is true of stories in the many languages (more than eleven!) in which South Africans tell and write stories. This point is best suggested by the advice offered by the poet, William Blake, who said that so as

> To see a world in a grain of sand
> Or heaven in a wild flower, [you should]
> Hold infinity in the palm of your hand
> And eternity in an hour.
> ('Auguries of Innocence')

At this stage, I can think of no better description of what a short story can be than that: a short story is something infinite that can be held in a human hand and something eternal that can be read in less than sixty minutes.

A GRAIN OF SORGHUM
Johnny Masilela

THERE IS AN ABUNDANCE of frogs in the Winterveldt which fill the countryside dusk with their forlorn croak. They live on the banks of a shallow reed-bordered wetland area beyond the enclave of withaak branches around our kraal of mud huts.

We place withaak branches around our huts to prevent the goats from lifting the drievoet pots with their horns and spilling the cooked food all over the log fires. The goats also have a habit of standing on their hind legs and nibbling at the leaves of the pawpaw trees Grandfather grows behind his hut. As for the frogs, they always wait for sunset and when the sun transforms itself into the brilliant golden wings of the weaver-bird, they start croaking their nightsong.

The crickets, whose song is not as pleasing to the ear as the chirping of the nightjar or the dikkop, join in, followed by the high-pitched laughing howl of the hyena from the slopes of the distant Soutpansberg.

It was these cheerless sounds that would send the nightjars and dikkops flapping their massive wings and taking off in fright into the dark skies.

Mama and I sat with our legs stretched out on grass mats in the hut where she did the cooking, half listening to the frogs and the crickets and the dikkops and the nightjars and the howling hyena.

But on this hot summer evening Mama was not cooking.

Grandfather was away visiting, and often when Grandfather was away, Mama did not cook.

We could have had the lunchtime leftover maize porridge and Mama's favourite, sour milk, if I had not helped myself to all of it behind the chicken pen earlier that day.

"A whole gourd of sour milk. You tell me. A whole gourd of sour milk. Now there's no sour milk left."

Mama was breaking wild morula shells on a grinding stone by her side. With a calloused hand she lifted the stone and struck it on the side of the morula. Then she used a piece of wire to scrape out the seeds from the shells, which she dropped into a broken calabash.

Mama's once beautiful hands were rugged like the soles of a herdboy, after many years of working with the plough and hoe, and doing washing for the white man who bred cattle on the other side of the dirt road to the Soutpansberg Trading Store.

"You just tell me. A whole gourd of sour milk. As if you're the only one who likes sour milk."

There was a distant twinkle in Mama's eyes which made her look different from the other mothers of the Winterveldt. And because of this strange little light, the villagers called her by a name that brought a lump to my throat. They gossiped about a grain of sorghum that had somehow found its way into her head. I did not believe them.

Mama had a lovely tattoo running down the bridge of her nose, and two more tattoos making a circle on either cheek. When she stood up she was the same height as a fully grown reed of sugar cane. Her stride was like that of a cattle egret. How could a grain of sorghum get into the head of one so beautiful?

Mama taught me not to grimace and to face the hills from where the sun rises whenever I took a gulp of herbal medicine. Such words of wisdom could not come from the lips of someone with a grain of sorghum in her head.

Mama herself did not like the stories about this grain of sorghum in her head. And so, from time to time, she would kick up lots of dust from the cattle and goat trails to make her point.

One day a group of us herdboys were playing morabaraba by the side of the road to the Soutpansberg Trading Store. Suddenly Kaalvoet Sithole came running through the maize fields, braving the prickly wag-'n-bietjie shrubs.

"It's not me! I never said it! It's not me!" Kaalvoet cried. Running after him, menacingly waving Grandfather's whip, was Mama.

Mama had overheard Kaalvoet talking to Katrina Masanabo. The topic of conversation? The grain of sorghum lodged in Mama's head.

Later that day it took the might of headman Vilakazi and his three wives to separate Mama — frothing at the mouth — from Katrina Masanabo. Mama had flung the big woman to the ground and butted her until an ugly purple patch appeared around the woman's eye.

Soon after this fight Mama stopped pedalling her rusty bicycle over to the cattle breeder to do his washing. Rumour had it that the white man could not have someone with a grain of sorghum stuck in her head washing and ironing his shirts and sheets and overalls, his wife's dresses and underwear.

That left Grandfather as the sole provider of the three of us. Neither Mama nor Grandfather ever spoke about my father, who I had only ever seen in a cracked photograph, eyes narrowed against the summer sun. It was said he had disappeared into the gold diggings many miles from home.

"Of course you drank all the sour milk so that I can starve. You just tell me, a whole gourd of sour milk."

A winding footpath slithers through Grandfather's place, past the farm of the cattle breeder and through the bushveld towards the villages of Khwadubeng and Motle in the north.

One day, as I was sitting in the shade of the mopani looking after the cattle, a laksman suddenly flew into the air from nowhere, chirping all sorts of summer songs, including those plagiarised from other birds.

Suddenly the bird nose-dived into the grass and came up

again with a grasshopper in its beak. It then did a kind of victory swoop around the top of a nearby withaak before coming to land on one of its branches. With a few deft movements it impaled its prey on a sharp thorn. Grandfather says that by so doing, the laksman signals the coming of someone from a faraway place.

I gazed beyond the withaak and saw an old man with a grey goat-like beard hobbling towards me with the help of a stick. I had never seen the old man before. He was on his way, I figured, either to Khwadubeng or to Motle.

Eventually the old man entered the patch of shade where I was sitting. Standing in front of me he removed his old torn hat, wiped the sweat from his brow with the back of his hand, and said, "I greet you in the name of our tribe, the Bahwaduba."

I mumbled back a greeting.

His eyes shifting to the can at my side, he asked if he could have a sip of my sour milk.

I mumbled that Mama did not allow me to share my sour milk with others.

The old man turned around, staggered a few steps from me, and stopped. Without turning to look at me, he spoke, as if to himself, in a trembling voice.

"I know you, my child."

"You know me?"

"I even know your mother, born of my old friend Tladi."

The name belonged to Mama's father who was buried a long time ago.

"Many harvests ago, when the baboki still sang praises to their chiefs from the hillside, I was part of a group of elders who received the herd of cattle so that your mother and father could be married.

"When she was brought here on a mule cart she found your father's people without their own plough and hoe and oxen, indeed without enough food to fill their own stomachs. Your mother went to Vilakazi the headman and asked to borrow a plough and an ox."

The old man cleared his throat and continued: "Men in your village could not believe what they saw when this strong woman — your mother — edged her way behind the plough, drawn by the ox. At the time of harvest the stretch of cultivated land was green with maize and brown with sorghum grain plants.

"Several ox-wagon loads were taken to the white farmer and bartered for money. And, as with our custom, the money was handed over to your grandfather who was able to buy his own plough, and the oxen you are today watching over. It hurts so much that those whose pastime is to fly brooms, have planted a grain of sorghum in your mother's head."

Still without turning to look at me, the old man slowly and painfully made his way through the footpath and disappeared into the bushveld. The laksman circled the branches of the withaak, singing a sad song.

Mama emptied a portion of the morula seeds onto the grass mat next to me and said, "Here's some morula seeds, eat."

As I began chewing on them, Mama got lost in her strange thoughts. Her eyes narrowed in what I could tell was deep resentment. Was she, for the umpteenth time, about to complain about the sour milk?

"You know the white man where I do the washing? He took me to the place of the sick in Pretoria. You know that?"

"Yebo, Mama."

"At this place a white man in a white coat spoke to me for a long time. A black woman in a white dress was saying what the white man was saying, you know."

"Yebo, Mama."

Her voice rising a bit, she continued: "They say there is something wrong in my head, the white man and the black woman. I scream at them and say, 'Is not true! Is not true!'"

"Yebo, Mama."

"When I say to them is not true, they all write, the white man and the black woman, things on a board they hold with the other hand. You know that?"

"Yebo, Mama."

"Then they bring a bucket and say I must fetch water from a nearby tap. And when I release the water into the bucket, it all leaks out through a big hole at the bottom. And I say to them, how can I bring water in a bucket that leaks. And they write quick-quick on their boards. You know that?"

"Yebo, Mama."

"You know I gave Kaalvoet Sithole a whipping for telling Katrina Masanabo I have a grain of sorghum in my head, you know that?"

"Yebo, Mama."

"Is not true that I have a grain of sorghum in my head. Is not true. Is not true!"

Indeed it could not be true. Not my beautiful mama.

MAGIC
Chris van Wyk

A Magic Show.
Date: Tuesday the 2nd of February.
Place: School Hall.
Entrance fee: 20 cents.
In aid of: The Seaside Fund.
Come One. Come All!

THE SEASIDE FUND TOOK a hundred Joburg children down to Durban every summer for one whole school term — three months. It was hard to qualify for this free train trip to a school on the beach called Transhaven four hundred miles away: you had to be all of the following: starving to death; not wearing shoes to school, even in winter; never bringing lunch to school; and coloured. Most kids, including me, were only one or two of these at any given time.

Kendrick Appollis was chosen in the year we were in standard two. He was all of the above, plus he never had a hanky. He was a third-year standard two boy and his mother had been in a bus accident and couldn't work — in case there was more space on the form.

If poor Joburg children went to the coast, I wondered when I was a little older, where did the poor children who lived at the coast go? Later I also wondered how a term of schooling was supposed to help these poor children. The old people claim that a dip in the sea takes away all the bad luck. But after the three months by the sea these boys and girls came back to school and back to square one, going barefoot with runny noses and begging sandwiches off the haves during lunch breaks.

Anyway, I asked my mother for twenty cents for the magic show. Whenever I asked her for money she said, "Otis you really think money grows on trees don't you?" To which I always wanted to reply, "If I did think that, I wouldn't be asking you for some, would I? In fact you'd be asking me because I just happen to be a better tree climber than you." But of course I didn't because that would've been the same as saying, "Don't give me any pocket money for at least a year."

She actually wouldn't have given me any money for the show, but I reminded her that when the school showed Steve McQueen in *The Great Escape* she didn't have twenty cents for me. In my eleven years on Earth we had established a kind of fiscal discipline: I could ask for money only for every other school function.

So I got the twenty cents, a grubby little thing with the old prime minister's face on it (who had been knifed to death in Parliament and was dead and buried) that she disinterred from a corner of her purse. Ma handed it to me with a reminder that it could've bought two loaves of bread, but what did I care. Bread appeared and disappeared in our home every day, the Magic Show came once a decade.

We filed into the school hall under the swishing cane of Mr Kelly who if he wasn't beating us up was treating us to a dose of his very smelly breath, the perfect atmosphere for his yellow teeth to rot in.

There were no chairs in the hall. If we all sat on the floor they could get in thirty or forty more of us. So we sat cross-legged in rows from the grade ones in front to the standard fives at the back. This was supposed to have the same effect as a movie theatre where everyone could see over the heads of those in front. It worked up to a point. And that point was me: I sat behind a boy who was in his third year in the same class so that while his brain was learning the same stuff over and over, his body was growing bigger and bigger. Now today I would spend the best hour of the year trying to look past those same ears his teacher accused him of not having — yes, it was old Kendrick Appollis.

But let the show begin!

Three men came strutting onto the stage, laughing and shouting. One was beating a drum, another blew a whistle, and the third man sang a merry tune. We liked it, we liked it. The singer stopped singing and told the two players to shut up so that he could speak to us.

He waved a big golden bangle at us and wanted to know, "What's this?"

We broke into shouts of "Bangle!" and "Ring!"

Our teachers, sitting on chairs along the sides of the hall, smiled at all the goings-on.

On stage the man swirled a finger at his own brain. This meant we were all mad. We cheered; it was a refreshing change from being called stupid.

He took a scarf and asked us: "What colour is this?"

"Yellow!" On this we were unanimous.

Then, in dramatic slow motion, he pulled the scarf through the ring. It turned green and we went Ooh! Instead of paying attention to what he was doing, he was looking at us and, with mocking bewilderment said, "What's the matter?" We pointed four hundred fingers at him and shouted, "Your scarf is green!" He said, "What?"

"Your scarf! It was yellow now it's green!"

"I beg yours?"

"Green!"

Only after cupping his ear was he able to hear.

He looked down at the scarf, but by then it was yellow again.

He conferred with his two friends and they all agreed: we were a crazy bunch. Try getting a magician to call you mad. I tell you it's the funniest thing in the world.

There was more magic. He took a cake tin and pointed out

a girl two rows away from me. She pointed to herself just to make sure. The magic man said, "Are you not Belinda Brown?"

"No, sir," she said.

"Then you're the one I want," he said.

Wow, did that joke get us slapping our knees and rocking our bums with laughter!

The girl got up, a little red in the face now, dusted lots of invisible fluff from her gym and went onto the stage.

"What do you see in this tin?" he said. She looked inside, looked up at the magician.

"Stones?" she said, as if she wasn't too sure. But with a magic man who could blame her?

"Show them, tell them." He handed her the tin of stones. "Rattle them."

She showed, rattled and told.

What was this guy going to do?

"Watch," he said.

He placed the tin of stones on a table and, as soon as his back was turned, his friends covered it with a sheet. But no sooner had they done this than he yelled at them to "Mind your own business! Who asked you?" and told them to take their stupid sheet off his tin of stones. Only now it was: a tin of sweets! Mints, toffees, nougat, coconut. And he gave it all to the girl who was not even Belinda Brown!

He repeated this trick with a tin of mud, which he turned into a chocolate cake, which he handed to Mrs Petersen, one of the grade one teachers.

I went home that afternoon wondering why he couldn't just have made tins of sweets and chocolate cake for all of us. God knows we had enough stones and mud on the school grounds just waiting to be turned into something tasty.

Well, whenever I think of that magic show, I think about my Auntie Leonie.

Hardly a week after the show, just as the talk of magic was beginning to disappear, Ma gave me some news.

"Auntie Leonie's coming to visit us today." This was a Saturday.

Auntie Leonie! She was my mother's youngest sister. She was a replica of Ma, except that she was taller, and wore glasses. Like Ma she was lovely. Even before I was ready for school she showed me how to hold a pen. Of all my mother's ten brothers and sisters, Auntie Leonie was considered to be the cleverest because she had gone as far as standard eight. Ma and everybody else, it seems, had dropped out in standard six, the beginning of high school. It must be all that studying that led to the glasses. Auntie Leonie was twenty-two years old.

"And she's bringing her new boyfriend."

"Oh really!" That was all I was allowed to say. Something like, "What happened to the old one?" would've been regarded as *ougat*.

In our little two-bedroom township house in Riverlea there was much preparation — shining the three front steps, wiping the sticky marks off the front gate, dusting off the coffee table in the lounge. Then Ma sent me to the shop to buy a family size Coke and a Fanta. And a packet of Bakers Romany Creams and Choice Assorted biscuits. Usually all we got was one bottle of cooldrink and a packet of Choice Assorted which were about seven cents cheaper than the Romany Creams — and then my siblings and I fought over the lemon creams — of which there were only two in every packet. (The Bakers Man can be so stingy, yes the Bakers Man can.)

Auntie Leonie and her new boyfriend arrived in the afternoon.

They walked in and from our kitchen I listened to the adult ritual of how-d'you-do's in our tiny lounge. "Arnold Rhoda," I heard my father say. "Related to Peter Rhoda who used to play centre forward for Gladiators?"

"My older brother!" I heard Arnold say. And then all four adults burst into polite laughter as if being the brother of Peter Rhoda was a funny thing.

"Where's Otis?" I heard Auntie Leonie ask. I smiled in the kitchen and got up to have a sip of water so that I could look

23

busy when she came looking for me. Seconds later Auntie
Leonie was in the kitchen with her boyfriend. I couldn't believe
what I saw. Arnold Rhoda was a short, stocky man — even
shorter than my aunt. And in every other way different to
what I had imagined. Dark of complexion, a full crinkly beard,
big white teeth. His small brown eyes glinted with a mischie-
vousness I usually only saw in someone my own age. A hand
popped out from a fawn corduroy jacket to shake my little
hand. I shook his hand and smiled back at him. I liked him,
from the word go. Auntie Leonie could see that I liked her new
boyfriend and beamed behind her big round glasses.

But this was only the introduction.

After the biscuits and tea and cooldrink, it is usually the time
when children have to disappear. This is when adults talked about
who's pregnant, who's still not married, who's pregnant and still
not married, and so on. But Uncle Arnie called for a pack of cards
and Ma knew it was safe for me to stay.

He made me pick a card. This was an old trick. I had seen it
done before. I picked the three of diamonds and put it back in
the pack. He shuffled the pack. He stopped. He thought hard.

"Is this your card?" he held up a two of clubs.

"No."

He threw it face-down on the coffee table. He showed me
another card. Again he was wrong. (This was not how the trick
went.) He flipped that one face-down too. He showed me yet
another card. This Uncle Arnie was so wrong, he wasn't even
getting the colour of the card right. Now there were three
wrong cards lying face-down between us.

"But why do you say no, no, no, when your card is there?"
(lying face-down on the table).

"But Uncle Arnie ..." I turned to my aunt who merely
arched her eyebrows behind her glasses. Ma laughed, Da
looked bemused.

"That's where your card is," the short man said, pointing to
the three wrong cards.

"It's not." I had known him long enough to put a little bit of
indignation into my voice. This short bearded new boyfriend
had shown me three cards and none of them was mine.

"Okay, what was your card?"

"Three of diamonds," I said triumphantly.

"Well, check those cards," he said, pointing to the three on the table.

I turned them up and there was my card, the three of diamonds! My face must've looked quite a mixture of amazement and disbelief. I had been tricked. But I could see that my parents had been tricked too. Only Auntie Leonie appeared unfazed. I asked Uncle Arnie to do the trick again. This time I watched his every move; even when he put his cigarette in the ashtray, put down his glass of beer which Da had poured for him, I kept my eyes on that pack of cards. But again he tricked me.

And again, and again.

His magic was not confined to cards alone. He showed us how to get a twenty-cent coin out from underneath an upturned bottle — without lifting up the bottle. Then he made that same bottle (the family size Fanta which was now empty) stand without support in a corner — halfway between the floor and ceiling. He also guessed correctly the number of matches in a matchbox just by shaking it near his ear — seven times in a row!

A year later, my aunt was Mrs Arnold Rhoda. They had a son and she was pregnant again. Uncle Arnie had acquired a house for them on the corner of the street we lived in and identical to ours. This was unheard of in those days when the waiting list for houses was so long that people who got married usually only got a place of their own when their eldest was in high school. I heard my father say, "Arnold," in admiration. "I tell you that one's got connections."

I was still very fond of my aunt. Whenever Ma sent me on my daily errand to the shop for bread, I popped in at her place to see if she wanted something from the shop too. Auntie Leonie still liked me. But she seemed always too busy washing nappies, hanging them out on the line in the bleak and tiny backyard, breastfeeding one baby, feeding another with a spoon, changing nappies. Sometimes so busy that she couldn't even remember where she put her purse or what she needed from the shop or to ask me if I had passed standard whatever. The years went by and she just kept on having babies.

Whenever I walked past their home on Saturday afternoons, Uncle Arnie was at home with his workmates and other friends who had come to visit. Always they would be drinking. The brown quart bottles of Castle and Lion, and Richelieu brandy, and Mainstay Cane Spirit — were a familiar sight on the coffee table. Music on the turntable — El Ricas, Trini Lopez, Johnny Mathis and the Flames — familiar sounds.

Another sound that grew familiar through the years was Uncle Arnie's favourite word for my aunt: "Bitch." Used in the following ways:

"Bring the steak, bitch. How long do we have to wait?" "We" was himself and his buddies.

"Bitch, more money for beer there. And move that fat arse of yours." This was meant to be a joke but his friends never laughed as heartily as he did.

"Bitch, the fucking child is crying, go and see what's wrong, Jesus."

Or just: "Ag, fuck you, bitch!"

Auntie Leonie didn't have another name for him. Arnie was what she always called him.

One night — no, about three o'clock in the morning, there was a knock on my parents' bedroom window. I woke up and heard my mother opening the squeaking window, and my aunt's voice, also squeaking, with fear. Her children were crying, in her arms and around her legs.

"Ag please, Jean, tell David to come. Arnie's gone mad down there!"

I could hear Da shake himself awake. He put on pants, a cardigan. And slippers! I was disappointed by the slippers. You couldn't kick a man with that. My father went out into the cold, barking night to see what Uncle Arnie was up to down the road. My father was an ex-Dazzlers goalkeeper. He was tall, athletic, and knew how to kick an object. But not tonight it seemed. Wide-awake now, and eavesdropping, I pieced together the story. First from Ma and Auntie in the kitchen where they drank a cup of tea and tried to get the kids to stop crying. Then about half an hour later when Da came back and told her to try and get some sleep — on the couch. It was okay, Arnold was sleeping it off.

He and his mates had finished two bottles of brandy. His friends had staggered off home at past midnight but he wanted more liquor. He demanded five rands from my aunt. She wouldn't give it to him — "Because I just did not have," she told my mother. He beat her up. The noise of her screaming woke up the kids and they all cried in a frightened bundle on the bed. He took a bottle of paraffin from the bathroom, went outside and splashed it all around the house. He tried to light a match ... "That's when I grabbed the children and ran up here."

There were more Saturday night/Sunday morning bangings on the windowpane. Lots more tears. Sometimes Auntie Leonie walked about with a black eye for days.

One day she decided that enough was enough. Uncle Arnie came home late one Friday night, drunk. He banged on the door waking up my aunt. She opened the door. He stood there, swaying from side to side. He had a friend with him. Somebody Auntie Leonie had never set eyes on before. A woman who could not have been a day older than twenty, in Levis too tight for her and a tatty, skimpy blouse out of which her breasts popped. A mixture of cheap perfume and day-old brandy fumes fluttered from her. She also swayed, and apart from an intermittent giggle, said nothing, showed no embarrassment or awkwardness for what was happening or about to happen. I don't know how my uncle put it to my aunt, but he told her that Carol, his friend, would be sleeping in their bed with them tonight. Then, the story goes, Auntie Leonie used Uncle Arnie's favourite word.

Auntie Leonie didn't say much else to anyone after that. But together with my mother, they planned the Great Escape. Auntie Leonie saved some money, borrowed some, sold some of their clothes for a few more rands. A few weeks later she went to Park Station, bought a third class ticket to Durban (children under seven travel free) where she would start a new life, without Arnold, without another man.

The day came. One Friday morning Uncle Arnie got up and went to work. This was the day when his wild weekend began and Auntie Leonie's nightmare started: Friday late afternoon until the wee hours of Monday morning.

The coloured people themselves had named Friday 'Bushman's Christmas'. It was the day most coloureds got their wages and when a kind of frenzy was ignited. On Monday morning many would not even have fifty cents for bus fare to take them to work. But what the hell; on a Friday afternoon when that first drink cascaded down your throat and splashed down in your stomach, its first effect was to make all Mondays disappear from the calendar — from here to eternity.

The Uncle Arnie weekends were not unique in Riverlea. Take for instance the Lunds and the Radcliffs opposite us. Mr Lund had married Mr Radcliff's sister and Mr Radcliff had married Mr Lund's sister, so they were closer than most families. Plus they lived next door to each other. Unlike Uncle Arnie and Auntie Leonie, these two couples drank together as a merry foursome, alternating their homes as the venue. They drank, joked, fried meat, drank, sang and became maudlin. Then an argument would erupt, usually from something minor: a spilled drink ("d'you know what the fucken stuff costs?"), the words of a song ("it's: Regrets I've had *a few*, not *a view*"), because one of them stayed in the toilet too long (have you passed out on the toilet seat again?). The guest couple then went outside and smashed all the host couple's windows, all around the little matchbox house, with half a brick each. The host couple would then stagger over the low wire fence and give the house next door the same treatment: tit for tat, butter for fat.

But back to the Great Escape. As soon as Uncle Arnie left for work, Auntie Leonie sprang into action, with an expression of resoluteness that had last been seen five or six years ago in her pre-marital days.

She washed the kids, she packed three or four suitcases with essential things, she filled a Tupperware box with cheese and tomato sandwiches for *padkos*. She came to say goodbye to Ma — I was at school, Da was at work. Ma gave her the train tickets that she had kept hidden for her. My aunt left the key with a neighbour — to be given to Uncle Arnold when he came from work that evening. Another neighbour, Mr Jardine, a pensioner, drove her to the station in his old Anglia.

Durban. A new life. Without Uncle Arnie and his drinking and swearing and beating and trying to burn the house down and trying to have three-in-the-bed sex. There were good dressmaking factories in Durban and an old schoolfriend who was also now living in Durban was looking out for a job for my aunt. For now she stood on Platform 14 in the centre of suitcases and bags with zips that didn't work and a child who was hungry, another who was thirsty, and a third who wanted to pee. The train came. And out of the blue, like the Jack of Spades in one of his card tricks, there was Uncle Arnold.

This was such a shock for my aunt that she cried and said, "D'you blame me, Arnie? D'you blame me?" taking off her glasses and wiping them off on the hem of her dress, putting them on, taking them off. How had he known she was leaving him? There was another surprise: he whipped out his own ticket to Durban and got onto the train with her and the kids.

They've been living in Durban for thirty years now, in a slum called Wentworth. Uncle Arnold got work on the docks refurbishing ships. Auntie Leonie worked as a seamstress. They had three more children. Every Friday Uncle Arnie comes home drunk and beats her up. He still calls her a bitch and she calls him Arnie. Apart from the fact that they all have a Durban accent, nothing much has changed; they're regarded by most people as just an ordinary coloured South African family.

SWARTLAND
Rachelle Greeff

THE FOWLS HAVE CREPT under the rubble and rusting ploughshares in the bone white yard. At the front of the farmhouse the fishpond is empty, lined only with a layer of powdery sand. The green scales of the cement fish beside the pond are flaking, and its once spouting mouth is covered with fever blisters. In the corners of the enclosed *stoep* swallow nests crumble. The screen door is shut. Behind the steel framed windows the heavy curtains are drawn.

The sound of the piano ripples through the dusty silence. In the *voorhuis*, on the upright Ibach, a bleached hen and chicken droops onto the keys. Against this potplant, and partially covered by it, is a sepia picture of a woman with waves in her hair, her skin like cream. Next to it is an embroidered text framed in black: 'And now abideth faith, hope, charity, these three; but the greatest of these is charity'.

A girl sits at the piano. She's tall for her age. Her shoulders are pulled back, her small breasts perky. A few pimples blemish her chin but will leave no scar because she doesn't fiddle with them — this her mother taught her years ago. Her hair hangs down her back in a long plait. The music on the stand is open, although she plays from memory. She is Beatrice, which means: 'she who makes others happy'.

Beatrice has a twin sister, Debora, who cannot attend school. 'Mountain stream, freedom, swallow' — her mother found the meaning of her name in a book in the town library close to the end of her pregnancy. Debora was delivered after hours of struggle. And therefore, as the mother repeatedly reminded Beatrice, she is bruised. They would have to be careful with her.

There were only the two daughters on the wheat farm. "For whom, I wonder, do I plough this land?" the father often grumbled, slamming the screen door as he went outside.

The arpeggios under Beatrice's fingers were written by Christian Sinding to evoke the bubbling streams of his land of moss and fjords. The sound fills the room where a peacock preens on the velvet throw on the sofa making it cool and sweet.

You can hear the music all the way down to the whitewashed labourer's cottage where Krakie, her hands folded on her lap, sits on a rickety bench in the strip of shade beside the door. As the day progresses she drags her bench round the house, always a few feet ahead of the cruel Swartland sun, her *kopdoek* a bright beacon marking her trek. Today is Sunday so she's off from after lunch until tomorrow morning. The rest of the week she cooks three meals a day on the Aga. The *baas* insists on three cooked meals a day, just as he once demanded of the *miesies*.

From where Krakie sits she can see the white cloths hanging on the washing line outside the farmhouse kitchen. She bleached them with her own hands. From a distance they look like nappies. Her own rags sag over the chicken wire in front of her cottage.

Whenever the child plays this piece, Krakie squeezes her eyes shut. Now the master is resting. And with him, Debora.

"Because your sister's not well," the father tells Beatrice, "she has to rest, as your mother said." His eyebrows are like tufts of burnt grass. He closes the door firmly.

Beatrice practises until the grandfather clock strikes four, then she puts on the water for coffee. She's talented, so the music she gets from the teacher in town changes often. But this piece she repeats every Sunday afternoon when her father and Debora lie behind the bedroom door — on the same bed where her mother's last breath rattled and her eyes turned to marbles.

The next morning a Chev police van draws up alongside the wire fence that separates the pepper trees, red-hot pokers and the fishpond from the rest of the yard. The only sounds are the screeching of the cicadas, the windmill's repetitive creak and the lilting chords of the Sinding piece.

When no one comes out to greet the two constables, they walk up to the screen door and push it open. *"Oom? Oom Jaap?"* they call, but there is no answer. In the gloom their squeaking shoes follow the music. They find the two girls sitting at the piano. One playing, her eyes closed, and nodding to the other who turns the pages. The policemen, somewhat sheepish in the solemnity of the moment, wait quietly until the last note falls silent.

Serving them coffee, the way her mother showed her, Beatrice answers their questions in calm detail.

They summon Krakie. "There was blood, but then it stopped. Even before she was in the family way I could tell something wasn't right," Krakie tells them, rocking like one with a baby in her arms.

The farmer finally begot an heir. This infant, like his young mother before him, was also trapped in the birth canal. But he was even weaker, he never even cried.

The constables also learn that Oom Jaap didn't wake when his daughters crept softly up to his bed with the 12-bore shotgun.

But the name of the piano piece, 'Rustle of Spring', that they will never know.

COMPRESS
George Weideman
(Translated from the Afrikaans
by Chris van Wyk)

THE AIR-CON HAS PACKED up and the December wind burns my face. The mountains are treeless. The plains are treeless. We drive and we drive. I don't know when we last saw a house. A hot wind forces its way through the windows. My old man could at least have chosen a better place to run away to. The speedometer needle slides beyond 140.

"Slower, Joe, you're killing the car."

"What does Ma know about cars?"

The day I got my licence I overheard the guy from the Traffic Department say he'd never seen anything like my driving.

Beyond the speeding nose of the car, a crow flies up from a carcass. Probably a rabbit that had gone to meet its maker. In the night.

One of these days I'll be as free as that speck of a crow in the sky. Free of Ma's nagging.

"You never listen, Joey."

I hate it when she calls me Joey. With so many Johans in the family Pa began calling me Joey. When I was still a *lightie*. I want to rather not think about Pa. Fuck the old man, it's his fault that we're now driving out here.

Namibia. Do people actually live here?

A freak wind — probably from a ravine — tugs at the car.

"Joey!"

I look at her and laugh. The car is a model of German perfection. I just cannot understand why the air-con has packed up. Maybe the gas leaked out or something. Soon after we had left the border post we realised that there was no cool air coming in. I checked that the thermometer was normal. On an eleven o'clock news bulletin — on a local radio station — the newsreader said that he could not believe it but their correspondent in the South made it known that soon after sunrise the temperature was already thirty-six degrees. Yesterday at three o'clock the mercury was apparently standing at forty-eight in the shade. Is it all they can talk about in this country? For the umpteenth time I try again to find a decent station — in vain. Now there's just a hiss, not even a crackle. Ma shakes loose her red dress around her thin legs and rattles another cigarette out of the packet. I see only now how thin she's become. She struggles with the lighter. Again and again she squeezes it back into the socket.

"Now the bladdy thing won't work."

I take the lighter from her and rub the ball of my thumb where the glow should be. It's cold. I squeeze it back into the socket. It doesn't jump out. I pull it out and give it a shake. Not even a hint of a glow. Ma scratches about in her handbag. Even turns it upside down. But among the little combs and folded tissues and all the other rubbish there is no lighter. Let alone matches. There is the photo. I know that every now and then she gives it a glance.

"What do I do now?" There is panic in Ma's voice. She tries the lighter again.

"Ma can stop smoking. This is Ma's chance."

The look she gives me! Shaking, she packs the stuff back into her handbag. Pa's photo lies on her lap. It's his fault that we find ourselves on this road, the old man's. I was ten when he disappeared. Without a trace. Early one Saturday morning he packed his fishing gear into the back of the station wagon — a Saturday morning custom. I heard the dog barking excitedly — and I lay listening to the drone of the engine until it disappeared into the distance. I never realised that he had loaded in more than just fishing tackle.

The mountains fold away on either side. An unending

expanse stretches into the distance. Over the stony plains the heat sweeps as if over a giant stove plate. It's only mad people who can live here. Or drive here.

About the separation affair I don't remember much. Maybe the words were harsher, the reproaches more strident than before.

In the distance a figure jumps up. A mirage makes it look as if the person is dancing or floating above the tarred road. When the car flashes past I see that it's a woman with a baby. She makes a feeble gesture, almost like a greeting. Out of the corner of my eye I see a man come running from the veld. In his hand something is swinging which sparkles in the sun. A bucket? He waves desperately with his other hand. It's not a greeting. A donkey cart stands a short distance from the road. The donkeys' heads hang. They look like statues. I glance at Ma. It looks as if she has dozed off. She has not spotted these people. I'm glad that she's sleeping. She would've told me to stop. And who would want to stop in this scorching heat? In the rear-view mirror I see how the woman turns around, how the man's arms flop down at his sides.

The road is particularly quiet. All of a sudden a crosswind tugs at the car. Ma's head jerks upright.

"Where are we now?" she asks sleepily.

"How should I know?"

"Don't you read the boards?"

She rubs her eyes, with a shaking hand, pours tepid water into a coffee mug. Swallows two headache tablets.

"And you could at least be a little more pleasant, Joey."

"I didn't say he should run off to this place."

"It's not to say your father ran away. There is such a thing as memory loss too."

I don't know why she wants to lie for him now. First he discarded us like you'd discard a bundle of rubbish on a rubbish dump. Then she struggled to get maintenance out of him. Then we heard he'd re-married. After that he vanished. Everybody thought he got drowned. Any fool could see that he had staged the thing.

A board flashes past. Ninety kilometres to the next town. Fuck!

We have to turn off somewhere here. To the right the tarred road leads onto a sand road.

"That's the one. I'm sure that's the one. You passed it, Joey."

"How was I supposed to know?" I slam on the brakes. The tyres screech, the car swerves dangerously. Ma gives me a reproachful look.

"From here there's still a hundred and twenty kilometres to go. That's what the woman said in her letter. From the turn-off. A hundred and twenty..." I don't know if she's repeating it because it sounds so unbelievable or because she's thinking about the letter again. There is something desperate in her voice.

The car swerves suddenly. She lets out a shriek and glares at me with big eyes. I have to reduce my speed and tighten my grip on the steering wheel. The loose sand is deceiving. It's not quite the same as a drive with your buddies on the beach in a beach buggy.

Dust swirls in through the open windows. Close them and we suffocate in the heat.

"Can't you do something about the dust?"

"I could stop driving."

"You know that's not what I mean. Jesus, Joey, do you think I'm enjoying this?"

The day Pa disappeared we thought his car had gone and got stuck somewhere. Or — worse — that he had gone and picked up a hiker. That he had been *moered* on the head. That night when his food was getting cold on the table, Ma became restless. When the boxing match started on TV, Ma phoned Uncle Wally. Pa was never one to *meiss* a fight. Uncle Wally said Pa was with him; they were going to phone but they were too busy chatting. Then Pa also spoke with Ma, he said it's over, he's not coming back.

Ma phoned family and friends and told them it was all her fault, that they had had a fallout. You fought day and night, I wanted to shout out, but I was in standard two.

A year or so after he remarried, Pa disappeared. Together with his fishing rod and bait bag, completely, as if a mysterious boat had picked him up and vanished into the blue yonder. That's how his new wife put it in her letter. One Sunday we drove out to his favourite fishing spot, the Big Rocks, with Uncle Wally. The springtide had long since wiped out all traces. The seagulls circled inquisitively above us and then flew away.

On Pa's birthday we went to place a wreath on the rocks and waited on the hill until the waves came and swept it away. Soon after that the Court declared Pa officially dead. And now, hardly nine years later, a creased letter arrived, in a primary school handwriting, full of mistakes. The name underneath — not a signature — said the writing belonged to Anna. It's not his second wife's name.

Sybrand is very very sick, the letter said. He will probably not be able to get up from the sick bed. He asked her to write to his wife and son and ask them to come and visit him, there's a lot he needs to tell them. At first Ma would not believe it but Uncle Wally confirmed that the letter was genuine.

"I'll take you there," Uncle Wally offered. But she said I do have my licence. Then Uncle Wally insisted that we take his car.

Ma read the letter over and over. We studied road maps. The letter mentioned only the name of the farm, and where we had to turn off. We don't talk about him anymore. We've already done that, since the letter arrived. Until this morning. Then the questions dried up. Ma became quiet at the border post. But the unspoken questions were eating away.

All I know is that my father, who I last saw in the year I turned ten, is busy dying from a strange, horrible illness. On a strange farm among strange people. In a strange, suffocating wilderness.

I have to break sharply a couple of times. Gates every five hundred metres or so. Ma insists on opening them. I let her. When it gets dark a piece of wire nicks her dress to ribbons and blood run down her leg.

"It's a sign," Ma says. Ma and her signs.

"About what?"

"We should never have come. It's useless."

"But we're nearly there."

"I know," is all she says. And sighs.

Something somewhere gives a terrific scream. Ma grabs my wrist.

"Maybe a jackal," I say, not sure.

The wide, still, darkness swallows us.

The farmhouse with its solitary lantern light hidden among a scattering of trees. On the stoep a woman with unkempt hair.

"I think you're too late," she says.

Ma squeezes past her. The house smells as if it too has stood shut closed in the heat. Everywhere Ma flings windows open.

The man, whose face is hidden deep in the stained pillow is not my father. My father is a big strong man with a can of beer in his hand and his feet on the coffee table in front of the TV. My father is a man who smells of smoke and after-shave lotion, who ties my boxing gloves and sings with the car radio: 'I will love you always'.

This man's eyes are dull, his face is decrepit and full of sores; his hands are like the pale roots of weeds.

Ma bends over him and calls, "Sybrand! Sybrand!" And later she goes and sits, clutching at her handbag on her lap. His eyes stare beyond the ceiling; his breathing comes in jerks.

"He just lies there," says the woman, who brings black coffee on a stained tray.

I can't look at him. I look at the flickering flame of an oil lamp. And at an orange-red flower in a vase.

"Don't you want to go and see what's wrong with the car?" Ma says. She has put her hand over Pa's worn-away fingers as if she wants to hide them.

I put the lantern on a rock near the car. The yard is desolate. Near the stoep are two tufts of grass; could that be where the flower came from? The wind has subsided; I walk in the foot-path around the farm among the scattered bluegums. The path is cut off from the veld by a row of white limestone rocks. Above my head stretches another path that in this bright light looks as if it too has been paved with limestone rocks: the Milky Way.

After the funeral — there were only about eleven people — we drive back. It's still windy and hot. Ma, who looks as if she hasn't been sleeping these past few days, doesn't say a word, except to say that her calf is sore where the wire snagged her. It's swollen badly and it's red. It doesn't look good. We make slow progress because this time I open and close the gates. And then I have to slow down even more: a tiny hurricane swirls from the veld, swerves suddenly along the path towards us forcing me to stop. Everything is covered in a red dust blanket. Quick! The windows!

When the windows roll closed the sweat breaks out on us like blobs of grease. The sandstorm shoots grains of gravel onto the car. I can almost hear how the paint is being scraped off the car. In the rear-view mirror darkness settles as if night has come. I press the button that controls the windows. Nothing happens. I wipe the sweat from my eyebrows. I press again. The windows stay where they are.

"Why don't you open them up?"

"The fucking things don't work." I try again. Nothing happens. We are sealed in as tightly a pressure cooker.

"Now what?" Her voice is hoarse. With clammy tissues she wipes the sweat from her face.

"We have to get out before we suffocate. I'll try and see if I can find the problem."

"I thought you checked the other night."

"With a lantern light? Ma must be crazy."

I tried yesterday; some or other electrical fault. The nearest garage is about two hundred kilometres away. "Here we just work on the cars ourselves," a man at the funeral told me. "But we don't drive such fancy stuff."

Suddenly I have a crazy idea: the car's brain has ceased up because of the heat. The bonnet doesn't budge when I pull the lever. I get out, slam the door shut, pull it open again.

"What has become of you?" It sounds as if she's talking to Pa, a long time ago. I try getting my fingers into the grooves of the bonnet. Even a crowbar would not have made it move.

With the doors open a warm wind blows over us. At least it evaporates the sweat. At least one can cool off a little.

"We don't even have water." She holds up the water bottle; there is less than a cupful. "What are we going to do?" I wish she would stop talking. Ma looks out across the plain. I follow her eyes. There are no trees, not even bushes. Only burnt-black tufts of grass. As if it rained here once a long long time ago. The only sign of life is a singing telephone line. Like the dust road, the gleaming lines stretch out into the unending distance. The only shadow is here underneath the car.

I suggest that we sit in the car; the doors are flung open like the wings of a disabled insect. Even though there is no air here, it is more bearable than standing in the sun.

"If it gets cooler I'll go and find some help."

But where?

When the donkey cart appears, Ma's lips are thick with fever, her forehead is packed with pearls of sweat. A red stripe shoots up along her leg. I tried to wipe off her cheeks and neck with some damp tissues but now the water's finished.

The man and the woman speak quickly in their language; it sounds like pebbles against a sheet of zinc.

While the woman makes Ma comfortable and packs out all kinds of salves from a little box on the cart, I try to talk to the man. He speaks Afrikaans with a peculiar accent, just as quick and easy as his own language.

Then his wife calls him. "Xiriri!" she shouts, or that's what it sounds like.

But it is not his name. He explains that it is a plant and that there is a small strip of rain that fell a few kilometres back.

For the first time in my life I ride in a donkey cart. The man, his heart-shaped face full of wrinkles, asks if we have come from the city or if we've come to visit. I'm not so sure what I should say.

Among the bedding on the cart a bucket shines.

I say: "My father's dead, we've come to bury him."

He gazes silently ahead of him, speaks in his click tongue with his donkeys.

"My daughter, too," he says. "We buried her this morning. Something poisonous bit her."

Again I see the woman at the side of the road; the man with the flailing arms.

"If only we'd got some of those leaves in time," he says, after we'd spent hours — or that's what it felt like to me — along the sandy bed of a dry river, "but it's so dry."

Back at the car his wife makes a kind of compress — that's what she calls it — with the leaves.

"That will draw out all the nasty stuff," she says, her hand on Ma's forehead.

YOU ARE THE DAUGHTER
Rayda Jacobs

AOUDA STOOD WITH HER two aunts around the metal katl, listening to the toekamandie's instructions. In this room the toekamandie was in charge.

"We don't talk about what we see in here," she said, "not even with family. What we see stays in this room."

Aouda couldn't bear to look down at the corpse. The beds and dresser had been taken out of the room, the curtains drawn, the air close. In the rest of the house, mourners sat on benches, whispering under their breath.

"One will be at the head, one at the feet, and one on either side."

Aouda stood at the head of the katl and looked down at her mother's grey hair, the ends creeping out under the sheet. Did hair straighten in death? Her mother's had always had a wave. Now it lay flat and metallic against stainless steel.

A few weeks before she died she said: "Listen, my girl, it's in that cupboard over there. In the box."

"What, mom?"

"My kafan."

She had looked at her mother, stunned. "What're you talking about?"

"I'm talking about my burial cloth. You mustn't be afraid of these things."

"You're going to live a long time, mom, don't talk like this. It's bad luck."

But her mother had never been afraid of anything and had gone to the shop and bought the white, winding sheet in which her body would enter the ground. "When it happens, my girl, the toekamandies will come to you. You're the daughter. They'll ask if there's anything in the house. You must know where it is." The toekamandies had come. They'd asked. She had taken out the box from the bedroom cupboard.

Now, the kafan was laid out on a side table, lined with cottonwool and dried rose leaves, stitched on one side, open on the other for the body to be inserted, like a letter into an envelope. Her mother, who didn't like perfume, tight clothes, and small spaces, would go sealed and scented into her grave.

"We'll start with the washing of the private parts," the toekamandie said. "It's better for one of the family. Aouda?"

Aouda looked at the woman who'd spoken. What went through the mind of a toekamandie, she wondered. What special thing did she possess? The task of washing and dressing the dead had nothing glamorous to recommend it except spiritual reward. Was it to be constantly reminded of the swiftness of life? Did toekamandies feel closer to God? She had always thought that the washers of the dead were old women, but Moena Toefy was a spirited woman in her thirties, who besides reading the Qur'an, also read Toni Morrison and Leonard Woolf. Moena was different to her husband. All he did was read the sports pages and the classifieds in the Saturday paper, his life revolving around blown gaskets, brake linings, and clogged carburettors, lying under a car with oil dripping onto his face all day long. But she owned a library card, and when she wasn't at someone's house washing the dead, or filling home orders for cake, her head was bent over a book in the overstuffed chair by the window in the late afternoon sun, and no child with a snot nose or a complaint or a hungry stomach dared disturb her. Moena had talents Aouda wished she had, and it was said that when Moena recited from the Qur'an, the heavens opened and the angels themselves stopped to listen. She knew all this about Moena because Moena was a distant relative and she and her sisters were always there when there was a marriage, birth or death, praying louder than anyone else in the room.

"What do I have to do?" Aouda asked.

Moena handed her a pile of linen strips. "Wrap these around your left hand. The sheet will remain on the may'yit at all times. Make sure you cover your fingers. The hand mustn't touch the private parts. Wash it three times, each time with a clean cloth. On the third wash, check to see if there's anything showing on the cloth. If there is, wash it again, ending on an uneven number."

It was strange hearing her mother referred to as the may'yit. The may'yit had always been someone else: her grandfather, her uncle, her best friend in a drowning accident. Mothers didn't die. They were indestructible. There forever.

"Can you do it?" Moena asked.

Aouda's eyes filled. She moved to the foot end. "Yes," she said. She, who had always been so afraid of death. Her tears dropped onto the sheet. She wrapped the cloths around her hand and dipped it into the warm water at her side, rubbing Sunlight soap on it. This soap left no scent on the body. She slid her hand under the sheet.

Oh, Mom, how will I go on without you? I'm so glad I told you I loved you, Mom. Some children don't get the chance, or can't say the words. You were more than a mother to me. I could tell you things. You always listened, always gave the best advice. Still, Mom, there was something I kept from you. I never told you about him. I never told you when I remembered it for the first time. Where I was, what happened to me when the memory came. I didn't want you to know. Just in case you knew who he was. Just in case he was close to you. Just in case you had to choose. I was two, Mom. In nappies when he took me out of the cot.

She looked at her aunts working on the arms and the hands. Auntie Rukeya, only a pucker between her brows to show the gravity of her grief, her hands working expertly under the sheet. Auntie Gaya, the youngest, weeping openly. The death had been a shock. Her mother hadn't told anyone what the doctor had said that rainy July afternoon, and hadn't gone back, not wanting to hear anything more, protecting her and her brother to the end. From what? From their guilt — remorse that they had perhaps not appreciated her like they should've while she was alive? That it might be harder for them to accept her death than it would be for her?

Remember the house on Harrow Road, Mom? The skipping ropes, the park, the pine trees on the corner where the children came after school to play? Those should've been happy days. When girls play with dolls and believe in princes who will protect them from witches and dragons and nasty men. There were many times I wanted to take you there, Mom, to tell you about me at that time. I was little, but knew already that something was wrong. I didn't know what. I didn't believe in Snow White and Clever Gretel, and if I was taken in at all by fairy tales, it was always by the cruelty to the little girl.

The water dripped down from the katl through the small drain into the plastic bath. The slow drip, dull and heavy, substantified the foreverness of death. The end. The end of life. The end of worrying about the end.

He wore a hat. I remember the colour, brown, the pattern of the wallpaper in the room, blue and pink flowers, the glass he slid himself into — up and down, up and down. Afterwards, the glass is milky and clouded. I can't see his face. It's hidden from me. But I feel his tongue, wet and cold. My little legs are pressed together, but he holds them apart with one hand. My eyes burn into the wallpaper; the pink little flowers, the blue little flowers. In another part of the house a woman is singing the 'Tennessee Waltz'. I don't know why I can't see his face. Sometimes I reach back to see if some small thing will come to me, and wonder, still, what I would do if I knew who he was and saw him today. The man who'd robbed me so early of laughter and innocence. I think I'm capable of putting a gun to the spot between his eyes. I wouldn't hesitate with the trigger. I would watch as his brain burst out the back of his head. Watch as he died. Perhaps if we'd talked, Mom, I wouldn't carry around this old wound. Perhaps you would've been able to help. Or, perhaps it would've destroyed you to know. I know one thing. What happened that afternoon changed me forever towards men.

The sharp smell of camphor filled her nostrils. "You put grated camphor into the final rinse," Moena explained. "For the worms. It will keep them away."

Aouda wrinkled her nose. She didn't like the smell and didn't believe the camphor would do anything. How could you prevent rot? The maggots would come from inside; glutting, gorging, irritable as ants on a watermelon pit. Wasn't that the constant scratch at life from birth?

She watched Moena spread a dry sheet over the corpse and remove the damp one underneath. Together, the four of them rolled the body onto its side, towards the centre, and slipped the padded shroud into place. The sheet moved and she caught a glimpse of the face. A young face, ivory-coloured, the features softened in death.

Finally, the may'yit was wrapped. Moena took two linen strips, and tied one around the neck, the other around the feet. "They'll loosen it when they lay the body down," she said, "so the cheek can make contact with the soil."

Aouda's heart squeezed in her chest. Contact with the soil! She recoiled at the thought. Ashes to ashes, dust to dust. Cold against the damp earth. Boxed in under planks. If it rained the water would fill up the hole and loosen the graveclothes. A sand vault six feet under the ground. Your last act of humility.

She looked down at the may'yit. It was over. Forty years of wiping her nose; a mother's lifelong murmur of love. The house in Rondebosch would be empty. No mother waiting for her visit, asking how she was, had she sold any paintings, who was the new man in her life. The lessons had ended. Her mother wasn't ever coming back. School was out.

COUPLE ON THE BEACH
Arja Salafranca

A MIDDLE-AGED WOMAN SITS on the edge of the lagoon and watches a couple take photographs of each other. It is the beginning of a new year. It is low tide, and the waters of the lagoon have receded, leaving a vast expanse of wet beige sand. The couple stand in it with bare feet splayed, toes squelching into the coarse grains, taking photos with their expensive cameras.

It is nearly the end of their holiday together, and they are using up their film before they leave Knysna. They make an odd couple as they take photos. The woman is wearing a smart jacket on this summer evening; it is too smart for this seaside town, too smart for this season, and too warm too. The middle-aged woman wonders why she wears it, when her feet are bare and her jeans rolled up to reveal pinky white legs. She can't be cold. Although there is a breeze blowing it is not a cold night, the day was warm, and the heat remains trapped as the sun goes slowly down. Perhaps it is to cover her body, perhaps she has gained weight and wants to hide behind her big black jacket. The middle-aged woman smokes a cigarette as she sits on the cement boulder and watches the couple. She knows all about gaining weight and hiding behind big clothes.

She has done it too. It is only now that she is older that she can afford to be freer, that she can wear anything and not be self-conscious and concerned that others, men, are looking at her, appraising her. She knows she is getting past the age of appraisal. She has read of the liberation that comes from middle-age — the loss of youth, menopause — she welcomes it.

Her hair is still mainly auburn, but lately she has been seeing the flash of silver streaks in it. They dart in and out
between the dark strands, as though playing hide and seek,
daring to be found.

He is tall and thin, as opposed to the female. She is shorter,
slightly overweight, her gloriously auburn hair long and flying
in the dusk's breeze. He is skinny and awkward in his body as
the woman is in hers. He is uncomfortable in the casual T-shirt
he's wearing, and the middle-aged woman wonders why he
wears it. Perhaps his partner, or whatever that girl is to him,
asked him to wear it. The middle-aged woman has a feeling
that he would be uncomfortable no matter what he wore. He is
that kind of person, awkward in his body, in his life, hanging
after this partner like a puppy dog eager to please her, compli-
ant and soft, willing to do whatever it is that would make her
like him, fall in love with him, something beyond this cold
dismissive need of hers.

But she won't let him go yet, she needs him, although she
does not like him. She needs him and that is her weakness,
that's what makes her hate him, and hate a part of herself too.
The middle-aged woman can see this as she smokes into the
pale blue dusk and watches the lagoon recede from this couple. She watches the roar of the sea at the heads as it foams and
dashes, as though the seas were a caged wild animal wanting
to get into this quiet piece of solitude, preferring the domestic
peace of the lagoon to the endless, deep, unfathomable sea.
Her boyfriend keeps wanting to take her on the sea, perhaps
on a small yacht. Time and time again she refuses. She is afraid
of the sea.

She clutches the cigarette between her fingers, looking at the
beauty spot on her little finger that a man once found so attractive years ago, a dark mark on the fleshy folds of her baby
finger. She watches couples take photos as the sky darkens and
fish burns in a house nearby.

The couple don't know where to go for supper. The woman is full from a sweet cinnamon pancake eaten late that afternoon. Her name is Ailsa. Her friend, her partner, her holiday companion, whose name is Mark, is hungry. Again. She doesn't know where all the food goes, or how it disappears on him, leaving him skinny and perpetually hungry. Back home in the tiny cottage they are renting for the week she tries to stall him. They watch TV, she puts more make-up over the day's make-up while he watches the news. She brushes her heavy hair again. It looks limp, it always sags in summer when it's hot, there is not much she can do about it.

"Hell, I'm hungry," Mark emphasises from the bedroom where he lies sprawled in front of the TV. It is their last night in Knysna, he wants it to be special.

Ailsa wants to get the hell out of here, go home as quickly as possible, be free from this friend who has shared her bed, her holiday, her life. She would like to go tonight, just ride straight through, back to Johannesburg, sixteen hours straight, to be home, away from this man who is as tangled in her life as fish caught in a net — as tangled and as messy.

"I'm still not hungry," she calls from the bathroom. "Can't we wait?"

They wait, talk is desultory, they make plans for the next day, deciding what time they should get up, pack, leave.

They eat dinner. They land up at the same place that sells the pancakes. This time Ailsa picks at a calamari salad, a salad that Mark will finish after she's stopped pushing her fork around the bowl, eating when she's not hungry. Only years later will she learn not to eat when she's not hungry. It's a simple thing, something she hasn't learnt yet.

The waiter serves them, beaming, bringing plates, taking away plates. Mark leans close to her, talking quietly. Ailsa thinks he does this deliberately, to make them look like a couple in the eyes of the world. She hates the way he does this, she doesn't want anyone to know they're together, she wants to shake him off like a bad smell. She leans back as though to tell the world that they are not really together. Mark makes small talk with the waiter as well, and Ailsa simply cannot shut off her disgust.

She looks away, distant, cringing. Mark's stupid, meaningless conversation falls awkwardly into the music and hollow of the restaurant. The waiter, she thinks, appraises her, looks her up and down, wonders why she is with this man who makes stupid, unintelligent conversation and drags her out to eat when she is not hungry.

There is dessert for him. She is so tired, so very very tired, it's early still and yet all she wants to do is to go sleep. Mark again makes plans for the next morning. He talks on, Ailsa adds a little to the conversation, trying to find something new to say, but it is impossible. They have said the same things now, to each other, for days on end.

It is exhausting being nice, not getting irritated. Ailsa hasn't wanted to fight, not this time, now that everything has fallen back on only the two of them. There have been irritations, dishes unwashed, not enough time for herself, a feeling of frustration and helplessness at his own helplessness. She is his life, she knows that now, and because she is his life, she cannot shake him off.

"I'm in love with you, Ailsa," he had told her months before as they sat in the lounge in her parents' home eating chocolate covered nuts in front of a fire. "I fell in love with you. One day a few months ago I woke up and thought, 'Hell, I'm in love with Ailsa!' What do you think of that?"

Ailsa had sighed, the bright lounge with glaring overhead lights and dim wall brackets, the flames crackling in the silence, the fire her father insisted on making every winter, hauling in logs and setting the stone fireplace blazing.

"I know," she had said. "I've known for a long time now, the way you look at me. But I'm not ready, Mark. I'm not ready for a new relationship."

Mark had looked at her then, the hard, sharp face dissolved into vulnerabilities, stripped bare of its usual arrogance.

How could she hurt him? How could she hurt him the way she'd been hurt and cast aside by the man she'd fallen in love with and then cast aside as easily as they'd come together. A year later, and she was left nursing a bruised heart, eating chocolate-covered nuts bought by a man who said he was in love with her, who had never fallen in love before and now said he loved her.

She needed him, she needed him for the friendship and for the soft pliancy of his weakness. As long as he was in love with her she could mould him or break him or twist his desires. She needed him because she needed people around her to stave off something unmentionable, and she needed, now, a man to say he loved her, and here he was, Mark, saying he loved her. And all she said was that she was not ready for another relationship.

Years later she would have said, perhaps, that she could not love him, that he wasn't her type — but on that night she could only suck chocolate off a nut and tell him she was sorry, and let him massage her feet for her.

He'd never even kissed a woman, the girl he'd asked to the matric dance hadn't even come to the after party with him. He'd plucked up the courage many times after to ask women out, but invariably they said no. He didn't know if it was because his stammer grew worse when he asked them out, or if it was because he was so skinny, or if it was the fact that he lived at home still, a man in his late twenties. His mother had told him to wait, she reminded him that his own father had only married in his thirties. There's plenty of time, she'd say, when he tried to talk to her about it. She did not help. She brushed hair from his eyes in a gesture of tenderness, and cooked his favourite foods and complained to him about her unfeeling husband, but she did not help.

He started noticing Ailsa after her break-up from James. They went, as friends, to movies and plays. They ate supper, as friends. This was even when she was still with James. He couldn't believe it was that serious, if she could go out to supper with him one night, the next with James while still hoping that he, James, would fall in love with her.

Sitting in the office they both worked in, she'd wonder aloud to him, asking if he thought James liked her, and then she'd describe James's actions and words. Or, she asked, did Mark think she was simply a friend to James? Mark had no answers.

It was only long after she finally asked and found out the answer to her questions, and spent long times behind locked doors, emerging tear-eyed, clutching the Valiums the receptionist pressed into her hands and life.

He first noticed her kindness and gentleness. Her soft shy way of talking and her fear of hurting anyone. He noticed the way she ate, delicately, with her small hands fisted around a spoon, or cupping a cappuccino, the way she wiped her mouth, the way she took care not to let the food spill, or catch in the corners of her mouth. He noticed this and thought she was a nice person. She took the time to listen to him, to go out with him. Here, at last, was a woman who did not run away, or make excuses that she was involved. She stayed and listened. They saw more movies, and one night, after drinks at a neighbourhood restaurant, he told her his greatest fear about having sex. He thought his penis was too small, and Ailsa stared into the darkness of the car, and said she'd only known one man, and his penis hadn't been that big, and that it didn't matter anyway. And that there was so much more to sex than a large penis. "Besides, when it gets big it gets big enough!" she'd laughed into the inky morning as they sat in the car. She hadn't yet asked him into the house, and later he was glad, would he have felt so free, so uninhibited in the house where her parents could have heard him?

The next morning he phoned her and thanked her for their talk. It felt like a veil was lifting, like light was coming in through fog and murk. He felt grateful too, grateful for her kindness, for the fact that she listened to him. But he didn't understand it.

He fell in love instead. That's what he'd tell people years later, himself, another woman. That he had fallen in love with her soft gentle brown eyes, and the long lashes and the thick wavy auburn hair, and the beauty spot on her little finger. He stared across at her day after day in the open-plan office and walked with her to the shops at lunch time and got close enough to her to smell her sweat and perfume mingling in a heady mixture that made him dream and fantasise in his narrow lonely bed in his own parents' house. And then he fell in love, simple as that.

He could not tell her, although he tried. He found out what her feelings for James were, and found out she was still in love with him, she was obsessed by that love, that man whom Mark had met only once.

Mark spoke about a woman he really liked, and she said tell me more, and he tried to hide it and eventually it came out. And she could not reciprocate his love for her as she ate his chocolate-covered nuts and let him take off her boots and knead her feet into submission. He kneaded and caressed and looked at her, wanting to kiss her and touch her breasts, he'd never touched breasts before, but had to make do with tepid coffee and the smooth curved muscles of her feet.

On their last night on holiday, away from Knysna, they find themselves booked into a grim, one-star hotel in a small town in the Karoo. It is clean, but plain. There are no lamps and the beds are two singles pushed apart. The bathroom is white and clinical, the curtains threadbare. The mattresses are lumpy and once more, Ailsa's supper sits hard and rocky in her stomach. Again, she ate when she wasn't hungry. A half a day riding in the car, the sun beating down, trying to get sleep, feeling exhaustion snatching her, trying to get away from the situation, the holiday, the man driving the big car through the sun-baked Karoo desert, the endless miles of scrubby, shrimp-like plants crouching over the dry earth. They ate supper at an American steakhouse, the only restaurant open in town on a Saturday night. A Chinese restaurant was closed, and a grand elegant hotel that Mark wanted to go to was expensive and had a set meal. Anger had hovered in the air, Mark had said he simply wanted their last night to be special. "I'm not going to spend all that money on a three course meal that I'm not hungry enough to eat!" she had retorted.

"Okay," he'd replied, but conversation died in the steak-house.

Still, after eating and coming back and undressing and washing face and brushing teeth and getting into their single beds, she lets him come into hers, and he is hard, as always, and she lets him have sex with her. Again, it is unsatisfactory, he comes too quickly, there is no joy for her. He tries to find her secret spot, and sometimes he gets it, but never for long enough. He always misses the mark, and she grows tired of his fumblings, and that is that.

The bed is too narrow. He lies against her for a while, his hard bony body offering little comfort, sinking away into the sheet and the pillows, there is always an elbow he doesn't know what to do with. He does not know how to hold her, or to run his hands around her soft hips and soft belly, to trace her scars with love.

Ailsa lies there and thinks this man is as cold as the one before. But, she doesn't love this one. He moans as he comes and she shuts off, his pleasure sounds like an irritation in the dark room. He comes outside of her (she doesn't want to get pregnant), and goes to the bathroom to clean himself up, turning on the hard white light. She watches his naked, limp penis dangling, body angular and bent as an old man's.

She hates him then, she tries to love him as he cleans her up, and hates him. She lies there passive in the white light streaming from the bathroom, and he cleans her between the legs, smoothing the white sperm away from her stomach into the wet toilet paper, and she doesn't even mind that he sees her naked, the imperfect body, the swelling of it, the scars, the unfeminine-like trail of dark hair. She doesn't mind, she doesn't care.

"That's probably the last time we'll do it," he says matter of factly as he drifts off.

He knows, he knows that was it, she's told him she is not in love with him. He knows that when the holiday is over she will finally find the strength in her to call a halt to this, that they will not have sex and she will not try to control her temper with him, or hide her irritation.

The sex had started a few days earlier, the night before the new year. Early in the morning before the next year she had forced him into her.

"Are you ready?" she'd whispered.

Yes, no, yes, no. "I suppose I have to do it."

He'd drunk champagne after they'd done it. They'd been saving it for the new year, but he opened the bottle and toasted the event. He couldn't believe he'd done it, kept exclaiming over it, blue eyes big, mouth agape, sitting up in bed with a wineglass while she lay there, thinking, Get off it!

It was a relief finally, even though he was quick, and she wanted something slower, something more. She almost called him James, then didn't call him anything at all, his name behind the other one, a name she had to grope for in her head.

She felt triumphant, she'd completed the cycle, stolen his virginity, forced him through that final border, showed him love and sex and kissing and lying in bed together. She'd broken her own barrier too, remembering sex a year earlier, the cold, silent night, the man who slipped off into his own single bed, the pimple that sprouted the morning after on her breast. Big and fat and white and filled with pus. She had squeezed it in the mirror, it spattered against her fingers, against the silver metal, as she clutched a towel around her, the day after she wasn't a virgin anymore. There was no blood that morning, simply yellow, oily pus that leaked out of her.

It had started earlier than this trip to Knysna though. It had been like a dance. After the night he said he loved her she'd agreed to go away with him. They both needed a holiday, he argued.

Over a long weekend they ran away to the mountains in the east, a deserted chalet in the shadow of snowy peaks, the pale watery beginnings of summer present in the heat of the day, the mornings and nights capped with cold. She let him caress her, it started off as a massage, a drink, the pale afternoon light coming in as he picked off her clothes, his hands moving further, getting warmer. No sex, he was a virgin, a Christian, didn't believe in sex before marriage.

But there were two bodies naked, the sordid details of an unmade bed in the waning afternoon, the silence of exhaustion as they forced food into their mouths in the hotel restaurant later, hair hastily combed, clothes piled up, putting make-up on. "But I don't want you to look pretty for other men!" And she rolled her eyes at him, choking on the cliché. Was he saying it to flatter her, or because he'd read it or heard it said? Or did he actually mean it? She put the make-up on, like she always did, and shoved the food in her mouth, conversation dead between them, the restaurant emptying.

"What if you have, you know, Aids?" he'd asked later, in another restaurant.

And she'd rolled her eyes again. They tried it the morning after that question, but they couldn't get the condom on, they didn't seem to know how, and she was dry and sore. He wasn't ready. She wasn't ready.

She pulled away, then pulled towards him, craving love, affection, dancing around his own wants the way he danced around hers. At times she even thought she saw that old hardness and sarcasm she'd first glimpsed in him, that had made her recoil from even friendship with him. She accused him, abused him. Told him it had to end, she wasn't in love. And the touching would stop for a while, and then start up again. She was starving, famished, she sucked and sucked at his dry orange, wanting more, wanting something else, disgusted with herself, with her need to love and be loved.

She was excising James's ghost, this was the way she'd get rid of him: by having sex with another man she'd be over him. Once she'd had sex with someone else she could get on with her life. She could forget James, forget Mark, be free to find someone new.

"I can't hurt you," she told Mark as they lay together.

"It doesn't matter. You've already hurt me. I fell in love with you and you can't reciprocate. So you have hurt me."

"I don't want to be like James."

"It doesn't matter."

James lay beside them, a ghost with presence and shadow and a history. Mark asked her all sorts of questions about James, what he was like, the way he treated her, what she had loved about him, as though he could appropriate the other man's abilities and qualities and thus make her fall in love with him.

The dancing continued. She could not let him go, he came to fill up all the crevices of her life, till she knew she'd never be alone if she didn't want to. He'd be there, as easy as an old armchair, she could phone him at any time, they'd see a movie, go to a play. There was no need to phone anyone else. The blanket grew tighter, it was secure, no need to risk being hurt with anyone else. One night, driving home with him, she stared at the black streets and heard him talk into the darkness, and again felt that frustration, and thought, maybe this is it. Maybe I must accept this. Maybe there won't be anyone else. He is not a bad man, simply a boring, stupid man.

The time passed. She pushed him away again. She wouldn't let him touch her, it had to stop. He was simply getting hurt.

On the last day of their holiday she is happy. She points her camera at the flat Free State farms and bubbly storm clouds and takes pictures of the sun radiating out as it dips and dives in yet another dusk. They have coffee in a restaurant attached to a highway garage. Mark watches as she laughs and gets enthusiastic. He smiles with her, the tensions of the last few days dissolved. He is tired, but he is happy. He wishes she could have been as happy a few days ago, back in Knysna. He does not want to go back. He goes back to work the next day, she won't be there.

He'll miss her in bed at night, the warmth, the miraculous warmth of another body, and her smell, that sweet smell that lingers in her hair, on his hands, he cannot get enough; or her buttery feel as he slides his hands along her hips, her stomach, doing as she asks him. It is all overwhelming as he puts his hands lightly on her, barely touching her. Only when she protests does he cup her stomach or her breasts, trying to give her what she wants, what he cannot give.

It feels like going back into darkness, although he feels changed. She flirts with the waiter in the restaurant. She is twenty-five, the waiter is a teenager. She feels older, finally like an adult, leaves a tip, spoons ice-cream into her mouth and tells him she's going to diet when they get back.

"I like you the way you are!" he protests.

I'm not doing this for you, she thinks. He watches her flirt, eat ice-cream, take pictures. It is like watching something fly away from you, like watching bubbles dissolve in the sunlight, like candyfloss melting on your tongue. A vague sweetness remains, a thick rough fur left on your teeth.

The sun goes down, you try to capture a sunset, the clouds come out blurred, an arm pokes out the corner of a photograph, fat and white. There is one perfect photo, with the light radiating out from the clouds, and the clouds spill out into the frame. One perfect moment, before it all disappears.

A middle-aged woman watches as a couple take pictures of each other. She has lived here for many years, It is quiet and she can paint in peace and every few years she has a boyfriend. Her paintings sell well enough for her to make a living. When the tide goes out, she goes down to the lagoon, smokes on the cement barrier, or walks on the sand, trousers rolled up, feet splayed in the coarse sand, the way she did on her first trip here years and years and years ago.

She had a dog when she first moved here, used to take him for walks but he died. And she has simply continued the ritual of her evening walks. It's a habit, a break from the day's work, a walk in the fading light, harsh lamps don't give her paintings the same look, she prefers to paint by daylight.

She has a boyfriend waiting in her house. He is younger than her, this season's lover. He lives far away, in a big city. He is a good lover, but now, so is she. She has finally learned to be loved, the men she knows know how to find her spot and take their time. She has sex, she has lovers, she has a canvas opened wide against the window that faces one of the hills of brown and green vegetation. There, in the landscape and gentle lights, she paints the hard angular paints that shout anger and despair and hard modern living.

Sometimes her daughter comes to visit. She expects her mother to paint soft gentle flowers and landscapes, to mirror this land she lives in. But she doesn't. She paints from long ago, when she was young, and she remembers what that feels like.

She paints young people — angry young people who don't know where they're going, who are still finding themselves, who wear hard bright colours and stare out of the canvas with hard accusatory looks.

Her latest painting though is different. Unlike the others it is a soft gentle painting done in pastel blues and pinks and light whitish colours. A couple take photographs of each other on a beach. There is a tall skinny man who holds a camera taking photographs of a short woman with auburn hair blowing in the wind, smiling uncertainly into the orb of his lens. They wear old-fashioned clothes, jeans that flare at the ankles, tie-dyed shirts, it is a long time ago.

Somehow, though, the lines are jagged, the man stands too far away, the woman is too uncertain. There's a sense of unease in the picture, of disturbed lives.

Sitting on the cement platform a middle-aged woman edges into the distance, smoking cigarettes, watching the past unfolding before her. The middle-aged woman wears a red top, it too is jarring, like a flash of blood.

It is all intermingled as Ailsa puts the final touches to her latest painting, making the red of the top harder, more violent, more bloody. The past doesn't fade, it may lie sleeping and then it comes seeping out through the cracks in your life — in a painting, a piece of music, a movie that reminds you and perhaps makes you cry, makes you go back through the tunnel of memories and time. Till you stand in the vortex, watching a younger self, wishing you could give advice, tell her where not to go, where she went wrong, how, if she leaves half an hour earlier, or attends a certain dinner she once refused to, she would meet a certain man, not this one, not that one in the kitchen, simmering ratatouille. But it's all impossible, to reach back as she reaches forward, asking, always asking questions of her older self, at twenty, at thirty, now at fifty, she tries to peer at her self of sixty, seventy. It never works. The future woman walks away, face in shadow, body turned away, refusing to answer questions: "Live your own life!" she would be saying if she could talk. Instead you're left with the present, even as it dissolves rapidly into the past, memories swirling away.

Ailsa sighs, catches a piece of her auburn hair, pulls out a silver strand and holds it to the light, fascinated as always by the luminosity of her white hairs, the absence of pigment and the way sun shines right through.

CAT GOT YOUR TONGUE
Ken Barris

As THE BOY WALKED, a pale fire played about his mouth. He smiled at its heat. He felt loose and naked in his power. People passed him on the street, not noticing the flame: the sun was directly overhead. The only thing that afflicted him was the pain of his two missing fingers on the left hand. Not pain exactly, but he was bothered by their ghost presence. His thoughts turned over slowly but he was more alert than dreamy. A slow calm alertness that happened by itself.

He said his name aloud in faint golden letters of fire that the sunlight passed right through: Cain. That was his new name, since he had begun to change. He walked on for a long time, climbing the steep road that led out of the industrial district. Each step was a link in a chain of time that spelt Cain.

He was thirsty and his shirt was soaked at the small of his back. He stepped into a dark store. It took a while to adjust to the gloom. A Chinese businessman watched him with tired eyes, saying nothing. Cain went to the fridge and took a Coke. But there was no money in his pockets, no silver. He remembered money from before he had begun to change, but it didn't matter now. So he left. The owner of the store stayed where he was, his eyes more tired than before. He tried to remember something he had noticed, but it didn't matter anymore. Cain drank the Coke gratefully as he walked.

The sun came down slowly through the long afternoon. By the time it was staring into his eyes, he had left the town and was walking down the uneven road that wound through acre after acre of impenetrable black wattle. Sometimes a car shot by, the draught of its passage tugging at him. Only the odd vervet monkey sought Cain out, begging or watching him wisely, yawning, scratching itself as he passed. He thought one might accompany him, and so the next one did, jumping on his shoulder. It smelt warmly stained, very alive. Its black fingers clutched hard and it twitched finely at times, almost vibrating. When he was tired of the weight and the twitching he let the monkey go.

The moon was at its height before wattle gave way to pasturage, and he slept at the side of the road, in the thick damp grass. He dreamt his name, slowly, winding in and out of its architecture, through the empty chambers and crouching doorways of its letters: CAIN. Inside that building he was an ordinary boy. No flames played about his mouth. He ruled no monkeys or storekeepers. There was only a boy looking back, frightened and alone. There were many things he didn't want to remember — how he had lost his fingers, or why he had changed. There were images that he fought against. There was a tearing thing he remembered. He kept still and quiet in himself, not letting the images see him.

He was hungry when he woke up. Fire played about his mouth. He walked on, leaving the road. He came to a stream and washed himself in the ice-cold water, shuddering. He drank deeply. Later he came across a prickly pear thicket, left there by a farmer decades before to separate his fields. But there was no farmer now and the fields hadn't been ploughed for years. He picked pear after pear, carefully. He still had the knife; he had to wipe the blood off with moist grass. But there was no blood on the blade. It was something he remembered and thought he saw. Still, he wiped the blade many times. Then he cut the ends off the barrel-shaped pears, and cut each one neatly down the length. That way the thorny jacket could be opened. He ate the fruit slowly. Sound returned — the silver clicking of whidah as they swooped from bush to bush, crickets, and far away the drone of a chopper. He glanced at the sky and kept still until the noise of the helicopter faded.

Cain lay down and closed his eyes. His stomach was

swollen. He rested and remembered the noise his voice made speaking. He was speaking to the girl. He said: "This isn't my first life. I was born in the Bible times. I was Cain, you know the one who killed Abel." She had looked at him seriously, mirthlessly and said, "Sure you were Cain. I was Abel. You killed me. That's why you came looking for me in this life." He looked down at her feet and saw that they were beautiful and said, "You don't believe me." She didn't say anything. Her lips were pale, he remembered that. Her mouth was quiet, and she was waiting for something to happen. He didn't know what should happen. They were sitting on the beach, and it was getting dark, and the waves were beginning to wash up the sand towards them, reaching up slowly and falling back but still climbing on. Later, when he tasted her mouth it made him think of a fruit that no one had discovered yet, too ripe to bear. The memory made him stand up and walk on, leaving his voice behind but not the fire that still played about his mouth.

He walked all that day without seeing another human being. There were plenty of crows and hawks and other birds, and sometimes cows that watched him indifferently as he passed by. Then late in the afternoon he mounted a rocky plateau and came on a stone shack facing away from him. As he approached he saw that it stood on the lip of a shallow ravine, overlooking a calm and muddy river. A middle-aged man sat at a table on the crude porch, writing and sometimes sketching. He was bald and had thick glasses. He wore only a pair of shorts, and he was tanned, his skin leathery and dark. He looked up, surprised. He watched Cain suspiciously, his mouth slightly open.

His voice was gravel: "You walked here?"

Cain nodded, and waited.

"Cat got your tongue?"

Cain pointed at his mouth and shrugged. He didn't dare speak. He didn't want anyone to see the flame. Not yet. He didn't know what would happen then. He didn't know how much flame would shoot out if he spoke. How far, how hot.

"Mute? Can't speak?"

Cain nodded again. His fatigue poured out through the gesture. It was the fatigue of too much power not used enough. The man thought it was ordinary fatigue.

He said, "You're tired? You want something to drink?"

He nodded gratefully.

The man went into his shack and came out with a beer which he passed to Cain. It was tolerably cool. "I've got a paraffin fridge in there. It's not too bad." Cain drank deep, then raised the bottle to the man in appreciation.

"Name's Tubal. Don't suppose you can tell me your name. Wait a minute." He fetched Cain a notebook and pen. "Here."

Cain took these artefacts and held them passively. He shook his head.

"You can't write? What do you use to communicate? Smoke signals?"

Cain could write. He didn't want to; he needed to keep things simple. It was safer for everyone that way. He shrugged.

"That's fine," said Tubal. "I don't need to talk to anyone. That's why I'm here in the first place. Most people talk all day long, I don't. You can stick around if you want to. Beer's in the fridge. Help yourself. If you're hungry, open a can of beans. You'll find it there, inside." Tubal dismissed Cain as if the boy were a thing he had forgotten about and went back to his table. He stared out into the distance, then began sketching and writing again. Cain sat down against the wall and slowly drank the rest of his beer, guarding his light. He wondered what would happen to Tubal.

Tubal looked up. Cain was standing beside him, peering at his work. He laughed: "You can't write, but you can read? I thought you didn't add up." There was stone in his laugh. "Even if you read this, I wonder if you'll understand it."

Cain read silently: 'Fire is the generative element, and from its transformations all things are born. Condensed fire becomes steam; steam becomes water; water, through a further condensation, becomes earth.' The handwriting was firm, clear. He didn't understand it. There were drawings of a strange device, an arrangement of spheres and crystals, marked here and there in the characters of a language Cain had never seen before, perhaps Hebrew or Russian.

"You're reading Heraclitus, boy who can't read. I study the philosophers. I'm not a philosopher myself. I make things. I think of things to make."

Cain shook his head and stared down at the river. Something dark rose to the surface and sank again: a big catfish, bigger than a man, its mouth as wide as human shoulders. He looked back at Tubal. The older man was staring at him, shrewdly. It was hard to meet those eyes glinting through pebbles of glass.

"You're a canny one," said Tubal. "Not all here. Or something's here that you're not admitting to." Cain started, because he felt Tubal's gaze go right into him, solidly. "One of the two," said Tubal. "One or the other."

Cain went back to his wall and sat down. Tubal continued staring over the river, chewing his bottom lip. From time to time he scratched in his book, then rested. He said: "With this organ I aim to turn vibration into fire." Cain said nothing, gave nothing away. He thought: fire is my self. Tubal said: "A vibratory technics. That is the future."

After supper Tubal threw more firewood on the coals and the flame climbed hungrily. They stared into it, blinding themselves to the night. They could hear the night though, the tangible silence as well as the sounds of insects and more complex predators. A log of Port Jackson willow hissed and spat in the centre of the fire. Tubal remained in his shell, contentedly drinking whisky. Cain could feel Tubal's indifference, as if the older man were cased in a metal almost incorruptible such as bronze. Now that he was with someone, Cain felt lonely.

Tubal said, "Tell me your story, boy. I know you can speak."

Cain felt the arrogance in the word 'boy'. He could taste it: boy. Tubal's voice was gravel, rustling fragments that ground against each other. Cain pointed to the fire, and slowly his arm subsided. That was his story. Tubal didn't see the movement. It meant that all the leaping parts of the fire were separate and died rapidly but the fire lived on at least for a while. The word fire was a complete lie: the word was the same for all fires, and every fire was different, even to its own parts and to itself. Cain didn't know why that was his story.

"Cat got your tongue," said Tubal. "They said that when I was a boy. In those days when you were in trouble you kept quiet. You were ashamed. Then they said: cat got your tongue."

Tubal offered the flask, but Cain shook his head. He didn't like spirits. "What happened to your hand, boy? Your fingers."

Cain carefully took out his knife. He opened it and made slicing movements next to the mutilated hand.

"Someone cut you?"

Cain shook his head. He carefully folded the knife and put it back in his pocket.

"You cut yourself?"

Cain nodded, staring at the ground. He didn't want to look at Tubal's eyes, onyx behind the glasses and very small. "You were ashamed," said Tubal. "Very ashamed." Cain looked at the eyes then, but turned away at once. He felt trapped. Panic rose in his heart. Tubal held up his left hand. The two outer fingers were missing. Cain's head swam. Tubal laughed: "Nothing to do with shame. I was trying to make shelves. I cut them off on a circular saw." When he laughed, Cain tasted brass, unpolished brass. "Now I don't really make things. I think of things to make. That way nothing gets cut off." The logs in the fire collapsed, and sparks flared up, drifting some distance like burning insects still alive. "You remind me of myself," said Tubal, "when I was younger." He lay back on the ground and wriggled his back, finding a more comfortable position. "It's all got to do with sex of course." Then he lapsed into silence, while Cain kept very alert, very still, waiting and ready. A giant moth blundered out of the night and flew around him. He jerked his head away angrily. He was still clutching the knife when he fell asleep.

Things were different the next morning, down at the river.

Tubal had sent him down to fetch water. Cain squatted in the clay and stared at the water. He didn't feel calm, but the water was calm. Only then a murky black cloud rose in the centre of the river, and slowly moved towards him, or clarified itself in his direction. It sank briefly, then rose rapidly to the surface and then the mouth of the catfish broached. Its whiskers were easily further apart than the breadth of his shoulders. They stirred on the surface like slender water snakes, with a rotten intelligence of their own. The fish seemed to look at him; involuntarily, he scrambled back. The catfish sank down into the cold yellow water, and waited. He knew that it was still there, he could feel it in the yellow river, he could feel its cold blood and the lazy scudding of its tail against the current.

Cain still had to get the big plastic bottle filled. He forced himself back to the water and squatted, and forced the mouth of the bottle under. Water began to gargle in, rhythmically, as if it were being swallowed by the bottle. He kept an eye out for the catfish. He didn't think it would come in this shallow.

The bottle was nearly full. He had forgotten about it. It lay there on its side in the muddy warmth. He was thinking about how he had changed, and what he had done to the girl that night on the beach. After he had tasted her — after he was finished — her feet were pale, and still beautiful. Only they could not move. He wiped the blade carefully on her skin; but that was not enough. He couldn't get her blood off the blade, though he wiped it many times. He knew therefore that he had made God angry. God needed to put a mark on him. There was no question about it. He found a rock flat enough to use as a cutting board and rested his left hand on it, the fingers splayed out.

The catfish rose again, slowly. It was nearer now, maybe three yards away. Its muddy eye cleared the surface, glinted briefly. The fire in him ebbed, almost went out because of the terror the fish inspired. I could feed myself to the fish, he thought. River water lapped around his feet. The fish sank back, and became a cloud again. He could see its darkness. He straightened up, screwed the lid back onto the bottle. He thought for a minute that the two fingers were still in his pocket, that he could give them to the monster; but he had buried them, somewhere on his journey, a long time ago maybe. He turned back and began the steep climb, dragging the heavy bottle of yellow water.

Tubal was at his table, working at his papers and sketches. He stared at Cain, watched him contemptuously as he dragged the water onto the porch and let it thump down. "What's your name, boy?" asked Tubal. Cain shrugged. My name is fire. My name is burnt out. Silence filled him, a rage that was different, even to its own parts and to itself, and fire played around his mouth silently.

Tubal said, "You've walked out of the past, boy. You've walked into the future." He raised his maimed left hand: "You're my past — I'm your future. Maybe that's your name." He turned his head to the side and spat. Cain wondered what would happen to Tubal. His broken hand gripped the knife inside his pocket.

Cain sat against the wall of the porch, in the mounting heat of the morning. When Tubal wasn't looking he raised his face to the sun, and released a single jet of flame. It was invisible against the harsher cosmic light, but he knew its heat and when Tubal wiped sweat off his forehead, Cain smiled. He drank yellow water from the river to cool his mouth down.

The old man worked on his blueprint for a new vibratory technic and stared out across the river through his thick glasses. Cain fell asleep and dreamt a name for himself, spelling out progressions through the bronze halls and arches of the letters: TUBAL-CAIN. Inside that temple he was no longer a boy silenced by a monster catfish in a river. He was a maimed artificer who worked with fire and crystal and suffered little affiliation with the present moment.

A MOTHER, HER DAUGHTER, AND A LOVER
Roy Blumenthal

Prologue

A BIRD HUMS A descant to the melody of tyres on tar, the cars below. During a particularly powerful crescendo in the song, the bird swoops, flies, to a duet with the bass voice of a passing bus. It sings, the bird, a flute of wine, a vial of honey, then sounds a single percussive note against the speeding windscreen.

1. Spread
You taught me
about longing
when you sat
like that.

I SIT ON THE ground, one knee raised, elbow resting on that. Mother and daughter sit on chairs. All three with hands touching faces — a fist, a finger, a palm. A mother, her daughter, and a lover. And a choice.

"Open your eyes," says Katerina. I hear the smile hiding in her throat. "Come on, Geoff," she says, "open your eyes!" I feel my confidence oozing away, like a modest girl's breast oozing through her covering fingers when a boy walks in on her nudity. Bread dough and nipples and a bra on the floor.

She's definitely smiling. This is my first time naked with her. And her little ruse is as naked as she is — I peeked when I felt the breeze of her jeans whipping the air as they fell. I'm already naked. I had grown tired of pleading with her to strip with me. And so I closed my eyes when she told me she had a surprise for me.

My eyelids are mostly closed. The blob of her outline moves closer to me. I stand like an embarrassed soldier on a parade ground, ready to receive a medal for a routine bravery. And her hands clasp around my head, tender, touching the base of my skull where the hair ends. Her nipples hardening at this touch, blushing to a blurred dark brown. She caresses my hair and I open my eyes to the surprise of her body. Softly lined. Stretch marks where her daughter had burdened her.

My erection. The same blush as her nipples.

I push her hands away, and she resists, too slightly. I close my eyes again, search along her arm — from the hand towards the armpit, softly, with my fingertips only — for her face. She puts both hands over my eyes and puts her lips over mine. We are bending toward each other, our bodies separate. And then she puts her nipples against mine. We kiss.

2. Wet

> *You leaned over*
> *to read my screen*
> *and doused me*
> *with a wet dream.*

"GEOFF IS A FRIEND of Anja's," Katerina says. "What are you studying again?" The corona of her eye is speckled green and brown, a rather becoming connection of colours, moving well with the light brown of her hair. Funny that she would choose a red blouse.

"I'm not studying any more," I say. "But I have done a drawing course. I write."

We're talking to a big man with a vast beard and a pony tail. Some kind of chef. The exhibition is his girlfriend's. "Oh," he says. His eyes glaze a little. "How's Anja?"

Katerina answers. "She moved out of home last month. Lives in Yeoville now. Foolish."

"She's very in awe of her mother," I say to the man.

Katerina says, "Actually, she's very jealous of me. Accuses me of all sorts of things."

The big man nods at us, and a figure trips past us. He moves off to a different spiral of concentration, his body coiling like a dancer's. Katerina and I wander off to study a peach-coloured tapestry. The colours are almost all the same. Just subtle gradations. An important work? I look into her eye, searching for flecks of peach.

We are standing close to each other, closer than party-time protocol would allow without consequences. She has talked about our age difference, talked about being seen with me. She calls it 'The Age Thing'. But tonight she doesn't flinch. She is the one standing close to me. A test?

I drank too much at the opening. Katerina was angry. "You can't dismiss this stuff by talking about 'taste'!"

I said, "I don't like it. I don't care how important this chick is."

"She's a woman, goddammit, not a chick! And it's not about

her. It's about her work."

"Yeah yeah. Full of craft. Attention to detail. Thanks," I said. The burly man was off to one side talking to an art critic, or maybe a food critic. He made all the snacks. Very good they were too. Best exhibition opening I've eaten at. I waved at him and pointed at the blank, subtle peach-hanging. "I'll take ten please!" I said, and Katerina slapped me. I went home alone.

Hangovers only suit a certain kind of person. I had to drink a litre of water this morning before I could stand properly. And then I had to wait for a few hours to get rid of the alcohol smell burnt into my tongue. And then I went to Stuttafords.

Right now I'm wearing a skirt. I look at myself often in the mirror to see if I'm still feeling comfortable with it. I look like one of those straight, thin, British women who don't wear well. The bulge of my crotch looks disconcertingly large as I survey myself. The thought gives me an alarming erection. It's lucky that I'm wearing underpants.

It's strange, this, my wearing a skirt. It was exhilarating for me to go and buy it. I'm very obviously male, and the shop assistants were curious. But I had already resolved to tell them nothing. Except that I wanted a functional calf-length skirt with deep pockets. "Who is it for?" asked one. Was it excitement that lifted her eyebrows?

"Please measure me for size," I said, and she paused an instant too long, like somebody pretending that they are mistakenly falling into a pool at a drunken party. She whipped a measuring tape round my waist.

They made me change in the men's change rooms. I couldn't make my erection go away. When I emerged, there were three sales assistants, all of them pretty in their own ways, all staring at my crotch. They were probably actually only staring at the skirt. I wanted to fuck them all, immediately, but I had promised myself that I would do nothing of the sort. Between the three of them, they had managed to find about thirty skirts for me to try on. And they insisted that I try them all.

The high waist is very uncomfortable at first. And so is the exposed feeling of my groin. It feels as if anybody can just come up and grab it.

3. *Waitress*
> *Smile sealed*
> *with lipstick*
> *and a stolen smoke;*
> *table cloth like paté.*

"ANJA?" THOUGH I WISH to speak her name aloud, I do not. Will not.

She says, "She's my fucking mother! How can you?"

I want to say, "But Anja, you and I have never had a thing, we've never even touched each other." But I stay quiet and she rants.

"You're fucking my mother and the whole town knows about it before I do!" She is sounding very shrill. When I go falsetto, I get to that pitch with difficulty. My throat feels very fragile that high.

I reach out, and my hand makes contact with her shoulder. She shrugs hard, and swats at me.

"Don't touch me!" She spits a little as she screams the words, and her voice slides over into ragged danger.

I touch her again, this time pinning her shoulder in my hand. She flails, and hits at me. I hang on and then, as she whirls at me, striking at my face, I slip my other hand under her blouse. She stops moving instantly. I've not seen her astonished like this before. My fingers knead at her breast, and she is rigid. Her mouth is open, and I can see the top of her gums, little pink nodules wet against the white of her teeth. She has whiter teeth than her mother.

I release her shoulder and slide my free hand under her skirt. A hand up her skirt and a hand up her blouse. And she is making tiny gasping sounds as I move my hands over her.

Her skin. Smooth, unwrinkled. They're so alike, these women. The same responsive nipples. The shape of the hair at the nape. They share a nape.

She leaves. Ricochets in her footsteps.

I frown and a distant headache starts and my hand reaches to touch, to explore. But I forget. My hand forgets and falls to my side. I must type something, before this passes out of my experience: *Her echoing ricocheting cold stone floor footsteps tread in me and squishing damaged sounds playing through head inside brains wormy squishing. She put bare hand into skull into my skull mine? takes handful slimy red squeeze little rhythm humming. Locked on chair. Room small.*

> *4. Bomb*
> *I wake to a blurred mosquito*
> *in the shut night.*
> *Then, a second waking:*
> *a thunderclap*
> *snaps on sirens*
> *to light my curtain.*

I'M LISTENING TO ELVIS Costello. The song is 'Inch by Inch' on *Goodbye Cruel World*. It's difficult to concentrate, but I'm trying hard.

The song has changed now. To 'Worthless Thing'. I'm wearing headphones. The sound of the music, the clatter of my typewriter — yes, a typewriter, a real, Olivetti-portable-circa-1943 typewriter — and the vibrations from the passing cars and trucks are doing strange things to my sense of balance.

An empty block of flats in stark, raw concrete bleaches the green of the trees. The building catches my attention because there are many windows with no curtains. There are weeds growing from the roof, which I only see once I put my glasses on. "Katerina?" I say. "Look at those weeds!" They're impoverished weeds, pale and thin, looping over into topographical nightmares in their attempts to escape. They want to join the green of the tall trees beside them. The trees reach up three storeys higher than the flats. "Katerina?" She is old enough to have seen these things before.

She has stepped into the room. I reach for her, to kiss her. I notice that her blonde hair is across her face, like bars.

I have ordered flowers. Not just for her. For me too. The smell of a manipulated red rose. That thin, almost offensive prickling of perfume. And the colours. Fuller than lipstick.

Pock-marked paper. I look about my room, our room, wondering how to describe it, what to leave out. The earphones dig into my skull, and I adjust them. Elvis Costello is on repeat.

There is a green cotton scarf at the foot of the bed, lying on a soft brown and cream blanket. I see the lump of my feet lifting an envelope, addressed, ripped open. The typewriter, small but heavy, is on my lap. The pale blue towel hanging over the desk chair is dry. The come stains are yellowing in places. The desk has a case of cassettes. And four piles of books, about half a metre high. The walls are white with Spanish plastering, a mirror, two paintings I made at school, and a huge photograph of a man's eye, stolen from a midnight bus shelter. A pile of shoes is visible beyond the bed, beside the dustbin. A red clock, a yellow lamp, within reach, linked in morning function. An empty coffee cup on the floor. And a stack of clothes on the small pine bench. Almost unchronicled — the fluffy toys above the rough-weave curtains.

And lurking under the clothes in my discarded pocket, in the loneliness of my abandoned trousers, the note, the note from her daughter.

I sniff the air and think of the sound of crickets.

My typewriter is on my lap, small but heavy: *I waited on the roadside, noting the cloud banking around my horizon in the north. I said, "Shit!" and looked around to see if there was anyone around to offend by that. But there wasn't. Just me and my horizon.*

The temperature dropped and I wished that I still had the coat. I shouldn't have sold it.

I said the word again: "Shit." No real reason.
The horizon, my horizon, got closer with each step I took along
this road. I would soon be wet and possibly swearing freely, wearing
the shape of the words. And I knew that no car was going to stop for
me.
"Fuck you!" I scream, and steam is now in my breath. Hell might
be talking to me. And now I'm shaking all over. Cold, fear, exhilara-
tion?
I'm probably going to freeze to death tonight. Last winter at least
I had a coat.

5. Encounter
  Hair bunned tight a
  scarab at her crown
  liquid english in her mouth
  to say "my name
  is Anja".

ANJA'S SUNGLASSES MUST HAVE cost
a fair amount. Her black hair suggests coolness and comfort;
her perfect lips invite ice. "I want you to make a choice," she
says. Her voice is even, low. No sign of the shattering she gave
it last week.

"So you were a virgin," I say.

"Me or my mother."

"Come in if you like." She stares at me through her sunglasses, past the open door. "I'll leave it unlocked," I say, and
pull it closed.

I sit on my balcony, waiting for Anja to come inside. I have
an old wooden folding chair that lists to one side. The sky is
dimming out, losing its glare. A cloud is travelling this way; its
shadow distorts the road, cancelling out the heat haze. The
cloud is white, but it has dark portions which seem to swirl
and move in odd gyrations. It is a large machine fighting itself,
trying to arrest its own motion, defeating itself all the time.

And who can win when defeat and victory are the same?
Anja walks to her car. She doesn't look up. She gets in and
drives off.

> 6. *My waitress*
> *Anja with a smile*
> *spreading through her walk*
> *into her voice.*
> *I'm falling in love*
> *listening to her restaurant.*

THE HAIRCUT WENT OFF without a
hitch, but I have little segments of hair lodged in my collar.
They don't come out. I'm going to itch sporadically for the next
few years. Which is to say, whenever I wear this shirt.

Anja seems to be talking to me again. She has popped in to
visit. We are on the balcony, and she has just apologised for
standing on the landing like that. "It's okay," I tell her. I am
trying to figure out the smile.

She says, "My mother is going to have an exhibition."

"I know."

"Are we alike? In bed."

"She's a very talented artist."

"How do I compare?"

"I didn't know you were thinking of being an artist," I say.

She starts unbuttoning her shirt. A man's shirt, with cow-
boy embroidery on the shoulders and over the pocket.

"I've got some writing to do," I say. But it is already too late.

A bus goes past the window, and the cracks shudder under
their masking-tape anchors. The truth is that the cracks are
travelling away from the centre, looking for a way out of their
pseudocrystalline frame.

I've just walked back from the barber. A short walk. And
then a longer haul up the stairs. Anja said she counted the
stairs yesterday. I can't remember how many. She remembers
more than I do. And her mother remembers more than she
does.

My shirt is back on, and Anja has gone home. Or maybe she has gone to visit her mother. I pass my hand around the inside of my collar. I study my fingers and notice a fresh crop of the little hairs. Looking in the mirror, straining around, I can see little red rash bumps appearing. It is a white shirt with brown hair.

I'm waiting for the bus to come again. I too am travelling to the periphery of my frame.

> *7. I, poem*
> *Open on your page:*
> *you trace me with your fingers*
> *with your eyes:*
> *my face asks*
> *to blur against your cheek.*

HIS FIXATION ON THE *walking makes him pause and look for an excuse for the interruption. His head swivels to take in the road beneath him. He bends to retie a shoelace. There is a piece of grass — hard, yellow — stuck in a lace-hole. He doesn't notice it hard enough to remove it. He is puzzled at walking so long. He wants to feel tired, but instead he feels vague.*

A hike once with his schoolmates and a hailstorm, zero-degree rain, and exposure and near-death from the buzzing numbness of hypothermia. An unsuccessful attempt at lighting a veld fire.

He rises from the half-crouch and dusts his hands on his jeans. As he begins again to walk, he notices the yellow starkness of the dust he is on. Where beach sand looks warm and rich, this dust is just as fine, but hard, hard. He feels his eyes shift to avoid looking at the road. The yellow powder cakes into the corners of his eyes like sleep.

He stumbles through a pot-hole in this road and finds that he has been walking asleep or hypnotised or empty. He is trying to avoid the dust.

I've noticed a fixation. I'm listening for the sound of cars and buses and other traffic. Anja's car has a loose exhaust. Katerina's door makes a shooshing sound when it shuts, and she always closes it twice.

There are loud voices sounding from over the edge of my balcony, men's voices, unpleasant, but not angry, not aggressive. They stop as suddenly as they emerged. Maybe they've been eaten by the car door?

Toilet-rolls look at home in toilets. I once dipped a toilet-roll in a basin and then watched it as it dried. It seemed to dry like anything else, but slowly. It crinkled like a chicken's plucked neck. Eventually I put it in the microwave oven.

Passed a blob on the road,
about the size of a discarded
balaclava or an overgrown rag;
its colour was an oily blue, and
it seemed to my eye
to have a suede feel.
Passed another blob,
and saw it crawl and turn its head
to study a catseye on the yellow line.
Somebody tossing pedigree
puppies from a moving window.

> *8. Kiss me yes or kiss me no*
> *Say you love me*
> *or say goodbye.*
> *Kiss me fleetingly.*
> *Or slow.*

MY RESTING PULSE IS 56 beats per minute. I am having trouble with this clock beside my bed. It ticks in two different ways: a tick and a tock. The tick or the tock appears precisely on the second. Problem is, there's no discernible pattern — it's impossible to know which one it will be. Tick tock tock tock tick. Or tock tick tock tick tock tock.

Confessions of a non-Roman Catholic pre-ordained unadorned unadulterated shamelessly climaxing confession booth bug: "Her lips grazed the mesh and she inhaled the passions of an eternity of sinners. She tasted their spit and fed on silence. She spoke."

Katerina looks movie-good, which is to say, someone might well tell her that she looks like Jane Seymour's older sister. In about seventeen minutes she will be woken from this deep sleep by my defective red plastic alarm clock. It has a repeater function, so we can sleep in tense three-minute bursts.

Her car is parked under one of the tall trees. Car alarms can be set to go off in three-minute cycles. Car thieves don't fall asleep on the job.

I am writing on a loose sheet of paper, with a pen. She doesn't like me typing in bed while she sleeps. I will have to type this up when she leaves: *He breathed deeply, three times, and told himself to go ahead, to do it. His jaws clenched and he rubbed his hands against his trouser legs, smoothing the material, warming his legs slightly. The muscle bulge at his temple jumped around, a cyst joking about liberation. Another deep breath. A sighing sound. And then he stood, suddenly impatient, ready.*

When I first met Anja, I was waiting in a long queue at the car licensing department. Almost a hundred people were ahead of me, with a good double that number behind. The man behind me had sweat on his lip. And hair. A moustache. Black hair. I peered over the head of the fourth person in front of me to try to get a glimpse of the fifth person in front of me. I had seen her only briefly as I approached the queue. She had held my gaze for a full second before tossing her head and swinging black hair across her eyes. She used her left forefinger to flick it back over her head. It hung straight down until she flicked it again.

Later, after I'd gotten to know the two of them, I asked Anja how her hair came to be dark. "Such a contrast to your mother's blonde," I said.

"My father," she said.

"But you and your mother look alike."

"Ha ha ha."

"You do!" I said, and we made love again.

He waited a while to see if 'The Entity' would get her. But his mom wanted him to change channels, because she was frightened. But he held the remote control, guarding the buttons. He used his other hand to ward off a headache by pressing into his temples. He made his mother wait until 'The Entity' got her.

There was a silence, a lull in the normal music, a pause, a hole, and the television screen was throwing black light into the furthest corners of the room. Inside the screen, the woman looked in, silently, on her sleeping children. "I can't watch!" said his mom, and she pressed his index finger, which in turn pressed the channel change. The screen spewed colour into the room, and a man with a piano accordion played folk music.

He was sitting beside his mother, clutching his head in numbing fingers, blood rising under his fingerprints like a blush to his temples.

9. Cold
You swirl
in the mist
of your
outbreath.

"GOOD NIGHT, GEOFF," SAYS Anja. She is standing near the bed. She will bend down and peck me on the cheek. I have developed an almost unconquerable lethargy. It refuses to let me sleep, but it also keeps me immobile. The moment my eyes fuzz over, a sick feeling in my stomach turns to an agitation. I have a spastic colon. It is caused by stress.

"Good night, Anja," I say. She doesn't kiss me.

I have sprayed long-lasting insect killer on my floor to try to prevent a flea panic. There is now a dying moth flapping around in a bewildered haziness. It will flap until it dies.

Earlier, before we made love, I brought the dustbin from the kitchen into the lounge. I started clipping my nails, trying to get them down into the rubbish. But more often than not, they flew somewhere else. "Do that in the bathroom," said Anja.

She was on the easy chair, reading, but I couldn't see the cover of her book because my glasses were in the bedroom. I carried on clipping my nails. The one on my left ring finger was cut too close. I flinched, and Anja looked up. I carried on clipping. The finger is still sore. Tender, really.

I have made myself get out of bed. I am eating a late supper — cheese, tomato and salami on bread. I have decided to do some reading. I have noticed that when I'm alone my hand reaches down and plays with my crotch. The book I'm reading is *Great Expectations* by Charles Dickens.

I'm looking past my curtain into the reflective darkness. The constant blurred buzz of night-time traffic makes me think of holding a shell to my ear. The shell here must be big, outside my window, unseen.

Pock-marked paper: *"Where are you going?!" he screamed, twisting his head in a violent jerk. A tiny spot of saliva arced from his mouth. It landed on and clung to her dress, on the nipple. She lunged at the door, flinging it wide to smash against the wall. She strode out, leaving the door to bounce into an equilibrium.*

He stayed in his chair and listened to her footsteps crushing the pavement away. He breathed deeply and smoothed his trousers with uneasy movements of his thick fingers. A knot of movement in his temple played counterpoint to the tension in his jaw. He made a shaky sighing sound, and stood, and his hands continued their smoothing of his trousers. The friction warmed him.

> 10. *For I have left*
> *Her arm across my chair*
> *as I curl closer into myself*
> *to drive her away.*

HELLO. MY NAME'S BERT *and I'm a flower deliveryman. They asked me to say a thing with my experiences, you know, in the job. This oke said I must say it in the tape. But I'm shit scared cos I'm not a educated oke. He said any hassles they would fix, but still, I don't want to make fuck ups.*

I don't know what experiences to talk about, you know, I see so many people in a day. I do about thirty deliveries every day. I like my job because I see some nice people and I make them happy with the flowers you know.

But one day I got sent out there to Vereeniging and there was this funny house, like small, you know, and it had a funny garden. There was this strange thing there in the garden. Like there was all these dead trees which were planted, but they were planted in concrete, you know, like a washing line pole. All these trees had plastic flower pots hanging off them with ferns and creepers growing in the pots. It looked quite nice, because the trees were painted black and varnished. I never saw a thing like that before.

Hey and the one time this oke must of had a affair and his wife must of found out. Cos he had me deliver one rose on February 1, two roses on February 2, three roses on February three. You know. Until on Valentine's day I had to give her fourteen roses. And she looked like a really nice woman.

The feeling of restedness starts to saturate Katerina's sleep, and she twitches. Her daughter is a much more solid sleeper, but she doesn't stay much anymore. In due course Katerina will start stirring, even pushing her hands into the air without waking. Then she'll spring up to go to the toilet for her early morning piss. But for now, she is asleep.

"I'm old enough to be your mother," she told me last night.

"Clichés," I said.

"Geoff ..."

"Katerina."

"Nothing."

Her eyelids twitch and she starts to dream. I don't know what she's dreaming. But she will tell me when she wakes.

"Are you sleeping with my daughter?" she asked me.

"I'm sleeping with you."

"You've been fucking her, haven't you?" No smile. Her daughter smiles under pressure. Katerina looks dour.

"I want to model for you," I said.

She shook her head. "Too intimate. Can't see my subject properly if I'm fucking him."

When she returns from her piss, she'll tell me her dream. This is what I predict she will say: "*A thin man with olive skin and green swimming shorts steps up to me and leans forward, gaping like a contented fish. I ask his name and he replies in a silent fish gape. All I see is the chasm of his mouth and the shape of his eyebrows. Suddenly I'm standing in a shopping mall, plastic plantlife tearing away at my stockings in a placid, non-aggressive way. I'm carrying piles of parcels which I'm smiling about. Then, still smiling, I start tossing them away, as if I'm feeding a hungry mob of pigeons.*"

The eye movement stops, and she stops twitching. A frown has appeared on her lips. The clock ticks beside her. The frown disappears with a movement of her head, and her face re-emerges from her hair corona.

She will stay asleep until five minutes before the alarm goes off, and will forget to switch it off before rushing off to the toilet. She will be halfway through pissing when it does go off, and she'll rush back to the bedroom, panties at her ankles, to silence it. She will glare at me.

I am good at predictions. I will not predict when she will leave me or when her daughter will leave me.

> *11. February*
> *This new month*
> *finds an emptier bed*
> *to penetrate with its chills,*
>
> *a bed I can spread-eagle on*
> *to search the perimeter,*
> *to find the edges of my warmth.*

THE SEXUAL IDIOM OF the time is expressed in a revealing way. Women have taken to wearing vulva-shaped dresses, with all the right colouring. Stockings are striped, and seem designed to lead the eye up the leg, to the mock-vulva their owners are sporting.

Men have taken to wearing delicate haircuts which require precision tossing of the head.

I look over the edge of my balcony. This morning flatland is unbustling. A man is standing on his balcony. Right near the edge. He is masturbating. Silently. He has started moving his arm faster, and his face contorts. For a moment his eyes close. But now he licks his palm, quickly, but when he resumes he's moving more slowly, building up again. He's enjoying the vista before him. I've seen him doing this only once before.

There. His face contorts once more, and this time the silent scream pours onto the street, trickling down to the daisies potted below. He wipes himself off with a towel. His scrotum is very hairy.

His semen is clearly powerful. A woman in a vulva dress emerges from the house across the road and rushes like springtime to pick the daisies.

Somebody next door is coughing. In the last few days, Jonathan Livingstone Seagull has entered and left my consciousness. Behind my eyes are the seething red dots of sleeplessness.

I've been cleaning Katerina's oil paint tubes, forcing the lids off, scraping old caked rubbish from the tips. My nails appear to be torn and bleeding and bruised. She has abandoned her paint.

Anja is here. She thumps her fists against my chest and grabs my hands. "Can't you leave her paints alone?" she says. Her lips have taken the shape of her mother's, and I want to kiss her.

"Some lunch?" I say, pulling my hands back. She looks at me. That slight smile again.

She touches the side of her neck with four fingers. "I want you to touch me. With her wet paint. Paint on me."

"I'm going to make sandwiches now. They won't take

long." I walk to the bread basket. Before I reach it, I pause, reach for the withered flowers I had ordered so long ago. I pluck them from their vase, bin them. A smooth movement.

The storm outside hangs back like a suppressed cough waiting for the inevitable. I prefer not to believe in things inevitable.

The rain hits my window in time to my typing: *She hugged herself once, for a long while, to give herself comfort. Then she opened her knife and sliced longways from the inside of her wrist down to halfway to her elbow. As if tuning her classical guitar, getting ready to play, she inserted her index finger into the slit, found the artery, plucked it to emit a note.*

The sound did not please her. It was rather metallic, and slack. Looping the artery over her finger, she squeezed it delicately with her thumb. Then she twisted a loop into it. Rotating her hand she looped it again and then again.

Moments before the snap, she realised that the tension had been almost right, almost ready for playing.

My curtains are parted slightly, in the middle, near the bottom. A bit of window is peeking at me. I don't want to get up. I'm naked. The window is glaring at me, a shard of sly ice.

It is roughly time for me to go to sleep. The two people next door are out watching a movie. I couldn't make out which one they chose. They were talking too softly. But it should have finished at least two hours ago.

I must put a T-shirt on. I will be naked tonight, but I will have a T-shirt on.

My door jamb is not tight, and the draft from my window is making the door knock against the frame. A dull sound. Like a painter slapping a pallet knife against a wooden pallet. The draft is chilling my arm, ridiculing my nudity, sighing seductively.

12. Visit
I touch your photograph
too often
for my heart to heal.

I'VE BEEN SPENDING A lot of time on my bed. Lying down has become my occupation. The ginger cat from across the road is lying here with me, snoring. My typewriter is on my pillow, and I'm typing with one hand, at an angle.

"But I'm not going to abuse you." An off-hand remark. Except that it comes from the cat. A touch of sadness in the movement of the whiskers and the orange tail.

I don't like telephones. You can't really have a conversation at all, because maybe you're not really in the mood, or the other person on the line isn't. And neither of you can tell. The sound isn't attached to your body. And looking at the plastic mouthpiece and crying into it is not a happy thing to do.

There is a pencil lying on the desk, unsharpened, ineffectual. An eraser nearby confirms its impotence. Both are static, waiting for a person's hand to compel them into a dynamic system of action and interaction. Paper is outside that closed system. It is being raped by my typewriter: *Like countless amateur politicians, he is allowed to gabble about the 'state-of-the-nation' with complete impunity. "I think we should wipe them off the face of the earth," he said, shifting his eyes around to see if 'them' were within wiping distance. They were nowhere in sight. "This shit's been going on long enough. Somebody better put a stop to it." He fingered the knot of his tie as if it were the cause of the rash on his neck. "I'm normally pretty moderate," he said, and probed under the collar with a fat finger and a manicure, "but things are getting out of hand."*

I'm looking for dreams to enter my consciousness so I can analyse myself with awareness. It becomes difficult looking at my cassette cases. Here are the Bach Cello Suites, and here are

The Pogues. There is the broken Walkman lying beside them. Television calms me. All the violence, all the trouble. It all comes out fine in the end. Problems really are coped with. How do they get the scenes to change so smoothly?

I wait in the lobby, a lavish place with a lot of mahogany and burgundy and gormless prints of oil paintings. Overstuffed sofas line the walls, and tiny coffee tables pretend to be functional. A big man in a second-hand suit appears at the door. He hesitates, looks around, almost awed by his surroundings.

He comes closer and shakes my hand. Softly. We exchange names, and I forget his instantly. It is his face that interests me. Curly dark-blonde sideburns curve upward to join his eyebrows in a slab over the bridge of his nose.

We pass a silver mirror near the door, and the black dots of rust injure my companion's reflection.

I'm listening to the radio. Katerina is beside me, not bothering to feign interest. Just lying, calm, eyes maybe staring at nothing in particular. "Why are you here?" I say. Her mouth just pulls into emptiness. She seems to be finding it difficult to pretend to be happy.

Just before she goes, she says, "Have you met Anja's boyfriend? He owns a five-star hotel. Have you met him?" She leaves her oils behind. Maybe she wants to come back again.

> *13. After the Beep*
> *The only messages*
> *I'm sending you*
> *are those*
> *on my answering machine.*

THE FOYER DOORS SLID *open and I felt the chill of air-conditioning as I stepped out. My throat closed against the sanitised air, and I made my way towards the lifts. As I passed the reception desk, I noticed a face in the foyer turning suddenly away, as if it had been caught in the act of staring at me. I looked aside, keeping him in the corner of my vision.*

The face turned again to search mine. I looked at him, boldly, and our eyes met until the lift bell tinged. Our eyes had us fucking our brains out on an unromantic bed, he straddling me and sweating, his cheeks flicking in rhythmic jerks as he moved, my hair streaming over my writhing eyes.

I am hiding here. Nobody knows me and I can be alone with myself. I have walked back into the lobby after a short spell at the beach, and another man is staring at me. He seems to think I am staring back, judging by the furtive leer, the cocking of his brows.

I move to the lifts, press the 'up' arrow, wait. Their eyes are on me. Their mouths are open slightly, suggesting a kind of invitation, or the hope that I will accept the possibility of an invitation. There is a tinging sound coming from the lift. I step inside.

His gaze had caught mine across the foyer. My nostrils had, I am free to admit, flared, and I felt colour erupting on my cheeks and on the tips of my ears. I had sailed into the lift as the doors parted with a ting. Somebody got in with me. A balding man with a pot-belly. He smells of sweat and deprivation. He looks down at my skirt and immediately studies the ceiling.

I find myself stepping out on the third floor, and my heart races in the sudden panic that I might not remember my room number. My first impulse is to jump back into the lift and head for the reception desk, but the lift is already closed, sailing up the shaft like an over-sexed bellboy. After some moments of near-terror, I realise I am clutching my key. The number is on the tag.

LESIBA THE CALLIGRAPHER
Zachariah Raphola

LESIBA SCREAMED WHEN HE woke from his nightmare. As wakefulness took possession of him he was struck by three things: a sour taste in his mouth, the meowing of his neighbour's cat, and recollections of the dream. It was the third time in five years that the same dream had recurred. Each time he would be wading through a snake-infested pit. There was this one green and blue snake that would strike his heel, and his attempts to bash its head were always unsuccessful. He was not overly concerned about the bad omen it might carry. Rather he was irritated by the fact that it delayed the completion of his 'Book of Dreams', a diary in which he recorded all his dreams, past and present.

He was already at Chapter 102. Unlike previous times, when he would dismiss the dream, he started thinking about potential enemies among his friends: Peter, Sonto, Mandla and Eddie. The last was the one who was giving signs of growing into a rival. In the past they had clashed over women. There were also his work colleagues. Among these, Ketso, his departmental supervisor, was the one with the potential for trouble. Though married, he was determined to frustrate Lesiba's chances of *jolling* with Benita. He knew though, that Ketso was not a threat. The man was a bad dresser and a lousy smoker who was still stuck on BB Tobacco in the era of Peter Stuyvesant. He couldn't charm women or tell convincing lies. His only speciality was blabbing about his subordinates to the bosses. It was common talk that Ketso's position was more of an affirmative action gesture than a recognition of competence.

Outside his door, lording it over the whole township, there was *Bra* Shine, the one with the perpetually clean-shaven scalp, and *Bra* Morgan, who had a *panga* scar running down the left side of his face. Both were rumoured to be members of the local Big Five gang. Both drove colossal Be-My-Wife BMWs. Though they were forever associated with this or that crime, no life-valuing gossip monger was foolish enough to suck onto any of those rumours. Lesiba was one of these clever ones.

Jwalane was his common-law wife. She was based in Craighall Park as a live-in domestic maid. He saw very little of her. The few times she visited him in the township, she brought food parcels, most of which he was certain had been 'self-donated' from the madam's kitchen; another aspect of wealth redistribution on a small scale. He thanked his ancestors for such a considerate wife. It enabled him to spend his extra cash on luxuries like horse betting and regular church pilgrimages to different parts of the country.

It was only when he missed her that he used to consider getting himself *mmane-a-bana*. Those brought their own problems: money and the other men they were involved with.

He knew that men of his times — those of one or two generations before — were brave and passionate enough to kill over a woman, if not to marry her then at least to settle her with a dozen kids and spend the next ten years lamenting the lack of virgins to marry.

Jwalane ... could he depend on her? But then most women were loving and caring enough to spurn the advances of humble men besotted with them in favour of jackpots like *Bra* Shine and *Bra* Morgan who were so obsessed with money that they were prepared to kill for it — but not work to earn it.

He thanked his ancestors for their stinginess in not giving him even a semblance of wealth. He was certain that if they had, *Bra* Shine and his *bras* would've repossessed it a long time ago.

The dream of the snake-infested pit ... That was not the only dream he dreamt. There were others. Dreams that used to mount him and ride him to strange lands. Dreams that took him through streets paved with human flesh and bones. And there were times when bits of his own flesh would peel off to merge with the tar spread on those streets.

His reflections about the dreams were disturbed by the sound of an AK-47 rifle. There was no need to panic for he knew it was only one of the Big Five gang engaged in target practice in preparation for yet another bank robbery. With that comforting thought he went back to sleep.

Arriving at work the following day he found Ketso at his locker. On seeing him the latter hastily scurried away. The previous night's dream came back to mind. Lesiba resolved to give the locker a thorough search later. He went out looking for Mandla.

"Hey, *monna*, what was old Kickso doing in my locker?"

"Scouting for love notes from Benizo!"

"I'm serious, man. That *ndala* is up to something."

"Take it easy! He was probably after your lunch."

"I don't believe that. You know Kickso doesn't go for your smiley and runaways. He is a guy for pizzas and buffet tables." They enjoyed ridiculing their supervisor.

Lesiba gave his locker a thorough scrutiny. After patient searching he found what he was looking for — a coppery piece of tree bark. He wrapped it in a sheet of A4 typing paper and took it home.

His dreams that night were elusive. He could not pin any of them down. He would see faces and figures but they would lose their profiles the minute he tried to focus on them. The customary numbers that had helped him throughout the years to bet correctly with the Chinaman and on the horses were also elusive that night. It was then that he regretted having brought home Ketso's coppery charm. Once more the completion of his Book of Dreams was to be deferred because of a lousy error.

Three days later he dreamt that he had lost the ability to dream. That was not the only dream he dreamt. There were others: dreams that would unfurl curtains before his eyes and screen gory pictures of his death on a spit. Dreams that unreeled with scenes of his dismemberment by wild dogs. At times it was punishment for fondling altar girls. At other times for pickpocketing infirm beggars.

The dreams so shocked him that he resolved to go and consult a *nyanga* the following day. The man endowed with ancestral powers addressed him: "Thank your ancestors for leading you to me in time. Had you wasted one more day, I tell you, your enemies are already sharpening their teeth to feast at your funeral

"There is a man ...? A tall, dark complexioned man ...? There is a woman. Sometimes she steals your gourd and drinks from your stream. But I see her stealing from the streams of other men as well. Avoid her, her mouth is cursed and contaminated with the saliva of wild animals ...? There is a big tree ... The tall dark man sometimes hides behind its trunk, sometimes he climbs it. His shadow always hangs around you. He absorbs all the sun's rays meant for you ...? I also see pages written, many lines of parables. The parables float around you. Mostly you grab them, but of late they drift farther and farther away ... Angry shadows hover around you. They want your parables ..."

When the consultation ended, Lesiba was dazed. Arriving late at work, he told a lie: that his taxi had been involved in an accident. He noticed that everybody looked at him queerly. All were distant and aloof. Whenever he approached any of his colleagues they would disperse.

After his visit to the *nyanga* he changed the title of his book to 'Book of Dreams and Parables'.

That night he again dreamt of the snake pit. The snakes all had human faces, those of his colleagues, neighbours, and relatives. This time, though, he was able to make additions to his book.

The dream that would lead to his social ruin followed. It was a couple of weeks before the 1984 period of political turmoil. He called it Dream Number 109, as it was his practice to number them. He saw black smoke descending over

Alexandra. Men and women were choking and vomiting before falling down and dying in the alleys and gutters. An angel came and lifted him up above the smoke. He made the terrible mistake of telling the dream to his priest during confession. He could tell the priest didn't like it by the way he frowned. Much later he was called by the archbishop to clarify the matter. He was instructed never to tell other church members the dream and to renounce the part about the angel as blasphemy. He was not surprised, therefore, days later, to see the archbishop address a press conference where he told of the tragedy that would befall Alexandra.

When the insurrection erupted ten days later the archbishop was hailed as a latter-day Nostradamus. Journalists besieged his house and converts joined his church in droves. Lesiba secretly hoped to be promoted to the position of elder, but that never came. Instead he was ostracised and accused of aspirations to usurp the archbishop's position.

After that episode he learned to keep his dreams to himself. He resolved to keep the book a secret. He spent sleepless nights consuming ink and paper recording and revising the dreams. After recording sessions lasting several weeks he would go out gallivanting. It wasn't long before he fell victim to the consequences of that revelry: losing the power to record or retain his dreams. This worried him a lot.

He consulted one of the church elders.

"Your ancestors are angry. They are taking what they gave. Worse will follow. Stop your gluttony, stop your carousing," the elder cautioned. Lesiba pondered over these instructions.

Finally he concluded it was better to sacrifice the pleasures of life, not out of desperation to finish the book or a desire for the fame it might bring him, but because he knew that feeding some of the church elders with his prophecies was advancing his aspirations to the position of archbishop and the power and money that came with it.

He was nonetheless haunted by worry that he had not yet

dreamt the ultimate dream, the dream that might reveal his destiny. He started fasting. On the third night of his fast the late archbishop of Mount Galilee Christ over the Cross Church in Zion appeared to him.

He instructed Lesiba to part from Jwalane and devote his life to spreading the gospel. Lesiba spent days brooding over the instructions. Finally he sent Jwalane this letter:

Dear Jwalane

A couple of nights ago a strange dream came to me. You are aware of my many previous dreams. Like the time I dreamt your mother had been bitten by a crab. Then days later she suffered a paralysing stroke.

I constantly pray, Jwalane, that the dreams remain just that, but unfortunately they don't. Terrible happenings have followed each one.

My church elders have warned that unless I heed and obey this latest dream, my days in the world are numbered. Our late Archbishop, Baba Mandevu, instructed me to forsake all earthly possessions and devote my remaining days to gathering his scattered sheep before the seven angels of destruction descend on the earth.

Baba Nhlapho constantly preached in church that Russia and America possess strange birds above the clouds that will converge on the earth to announce Armageddon with terrible fires. He says all the waters from the world's seas will never put out these fires.

My wife, Jwalane, I know by obeying Baba's instructions I will be saving not only myself but you and the Lord's many many children. As a devout Christian I know you will understand.

Until we meet again in the Lord's Ark I pray and wish you the Lord's blessings and forgiveness for all your sins.

Your devoted brother in the Lord,
Lesiba

When they heard about the letter, Jwalane's parents called an urgent family meeting.

"Take the fool for a good *sjambokking* at a people's court," Jwalane's brother shouted.

"That is not our custom," Jwalane's aunt countered. "Call him and his parents to resolve the matter."

"I tell you, he is sick. With those nonsense dreams! I heard he's after the archbishop's chair."

"Why doesn't he just start his own little sect? Pretoria doesn't even bother registering them."

"You better all call him and resolve it or I'll sort him out. Nobody plays around with a sister of mine."

Meanwhile Lesiba's life continued. The frequency of his strange dreams increased.

There were dreams that blinded his eyes with an inferno stoked on the holiest shrines. There were dreams that would part like the Red Sea during Moses' exodus from Egypt and feed his enemies to the torrid waves. There were the dreams of necklace victims; they would emerge riding on chariots, brandishing Eiffel Tower-sized torches, charging after their executioners.

Sometimes he would dream during the day. That was when he was engaged in trying to interpret the dreams. He would close his eyes and see crowds of devotees prostrate before him, offering their reverence for the salvation he brought them. He started nurturing that dream into a probability; in time it matured into a reality. Only that reality happened to him alone.

When the late archbishop came again, he impressed upon Lesiba the need to double the tempo of spreading the gospel. He stressed that the end was around the corner. "And the Lord's ark has only a driblet. Look at your sagging belly; I instructed you to give up earthly pursuits yet you continue stuffing yourself."

"But how will I survive? I don't know the difference between fasting and starving."

"The One who commands will provide."

Yes, he recalled that the One referred to did provide for John the Baptist in the desert. The following day Lesiba sent a message to Mandla to collect all the belongings from his locker and bring them to him. Ketso relished the whole turn of events. When word spread around the factory that Lesiba had left work, he went about boasting: "Who did he think he was? He is only a sick fanatic. I tell you, no stupid prayers can withstand my *muti*."

Lesiba devoted his time to prayer and the interpretation of dreams. Multitudes started arriving to have their dreams interpreted.

"Please give me *muti* so that I can dream," some pleaded with him.

"I am scared of my recent dream. I dream about myself being run over by a bus packed with tourists."

"Let us listen to the giver of dreams."

After a moment's meditative silence Lesiba said: "I see you crossing mountains and rivers. Going to places where none of your people has ever been before."

"Oh please make it happen. I love to travel."

Lesiba would always say: "Let us ask the One who gives dreams to interpret them." They would then bow their heads while he communicated with his God. Sometimes the interpretations would happen quickly, at other times he would be forced to remain with head bowed for close on an hour.

Then multitudes of young men and women started sniffing each other's heels as they raced to his house. Sometimes he would have to suppress a chuckle during these consultations. The young men mostly asked for help to be brought into contact with this or that virgin whom they claimed to have seen in their dreams. Some lamented the failure of their prayers: "For six months I have been praying to meet and marry Miss Alexandra. In my dreams it happens, yet all my efforts to meet her have failed."

"The woman I constantly dream of making love to tells me I'm not her type when I propose to her."

The young women, too, came in droves.

"The man I love has a wife and two children. I have been praying for their death. It is now almost a year; instead the wife is getting fatter."

"None of the fathers of my five children want to marry me."

To these, Lesiba would say: "Be patient. The giver of dreams will unravel them when he is ready."

Widows came. They asked him to pray for them so that they would meet new husbands. Some of them would even confess that it was revealed to them in dreams that he was the man that they should get married to. Among them were beautiful ones, and he would feel tempted.

Not long after that he started having the same strange dream for three consecutive weeks. And there were others as well ...

Dreams that ripped the lids off coffins and tombstones off graves to reveal martyrs. Dreams of the blood of all murder and violent death victims, from Abel to those of modern-time carnage, gelling into giant waves and clouds that flooded the land and drowned all living organisms on earth.

He tried to shut off the dream, dampen it with the singing of hymns and of chants, but it refused to be expunged from his mind. The arrival of more widows, younger and more beautiful than before, started interfering with his telepathic frequency. Meanwhile the strange dream continued. He recorded it in his book as Dream number 128 and subtitled it:

Dream of a dozen orgies

In the dream I saw twelve men and women emerge from the Jukskei River. Their hands turned into knives and forks. They ran about sharpening these on rocks, brick walls and concrete pavements. They then turned and started chasing after each other. They sliced off each other's sex organs and roasted them on rocks along the river bank. They indulged in frenzied dancing and feasting. They ululated, while others started wailing, ranting, and scratching their bodies. They poured the blood into wine glasses and offered toasts to each other.

Women suffered doubly, for once they had sliced off men's dangling members they were left with nothing else. The men, however, came running back to slice off their remaining breasts.

Then the well-nourished men with full bellies cut the left-over breasts into thin strands which they dried in the sun to make biltong. They then held a contest to see who had the largest biltong supply.

A chanting Jwalane appeared. She ran, brandishing a panga, determined to slice off my penis. Divine clemency prevailed and I managed to break free from my trance before she could accomplish her mission.

This dream shocked Lesiba. He could not reconcile it with the reality he so wished for. He wondered whether the dream had any telepathic link with his latest legion of followers, the widows.

He had dreams of aborted foetuses sealing the fallopian tubes of females universally. Dreams of harsh martial laws and executions to counteract violent acts and solidarity protest marches of redundant gynaecologists internationally.

Mmadieketse, better known throughout the township as Cinzano Widow was a strikingly beautiful twenty-seven-year-old. It was rumoured that her thirty-year-old late boyfriend, a bank robber, had left her a fortune; a shebeen on East Bank, a tavern in Selection Park, a ten-roomed double-storey mansion in Mmabatho, and three cars — a Caravelle, a Seven Series S'lahla, and a 525I Gusheshe.

Of course Lesiba was not attracted by her material wealth. He heard that she was haunted by a curse of losing all her men. They were snatched from her either by a knife or a bullet.

Nor was he interested in another rumour that, at the age of fourteen, she had sold the life of her first boyfriend for a bottle of Cinzano.

"It is sheer luck that none of them has shown her his true colours. But, I tell you, she'll meet her match one of these days."

"*Ja*! She double-crossed them against each other. Once they take hikes six feet down she inherits their loot."

"That flat belly of hers is stuffed with jackrollers. Wait until they start coming out. The whole of Alex will be swarming with them."

Cinzano Widow was loathed by women. Maybe it was jealousy: few of them could match her magnetic charms in hitting jackpots. But wasn't the Son of Man, too, despised?

Late one evening she came to see Lesiba. He prayed fervently for her.

"Lord give me strength to guide this soul to salvation. Your stray lamb seeks your embrace."

"*Baba*, I am frightened. A Zionist prophet has warned that I will be knifed to death within days unless I repent. Please, *Baba*, pray for me."

"Talk to the One above. His ears are a sanctuary for wandering voices."

"All the men I have planned to marry have passed away. The last one was shot two weeks ago."

"The ears of the One above are alms for famished words. Let us pray for your soul, his soul, and the souls of all the departed."

As the two bowed their heads, Lesiba was aware of the woman's perfume. He was also aware that their heads were touching. In contrast to his audible praying, he could only hear her whispered murmur. It was then that he became aware of the minty fragrance drifting from her mouth.

"*Baba*, is it true ...?" she suddenly whispered.

"Shhh! Pray, my child."

"Is it true what they say, *Baba*?"

"What?"

"That because I did not observe *amasiko wethu* after the death of my first boyfriend, all men who sleep with me will die?"

"You undoubtedly have sinned, my child. But remember the One above forgives seventy-seven times seventy-seven."

Lesiba's prayer rhythm was disturbed. He stopped. He raised his face to find her looking at him appealingly. The deeper he looked into her eyes, the further he saw the desperate lost soul drift into oblivion. He reached out his hands to save it from getting sucked into the abyss.

"Open your heart and soul to him. Pray, my child. Remember to forgive seventy-seven times seventy-seven ..."

At these comforting words she collapsed into his arms.

Hopeless, her fragile body already resigned to spiritual widowhood at twenty-seven. As her body brushed against his, he felt like the baby Christ in Mother Mary's tender arms.

When he woke up it was one in the morning. Cinzano Widow was snoring softly by his side. Quietly he got off the bed and went to kneel at the door to say his absolution prayers. When he came back to bed she was awake.

"I must go, *Baba*."

"The world has grown teeth; I cannot allow you to venture out."

"I am okay, *Baba*. I feel cleansed. I know nothing will harm me." She kissed him before jumping out of bed and preparing to leave. He rubbed his eyes repeatedly for he saw what appeared to be devilish silhouettes hovering around her. They were making obscene and threatening gestures at him.

A heavy pall wrapped around him. He shook his head to chase away sleep, but like a sedated patient on an operating table, he drifted into slumber. He was in the grip of the pall when the late *Baba* Mandevu appeared.

"Heed! Adulterer, fornicator, where is my flock?"

"*Baba*, why do you frown on your devoted servant?"

"Go, sinner! For one extra night you could not resist the temptation of earthly pleasures. Where have you led my lambs? To the jaws of marauding wolves. With whom will I trust my flock when my appointed shepherds turn into wolves?"

Lesiba tried to plead his case but the archbishop remained unrelenting. "I have given you your dreams as your reward for leading my flock. But all this you scorn to appease your lust."

Lesiba tried harder to plead for his moral lapse. The late archbishop continued to disdain him. He then instructed Lesiba to burn the manuscript of 'Dreams and Parables'. Lesiba woke up and sat on the bed. He could hear the rain lashing the roof. His blankets were warm and comforting. He found the idea of destroying his valuable book unacceptable. He then concluded that the late elder had confused his commands. Maybe he had meant to instruct him to destroy all the newspapers and other books and magazines he read. With that comforting thought he went back to sleep.

Much later he was woken by the shattering of one of his windows. Reverberations of thunder followed. He turned to find the window bars mangled. The smell of burning paper drew his attention to the sideboard where he kept his 'Book of Dreams and Parables'. He saw only charred black fragments of what had been his treasured pages of concrete proof that dreams are part of reality. He tried desperately but could not decipher his delicate handwriting in that soot.

A CERTAIN KIND OF LOVE
Roshila Nair

WHEN I ARISE THERE are holes where my eyes used to be. And through the gaps, I can see. In the doorway to the next room the beginning of a crimson sunset declares itself with a gleam bouncing off something metal. A line of light as bold as the single strand of hair on an old woman's head is all that my defecting eyes can see. The rest are words. Doorway. Crimson. Sunset. Metal. Single. Strand. Of. Hair. Words I imagine, or perhaps, words slipping effortlessly as indifferent memories from a past I am not certain is my own. As I walk towards the line of light in the next room, I am there simply by the memory of words.

I step over the snoring man. Now, an innocuous man. A little while ago the man had plunged into me against my will. I had struggled against him, but I am much smaller than he is. My struggle seemed to prompt him further. I pleaded. No. No. No. No. His no against my no. The same word. As my head hit the floor repeatedly, as the terror glutted my nostrils, as my world split with dread, he looked into my eyes and shattered my soul.

The man spoke to me. Patiently,
because I am a child.
I saw a flash of white teeth,
red gums, a pink tongue.
The cold ground under my spine
would not give way,
would not shroud me.

I can still hear the man speaking.
I want him like this

All along, I had wanted him like this
I do not,
cannot know the meaning of no
young as I am
he is my friend
this is another learning experience
I must trust in his love for me
have faith in my trust for him
he is my teacher

When he finished,
he slid off me and fell asleep.

I never doubt the words I speak. The meaning of the words I speak are without doubt. I believe my words. Therefore I speak. No. A word without doubt. But he had the word, too. Whose word was it?

Nothing changes and everything changes. Can a word be like that? Long ago and far away, the word brought the first speaker into being. The word that travelled on angry tongues hungry for revolution. No. The tenacity of a word that clings with absurd clarity like a drop of water on a desert plant at sunrise.

I am not surprised to find the word lodging in me for I am no different from any other woman who knows she is alive. Words and memories. All that lie between me and my non-existence. The attempt to create my death a little while ago. The man snoring in the next room.

I walk towards the line of light.

And here at last is the diminutive black iron figure of the thinker. The hunched shoulders focusing its gaze on the centre spot of the invisible circle created by its looking. The unre-markable, crudely detailed head thrust forward. The square arms held intently across its fertile stomach. The nipples of the full breasts tugging the torso to attention at its feet. The unfin-ished feet planted stolidly a few inches into the circle. I am sucked into the mysterious point of view at the thinking woman's feet. An inch-long scratch on the left shoulder bares the shiny metal as the setting sun bathes the corroded body of the iron woman.

I pick up the small figure, warm from the sunset. The modest light shining from its left shoulder guides my fingers. Its heaviness pulls my hand down. The unfinished edges of its toes press against my palm with the logic of razor blades. The papers on the neat desk, kept in order by the thinker's weight a moment ago, begin to stir as if alive. A township breeze, hot and ripe with the smell of a dog's corpse on the dump, drifts in through the open window. I place the thinker on the neatly written papers again. The rustling stops. I walk across the room to shut the window. I reach out. My fingers touch the iron handles of the window. The glass pane carries the paraffin odours of its recent cleaning. I inhale deeply the pristine smell, which reminds me of something ancient.

My eyes have come back to me and I can see the dusty street outside.

A scraggy pair of boys. Their dusty arms linked. Stroll down the street. Alternately. Kicking an empty jam tin. Ahead of them. Each kick. Attempts to send the tin further. The rolling tin. Brings them to a rusting gate. Hanging on one hinge. The smaller boy. Untangles his arm. And. Scurries up the polished red stoep. Without a backward glance at his rival. The abandoned companion dashes the tin off with his left foot and chases after its clanking before the front door opens to yield a woman with a pink headscarf. She glares at the scuffed shoes cowering below her. The woman raises her arm to strike the boy.

High above the house roofs shimmering in the hot sunset, is the three-coloured flag of liberation we erected this morning. The victorious hoisting to celebrate the arrival of our freedom. The release of our beloved leader. The unbanning of our faith. How we sang with raised fists in the air. How the women wailed like demons stolen from their children. The red eyed men shouted in loud voices. How the roar of the children's feet loosened the earth's fury. How we knew we could never be defeated because victory made our voices truth itself.

This morning. In the sunlight glinting with the raised dust. I heard too the shock in our voices. Even we had doubted our freedom for a moment. Our laughter. Our songs of glory. The grandness of our freedom. Waiting like new bread to be broken. Oh the sweet bread of freedom. The promises we make to each other in our happiness. I never doubt the words I speak. I had come to the teacher to share the news of our freedom with him.

Through the window, I glimpse the electric cables from which the green, gold and black flag still sways serenely in the breeze. And there at the end of the cable, on the tarred wooden pole, sloping dangerously towards a house, hangs the extra large red panties. There had been much fun at its hoisting this morning. We had roared with laughter. Booitjies Forever, our local drunk, staggered about with exaggerated looks of consternation that the police would express when they spotted the panties hanging in their red glory. The red panties marked the favourite spot for the Commandant's water canon on his customary calls to the township. The purple rain meant to cool our fever, drown our chanting. Silence our promises to each other. Never.

I shut the window. I return to the desk and pick up the iron thinker and enter the next room. Returning, I place the thinker on the writing desk. I am careful. I do not wish to stain the neatly written pages. My right arm throbs from its labour. I enter the peaceful kitchen filled with the smells of its absent owner. Carbolic acid. Bleach. The lavender of floor polish. Lemon of wood polish. Paraffin. Smells of dignity. I return to the silent room and strike the match. It flares and catches. I leave without a backward glance.

I walk towards the sunset. The street is bright with the last minute fire of the day. In the glory of the ebbing fires, I can see the morning flags of victory and change. Twenty feet overhead. Above the cables. I stand under. In Heaven. A choir of angels. In frothy white bibs. Are already singing. In solemn voices. The praises of another sunset. The beginning. The world. And the son of Adam in the house of silence I have left behind.

The town dogs gather around me, snapping hungrily at my hand. I toss the flesh that I have taken from the man. The flesh that violates. A fight ensues. I walk on. Free. Free. Freedom. Free.

A group of boys are throwing dice nearby. I put my right foot forward and soar into the sky. I carefully unpeg the red panties. As I float down gracefully to the ground my bloody dress blossoms like a summer rose around my knees. I place the red panties at the boys' feet and continue on my way, free, in the retreating sunset of the crimson angels.

CHANGE
Barry Hough

THE CHILD WAS GOING to change everything. Tessa could almost smell the change just as she could sniff the promise of each new season before it actually dawned.

And Tessa feared change like she feared blood. In her particular history the two had always seemed to accompany one another. Change and blood. Blood and change. They were in tandem, like Satan and Blits, Oupa Meyer's fleshy pair of black stallions that had garnered him many wins at the country horse show. Like Sue and May, the giggling blonde twins at school who swopped boyfriends for fun and slipped into one another's identities so easily that they apparently even confused their parents.

Being of farming stock and having spent extended periods on her maternal grandparents' cherry farm in Clocolan, Tessa was acutely tuned to the cycles of nature — more so than most people, she was forced to admit. People mocked her when she spoke almost prophetically of the smell of rain in swirling dust devils and said that she could hear the sap rising in the cherry trees when she put her ear to the rough bark. That she was always right about the rain did not deter folks from poking fun at her — this crazy girl from Johannesburg.

As a child, Tessa learned with growing fear and horror that existence was change and that the transition from one state of being to another was punctuated with blood. Birth had its blood. There was often blood when the cows and ewes discharged the young from their wombs in spring. Death too had its blood. Tessa had once witnessed the slaughter of a sheep, the blood spurting out as its jugular was cut with a knife. She never ate meat again after that. In each lamb chop or sliver of biltong she saw, she recalled the animal's sigh of death and the dulling of its eyes. Change, the transition from life to death, stared straight at her with a gaze so powerful that it haunted her still, would haunt her forever.

Tessa had fled from the scene of that slaughter, to where her grandmother sat playing the piano in the parlour. Chopin. She buried her face in her grandmother's floral apron, sobbing. The old woman's hands fleetingly stroked Tessa's hair and then went back to the keys. It was then that Tessa came to realise that music smelled of roses. She stopped crying. She lifted her head and caught sight of the blown yellow roses in the big pink bowl with its copper rim. Tessa had found sanctuary. As she became older and learnt to read music and play the piano she realised that she could escape, albeit for all too brief periods, from the world which beat with the ebb and flow of blood. But even here in Johannesburg, where she was sheltered behind walls in a leafy suburb, where slaughter was less public, the knowledge that it still happened remained with her.

Tessa knew that her 'escape' was a lie. One morning she woke up to find blood on her sheets and pyjamas. Her first thought was that she had been attacked in the night. Although her ripening breasts with nipples that stared back at her from the mirror, and her mother had warned her, nothing could have prepared her for menstruation. It was as if all the blood and change she had ever experienced had contracted into this one fearful rite of passage, a process she would be doomed to experience for years to come. She could never quite shed the feeling that betrayed her, violently and with such sudden bloodletting. And so, even with the knowledge of a clock ticking beneath the curve of her stomach Tessa lied to herself when she escaped into her haven of music.

She had inherited the piano after her grandparents had fallen victim to yet another spate of farm murders. Although the newspapers had not mentioned the detail they had heard from the police that her grandmother, Magrieta Meyer, had been raped. Tessa could still smell the sweat of the ragged men who had delivered the piano. The perspiration shone on their black faces as they eased the unwieldy instrument down onto the floor of the music room. And for a brief moment, as she looked into the eyes of one of the men, she wondered whether this smell of sweat was the last thing her grandmother had smelled. The "thank you" caught in her throat and came out as a cough. Tessa's hand flew to her mouth.

The black baby grand replaced her own upright and she loved the grandness of the instrument, the way in which it almost filled the room. She thrilled at the stroke of the yellowing keys and had to agree with the blind piano tuner that the new instrument's sound was quite wonderful.

Tessa looked into the child's big brown eyes and read the approach of change. The child, Pulisa, had Dora's eyes. But without the smile, the shy gaze, the averting motion. There was a hunger in them, a hunger for knowledge and the future. Dora, who had been Tessa's nanny, was killed in a taxi accident on her way back from her home in KwaZulu Natal. Tessa and her mother Susan, had to identify Dora's body. Oh, the blood! The corpse had not yet been washed and wore a mask of congealed blood, black against Dora's dark skin. Dora's death left a huge hole in Tessa's life.

The child was Dora's legacy to Susan. It had been Dora's explicit wish that Susan should raise Pulisa in the event of anything happening to her. The child, a thin eight-year-old, came; against her own grandmother's wishes and despite Grant's advice.

"You can't replace Desmond," Grant had stated simply in his private school English accent. "I won't allow it." He spoke as if he were giving an order to one of his secretaries at his office tower of glass and steel.

"Damn you, Grant! It's not about replacing him, it's about what Dora wanted. And this rush of paternal feeling is new to me. You wanted to pack him off to boarding school, you never spent time with him ..."

Tessa escaped to her music room before the argument got to the point where Susan, red in the face, would scream, "You English ...!" The more she ranted, the more stony-faced he became. The pall of silence that followed usually hung around the house for days, like the smell of something rotten, after which it settled into the ordinary silence and lack of communication that characterised their marriage. Tessa often wondered why her parents bothered to stay married.

Tessa closed the heavy oak door of the music room behind her and inhaled the scent of the roses in the bowl with the copper rim. She replaced the roses regularly. The piano's keys were cool against her fingers as she played Chopin. Music never let you down. The pattern of the notes on the white paper remained the same. And although your tempo and interpretation could vary to suit your mood, the notes never changed. She relaxed as the music flowed through her. She forgot, or rather chose to forget the things that upset her.

She hated the newspapers and the way they reported the violence, poverty and starvation in the world. The news in the paper was also printed black on white, but unlike the notes of music, it changed every day. She did not want to know how many more cars had been hijacked, how many more people had been murdered, had committed suicide or had died from a drug overdose. And although she often had spats with her mother, for once she agreed with her. Damn her father for mentioning Desmond. The memory hurt

The day he died, election day 1994, had written CHANGE in her life in a banner headline. Although she and Desmond were too young to vote (she was twelve at the time, he seven) they went along with Susan and Dora to the polling station where they spent hours waiting in a queue. The day was festive and Susan and Dora shared the huge picnic basket they had packed with other voters in a spirit of what Dora called *ubuntu*. She explained it to Tessa as meaning 'sharing' or 'a feeling that binds people together in a community'. As they were walking home, greeting people in the spirit of elation that characterised the day, a car veered from the road and hit Desmond and two other children he had met at the polling station. The driver was drunk. Desmond died on the pavement while they were waiting for the ambulance. Dora mopped the blood that ran from his mouth as he lay limp in Susan's arms.

A thought attached itself to Tessa's brain and settled there like a leech. Was her mother trying to replace the void her brother had left with Dora's child? The idea was so monstrous that she buried it deep in her brain and tried to give herself over to the music completely.

She played Bach. The order of his composition, the precision of his harmony seemed to counteract the confusion and chaos of her own life. While she played she seemed to have enough calm to view the overwhelming statistics of tragedy within her own family. Within five years she had lost grandparents, a brother, and Dora. Bathed in lace-filtered light and the sound of Bach, the violence and loss that had marked her own life seemed like something in a book or a play, disconnected from her. The blood that had been shed within her own little familiar circle might as well have been the blood in *Macbeth*, one of her setworks at school.

Tessa gritted her teeth and kept on playing. In her heart she embraced first her grandparents, then Desmond, and finally Dora.

When she left the music room she almost fell over the sitting child in the passage.

"Nice music," Pulisa said and flashed a smile.

In the weeks after the child came to stay Tessa became keenly aware of her presence. It seemed that Pulisa invaded not only her space but her treasured silences as well. Tessa had learned from her grandmother that you can only appreciate music when you know how to listen to silence. It was a gift she had acquired. Pulisa's presence seemed pervasive, almost like that of a bat thudding and whirring into the darkest corners of your sleep.

"I felt like I've lost all my privacy," Tessa complained to Susan. She always listens when I play. She 's like a big ear plastered against the door."

"You always listened to your grandmother play."

"That ... that was different; I was family. And, Ma, does she really have to stay in Desmond's room?"

"What?" Susan flared. "Do you want his room to be a tomb?

Don't be so selfish. Pulisa has lost her mother, for God's sake. She's Dora's daughter, your Dora remember?"

Tessa retreated from her mother's attack. Susan softened. "Try and make her welcome, she's just a child."

Pulisa settled into the routine such as it was. Susan and the char mothered her and even Grant spoke to her on the rare occasion he shared a meal with his wife and daughter.

Tessa still cocooned herself in the music room and was not prepared to let Pulisa into that sacred space. She could not find a way to really relate to the child. Until one day. Pulisa found a shoe box with holes in the lid. Either Tessa or Desmond had once used the box for silkworms.

"What's this for?" she asked Tessa, her eyes big with curiosity.

"I'll show you," Tessa said, her voice full of relief. She had found a window into Pulisa's life.

End of September. According to Tessa's calculations it was silkworm season. She bought a mixture of zebras and white worms at a pet shop and picked mulberry leaves from a neighbour's tree. A few ripe mulberries tempted her. Mulberry-blood stained her fingers as she ate the sweet fruit. When she got home she washed her hands.

Tessa put a delighted Pulisa through the whole silkworm ritual and checked every so often that the worms weren't starving.

Between the worms, her new school, and learning how to operate the TV and video Pulisa's life was full. She didn't get in the older girl's way too much. Tessa was studying for her final school and piano exams.

She slept fitfully and when she slept her grandmother whispered to her. Sometimes Lady Macbeth stalked her dreams with bloody hands.

The exams came and went and Pulisa's silkworms spun themselves into cocoons. She seemed to lose interest in the fluffy yellow pellets.

Meanwhile Pulisa had discovered the Geography channel on TV and watched the nature programmes with fascination. Tessa noticed that she loved documentaries about insects and carnivores. The stalking and killing of prey kept her riveted while the creepy-crawlies and sharks scared her deliciously.

One balmy January evening they sat together watching a programme on elephants. Tessa loved these stately creatures but was sickened by the way they were hunted and culled. As she was ready to escape from the blood and gore of a culling, something suddenly caught her attention. A piano's keyboard flashed in between shots of tusks and ivory being cut. "Until quite recently the keys of good quality pianos were covered with ivory," the pleasant English voice announced. "A synthetic substitute has however been developed ..."

Tessa cried out. Pulisa sat quietly, ashen and wide-eyed. "How could I have been so stupid? I never made the connection," Tessa later said to Susan as they sat at the dining room table.

"It's my fault too," Susan said. "Pretty shoddy for a northern suburbs gal who is so outspoken on environmental issues. I feel quite foolish. Why don't you go to bed?"

Tessa could not sleep. When she closed her eyes she had visions of sheet music: Mozart, Beethoven, even her beloved Bach and Chopin all written in blood. She washed her hands twice during the night. Susan realised it was crisis time when her daughter had dark rings beneath her eyes the next morning. Two days later people came to pick up Tessa's heirloom.

"They are covering the keys with a new material. I'm so sorry, Tess." Susan embraced her daughter as the men loaded the piano onto the truck.

The music room seemed so large without the piano. Tessa stared out of the window for a long time. The silence around her was frightening. Like death.

Then she saw Pulisa standing in the door, a shoe box in her hand. "Look!" she cried, "I brought you something." She stood close to Tessa and carefully lifted the lid with its airholes.

Two moths fluttered whitely between the yellow cocoons.

Tessa knew that the moths would lay eggs and die. Pulisa would most probably be upset, like Desmond had been. And that she, as the older sister, would be called on to explain all about the cycles of change

A CHANCE ENCOUNTER
Farida Karodia

ANDREW WATCHED FROM THE veranda as Petrus, the gardener, cleared away debris from under the trees. They had worked hard to fix the old place. The reward, of course, was that both the grounds and the house were now almost restored to their former glory.

He couldn't resist gloating about their accomplishments, especially to colleagues at the university. On his second visit to view the property, he had taken along two of his friends for an opinion before making an offer. They were both appalled at the state of the house and garden. Andrew, however, had recognised its potential.

Eager to join Petrus, he finished his coffee. He derived a great deal of pleasure from the old garden. The stone terraces with their mature guava, loquat and litchi trees formed a canopy which dappled the sunlight. In the centre of the garden the pond stood empty. The only evidence that goldfish had once existed were the fish skeletons embedded in the cracks of the cement floor.

Andrew came over to inspect the progress Petrus had made on the trench near the west fence.

"Too much work," Petrus grumbled, clutching his back as he straightened up.

Petrus returned to his digging while Andrew took stock of what still had to be done. Not even Petrus's ill-humour was going to diminish his enjoyment of the garden. Working with the earth and the flowers had always given him a sense of peace and comfort.

The garden in Shaugnessy, a suburb of Vancouver, had been his salvation in the difficult months when his wife, Margaret, left him and took their daughter Justine with her. They had only been in Canada for five years when this happened.

The Shaugnessy house was part of another life. The past with his family existing in some other dimension, totally unconnected to the present which, since his heart attack, seemed to have an unbearable urgency about it, as if he was running a race.

There was so much still left undone. So many regrets lurking beneath the surface like a wound that wouldn't heal.

His life had been turned upside down by a single incident, an unintentional lapse at a faculty party one night. He would've given anything to erase what happened, to turn the clock back and alter the events of that night. The brief sexual encounter hadn't been worth all the heartache and misery it had brought to so many people in his life.

Now, left to speculate about how things might have turned out, he was haunted by self-doubt and questions. Margaret, ruthless in her condemnation, had blamed him for everything, including the fact that he had brought her to Canada. That she had made all those sacrifices for him and he had betrayed her, was something she could not forgive.

He and Margaret had tried to hold their relationship together for Justine's sake. In the end, though, it became too difficult. The incident was a wedge in their relationship and it ultimately destroyed what they had together.

Margaret had once accused him of being a lousy father. In retrospect he saw that there was some justification for her criticism. He had not spent enough time with his family; he was always working late; there were department meetings, papers to mark, extra duties to perform. All that extra time devoted to other people's children when he ought to have spent time with his own child.

After his divorce, Andrew transferred to York University in Toronto to teach International Law. This was where he met his second wife, Yvette, an English lecturer.

Andrew and Yvette were married the following year and endured a stormy relationship which lasted two years. At their divorce hearing Yvette had cited his work as the cause of their marriage breakdown. Meanwhile Margaret had remarried and had moved to Sydney, taking Justine with her.

Inured to the pain of separation, the recovery from the second divorce was easier than the first, in which he had lost his wife and his daughter.

A few months later he had the heart attack. Although recovered now, doctors had advised him to avoid stress.

A few weeks before the first free elections in South Africa, he had received an invitation to visit, for purposes of discussion and possible participation in a new government. His background in international law and politics was of great interest to the parties concerned. The challenges were tremendous. But he wasn't quite ready. There were still too many unresolved issues in his personal life which muddled his thinking.

It took five more years before he returned to South Africa, accepting a post at the University of Natal.

Andrew sat down for a few minutes. He tired easily these days, even though he pushed himself to jog at least two kilometres each morning. At fifty-eight he was becoming increasingly aware of his own mortality. The doctor's warning about the possibility of another attack was like a pall over his life.

Why was it, he wondered, that although he craved peace he subconsciously sought absolution? He had hoped to find vindication for all those years of unhappiness by coming back here. He had hoped to fill his life with meaningful activity. But little seemed to have changed. There was still the same emptiness. The same feeling of not being centred. It was as if he had shifted off his axis and was spinning out of control. Conscious of this lopsidedness, he waited for it to correct itself.

Meanwhile, he occupied himself with gardening. There was no challenge here, no need to excel in extraordinary feats or to meet deadlines. It was an opportunity to relax. He felt he could give himself over completely to the joy of working in the warm soil, his hands probing among the roots, surrounded by the smell of decaying vegetation.

He noticed that Petrus was watching him as he examined the bougainvillaea. "Where are the shears?" he asked.

Petrus brought them over and in his slow, halting way showed him which vines to trim and which to avoid.

With verve Andrew tackled the clumps of pink and burgundy flowers. Then, oblivious to everything around him except the clipping of the shears, he separated the trusses of flowers and with deft snips cut through the vines.

The cry of an approaching hawker slowly penetrated his mist of preoccupation. "Fresh fruit and vegetables. Get your peaches and your pears, your naartjies and your litchis. Fresh fruit ..."

Despite the distortion created by a megaphone, Andrew paused, listening. He abandoned the shears and, followed by Petrus's disapproving gaze, hurried to the gate.

A green van slowly coasted down the street, one rear wheel wobbling absurdly. Brightly coloured hand-painted designs decorated the doors with caricatures of various vegetables. BAMJI'S FRUITS AND VEGETABLES was emblazoned across the back of the van.

"Bamji! Bamji!" Andrew yelled. The van hiccuped and shuddered to a halt. "Bamji! Is that you, you old scoundrel?"

A bearded, bespectacled face poked out of the window. "Mr Davis, hey, Mr Davis! So you come back neh?"

Bamji made a quick U-turn and brought the van to a halt outside the gate. He opened the door with a flourish and leapt out.

"So you remember me eh, Bamji?"

"Of course. Where you been, Mr Davis? I heard you been to Canada."

"*Ja*," Andrew nodded. "But it's good to be home now. I see you're still in business. How've you been, Bamji?"

"So-so. Not too bad. I don't have to pull that old cart like a donkey no more," he said, appraising Andrew. "Shish, it's been such a long time, maybe twenty years since I last saw you eh?"

Except for a narrow skirt of greying hair, Bamji was almost

completely bald. He peered at Andrew through thick lenses, then with a broad grin patted his stomach. Andrew teased him, repeating the old aphorism about a man's girth increasing proportionately to his improved circumstances.

"Not me," Bamji laughed. "I'm not yet a millionaire like some of those other guys, but still I can't complain."

"How's your family?"

"Okay. How about yours?"

Andrew paused. "My wife and I are not together anymore."

"I'm sorry." Bamji drew his hand over his bald head, his skin leathery from the sun. For a moment the two men stood in silence.

"Did you ever hear from Lalitha?" Andrew said eventually.

Bamji smiled distractedly and shook his head.

"You mean to tell me you never found your daughter?"

Bamji scuffed the toe of his shoe on the sidewalk. He looked up and shrugged. "The last time I saw her was when I brought her here to you."

Andrew didn't say anything.

"I don't know why these things happen. God alone knows, eh?" Bamji sighed. "Life must go on."

"I suppose so."

"I had other children to worry about that time. I had six of them you know. All still at home — and now five grandchildren also."

"All of them living with you?"

Bamji nodded. "Will you be staying here now?"

"Yes, for a while anyway."

"How come you don't stay in your old neighbourhood. It's a very grand place."

"It's better for me here, Bamji."

"Let me know whatever you want, Mr Davis, I'll bring it over. On Thursdays I bring fish also." He climbed back into the van.

"I'll tell my housekeeper."

Andrew watched Bamji drive away and returned to the yard. He calculated that it was about twenty-two years since he had last seen the child. The image of her face was still so clear. He could see her eyes, large and intelligent, full of uncertainty. They were the strangest colour he'd ever seen — grey with pupils the colour of faded charcoal. God, it was a long time ago.

Back in the yard he picked up the shears and returned to his pruning. Seeing Bamji again, however, had brought back many memories.

In those days Bamji had hawked fresh produce from a small hand-pulled cart. Andrew recalled how father and daughter had struggled to pull the cart to the top of the hill where he and Margaret had lived. Then Bamji would arrive at their gate, sweating and out of breath, always complaining that he was getting too old for the interminable struggle.

The child sitting on the curb across the street, patiently waited, the skimpy skirt of her dress hooked over her bony knees. There was something in her attitude, a weary resignation that had touched him.

Margaret had collected old clothes for one or other of her charitable causes. The boxes were in the garage and he thought they might contain something decent for the child to wear.

"Why do you leave her to sit across the street, call her in," Andrew said one afternoon when he got home early to surprise Margaret and Justine — only to find that they had gone into town.

"She's alright there, she's used to waiting," Bamji said.

"I've got some old clothes in the garage."

"For her?"

Andrew nodded . "Why does she look so sad, Bamji?"

"Always she looks like that," Bamji said with a shrug. He followed Andrew into the garage. "My wife doesn't want her."

"What do you mean your wife doesn't want her?"

"She is not the child of my wife. I uh ... I had a little ..." He made a dismissive gesture as if to show that whatever it was, it was over and no longer of any consequence. "Her mother was a Zulu woman who worked for me." His gaze turned to the child who was now standing at the gate. "Her mother died three months after she gave birth. No one wanted the child. It was just an extra mouth to feed. I took her to my mother. But then my mother got ill so I had to bring her and the child to live with us. My wife does not like the child. She never has."

"She's only a child," Andrew admonished, opening a box.

"*Ja*," Bamji nodded, "but my wife doesn't think so. She doesn't want her. So many times she has chased her away." He shook his head.

"What is her name?"

"Lalitha."

"Call her in, Bamji."

Bamji called to the child. She came hesitantly, chewing on the edge of the frayed neck of her dress, bare feet splayed on the concrete driveway. Her grey, sombre eyes, like flints of steel, fixed on the two men.

"Come come, child," Bamji snapped impatiently.

"How old are you?" Andrew asked the girl.

"Maybe ten or twelve," Bamji answered, "I'm not sure."

"Come on, Bamji, she looks much younger."

"No, I swear to you, she's about that age. One of these days I'll get her married, but no one will have her. Look at her, look at her hair."

There was nothing remarkable about the child's face. She resembled the street children Andrew had seen begging in the marketplace or down at the docks. Her hair was thick and coarse, and as he gazed at her she self-consciously put out a hand to flatten the wild, unruly bush. But the eyes more than any other feature held his attention. Although they were large and full of heart-wrenching sadness, they were the colour of granite. Pupils dilated almost to the size of her irises gazed back at him.

Under his scrutiny she lowered her eyes.

"She looks like you. Really, Bamji anyone can see you're the father, except those eyes ... such a strange colour."

"My wife says she has the eyes of a witch. She is frightened of the child." He glanced away shamefacedly, then after an uncomfortable pause he said, "There will be no dowry for her."

Andrew gazed at her thin and angular body, wasted through neglect.

"I can't leave her alone with my wife for fear that she will beat her. What can I do, what can I do?" Bamji threw up his hands in despair. "She is so clever, I tell you, Mr Davis, she is the cleverest of all my children. She is doing very well in school, very well. It is a pity ... such a pity."

The girl watched nervously, her glance like that of a trapped animal, darted between the two men.

"Have you consulted someone about the situation?"

"Who? Who is there to consult? No one wants her. Everyone has a problem."

"Would you like a cooldrink?" Andrew asked the child.

She came forward with small, hesitant steps. Andrew thought of Justine and how fortunate his own child was to have a warm, safe home.

"She's a good worker, she works very hard. You want her?" the hawker asked with the same persuasive whine he used to sell his produce. He noticed Andrew's hesitation and pressed on with confidence. "She can clean house and cook."

"I have a maid," Andrew snapped. "Bamji don't you want this child?"

"It is not I, it is the wife," Bamji said, lowering his eyes under Andrew's steady gaze. "Tonight she'll sleep in the street."

Andrew thought about Margaret and the resistance he knew would come from her.

"I can't help you, Bamji."

Bamji shrugged, thrust his hands deep into his pockets and studied the dusty tips of his shoes.

The child's gaze fixed on Andrew. The look of trust and expectation in her eyes tugged at him. "I'll help you out for a few days while you try to find a home for her. Four days, Bamji, no more."

"Thank you, Mr Davis," Bamji said eagerly.

"How can I be sure this isn't another of your tricks?"

"No tricks, no tricks. I give you my word. My word is as good as gold."

Andrew laughed. "I don't trust you, Bamji, but for now I'll have to take your word."

"I have no money to pay you." Bamji's gaze returned to his shoes. "I'll bring her clothes … whatever there is."

"Don't bother. We have enough in these boxes. But first she'll need a bath."

"Thank you, Mr Davis," Bamji said. He spoke to the girl rapidly in Gujarati with a few threatening wags of his finger. Then he left.

It was not going to be easy to persuade Margaret who paid lip-service to liberalism. It was one thing to collect used clothing for charity, but another to get personally involved. To get down and dirty. He thought that if Elsie, their maid, made the child more presentable, Margaret might allow her to stay for a few days.

The task of transforming the child fell to Elsie who immediately voiced her reluctance. But after much persuasion the maid relented. The one thing she balked at, however, was handling Lalitha's lice-infested hair. In the end she sheared the hair off and burnt it.

When Margaret and Justine returned home Andrew began his explanations. But with constant interruption from Elsie to complain about the hair. Margaret's expression tightened as she listened to their story. He could see the disapproval in her eyes. When he had finished, Margaret got up and strode out of the backdoor to the servant's quarters where Lalitha was. With her head sheared like a concentration camp intern she looked even more waif-like than before. She was standing by Elsie's bed, her head bowed, obviously filled with shame at her appearance.

Margaret's eyes were hooded, her mouth a thin, angry line. "Andrew how could you have done this without consulting me?" she demanded.

"I didn't think you'd mind."

"What on earth are we going to do with her?"

He hadn't quite figured that out yet but hoped a solution would present itself.

"Are you daft, Andrew? She can't stay with us. How are we going to explain this child's presence in our home?"

"But she won't be staying in our home ..."

"I don't know what's come over you. You have a child of your own that you barely pay attention to," she said angrily.

Justine, who was about six years old then, had slipped into Elsie's room and was gazing at Lalitha. Eventually she sidled over and slipped her hand into the other girl's. This physical contact seemed to rouse Lalitha. She glanced up, uncertainty changing to defiance.

"She's only a child," Andrew said.

"Are you out of your mind? Look at her?"

There was little Andrew could do or say to change his wife's mind. Lalitha stayed on for a week. Margaret was visibly relieved when the girl ran away.

No one knew where she had gone. There were no clues. A missing-child report to an uninterested police sergeant yielded nothing. Andrew knew that if Lalitha had been white the police would've made more of an effort to find her.

Petrus touched Andrew's elbow and with a start he realised that he had been lost in thought. He stepped aside as Petrus gathered the garlands of pink and burgundy pruned from the vine.

Andrew thought of Justine and Lalitha holding hands that night. The irony was that both girls were lost to him; one disappearing forever and the other alienated from him. Justine was an adult now, married and with a family of her own, living in Australia.

He had tried to make contact with her in recent years, but it was clear that her mother had poisoned her mind against him. He wished there was something he could do to make up for all the wasted time.

In the case of both girls he had given up too easily. He

regretted that he had not pressed the police to make more of an effort to find Lalitha. When he hadn't heard from Bamji he had assumed that she had returned home to him.

All week long Andrew's thoughts drifted back to the past. And when he got to the end of the week he realised it was Justine's birthday the following Saturday. She would be twenty-eight years old. He felt an incredible longing for her.

He picked up the phone and dialled her number. There was no reply. He'd had the number for several years now, but afraid of being rejected, had never called.

He thought about his role as a grandfather and how much he was missing by not being there with the grandchildren as they grew up. The thought saddened him. Each afternoon when he got home he sought forgetfulness in the garden.

Occasionally he interrupted his routine with social obligations: a dinner party or the theatre. But most of the time he stayed home listening to music or reading.

Saturday, Justine's birthday, Andrew tried several times to phone. But there was still no reply. He busied himself in the garden, hoping to dispel the cloud of depression he was sinking into.

After mowing the lawn he asked Petrus to climb up on the garage roof to secure the trellis for the wisteria.

He went into the house and tried again to call Australia. Again there was no reply. Should he chance calling Margaret to find out where Justine was? He began dialling his ex-wife's number but thought better of it and put the phone down.

On the roof outside, Petrus lost his footing.

Andrew heard the cry and the crash. He rushed outside to where Petrus lay writhing and moaning on the concrete driveway. His left shin had snapped like a twig and was protruding grotesquely. Blood spurted from the wound. Andrew tied a tourniquet and made the man comfortable before phoning for an ambulance.

"Good thing you tied the tourniquet," the medic said. He peeled back Petrus's lids. "Poor sod's in shock. Let's get him to the General." He gave the gardener a shot for the pain.

The next day Andrew went to visit Petrus with a parcel of fruit and sweets. He felt responsible for the accident.

At the reception desk an Indian girl in a canary-yellow blouse, asked him for the patient's name.

"Dlamini," Andrew said.

She raised a brow and sighed with exaggerated exasperation. "There are about fifty patients with that surname," she said. "What is his first name?"

Andrew stared at her blankly, mortified that at this momentary memory lapse he had blacked out the gardener's name.

"Sorry," she said with a mocking smile and turned her back on him to continue her conversation with her friend.

Andrew felt his chest tightening and took a deep breath. "Miss Moonsammy (her name was pinned to her bosom) either you help me find him or I'll raise hell right here."

Startled, she swung around.

"The ambulance attendant told me that this was where he was bringing him."

She glared at him.

"This is the General Hospital, is it not?"

Her colleagues, anticipating a scene, drew closer.

Lips pursed, she said, "Do you know what the matter is with him?"

"Broken leg."

"Male orthopaedic surgery. Fourth floor to your right."

"Thank you."

He used the stairway instead of the lift, holding his breath against the sharp smell of urine and antiseptic. On the fourth floor he turned right and found himself in the midst of bedlam. Suddenly he remembered Petrus's name and clung on to it as if his life depended on it as he stepped over mothers squatting with their infants. Some of them were breastfeeding, others were tending their babies with a vacant-eyed resignation. Adding to the chaos was the persistent drone of crying children.

"Excuse me," someone called behind him. He flattened himself against the wall as a large trolley rolled by. He found a ward and approached a woman sitting at the entrance desk.

"Where is the male orthopaedic ward?" he asked her.

Without looking up she pointed him in the right direction.

In the ward a young nurse glanced up curiously as he entered.

"Good morning. I'm looking for a Petrus Dlamini. He has a broken leg."

"Lemme see …"

"Where's Nurse Khumalo, Alice?"

This voice came from behind him and was addressed to the nurse in front of him. Its authoritative tone made Andrew turn around. The woman wore a white uniform and maroon epaulettes. Their eyes met for a brief instant, hers like flints of steel. Several pictures flashed through his mind. Years of experience and self-assurance deserted him in one hesitant, questioning utterance of her name: "Lalitha?"

There was not a hint of recognition in her eyes as she gazed back at him.

"Don't you remember me?"

He could see her struggle to place him. Then he saw the flicker in those steely eyes.

"Of course." The words were spoken without warmth. "Mr Davis." Almost as though she resented this intrusion from her distant past.

He marvelled at the change. She was self-assured — so different from the little girl perched like a bird ready to take flight. Now she was grown up, a figure of authority in her white uniform — and right now, slightly irritated.

He smiled because he couldn't trust himself to speak.

"You've come to see a patient?"

He nodded.

"And he's not here?" she asked the nurse.

The nurse consulted her list again and shook her head. "No, Sister."

"He may be on the other side. I'll take you there."

"What an incredible coincidence," Andrew said, walking beside her.

She glanced at him, her brow arched.

"Just last week I met your father. He's still selling fruit and vegetables."

She ignored his comment and walked ahead briskly, smiling and nodding at patients.

"He has a van now."

Still, she did not respond.

"He thought you were dead."

"You'll have to excuse me, I'm in a bit of a rush. I'd rather not discuss my father and I'd appreciate you not saying anything to him about seeing me."

"Of course. I'm glad to see that you're well."

"Thank you." She smiled absently. "The patient should be in this ward," she said, standing in the open doorway. "Now I have to go. Goodbye, Mr Davis."

"I thought of you so often, wondering what had happened to you." She was about to walk away and in an involuntary gesture he put his arm out to restrain her.

Startled, she drew away.

"Sorry," he said with a wry smile. "I'd like to talk to you." He held out his hands imploringly. "Please have lunch with me."

She shook her head. "Look around you, look at the chaos."

"When will you have time?"

"I don't know."

"I have to talk to you …"

"Mr Davis, please …" She gestured to the ward, a long, narrow room with about twenty iron beds on either side. "I really must go. I'm very busy, as you can see for yourself."

"Lalitha, you can't blame me for what your father did."

She had started walking away, but his remark stopped her. Uncertainty replaced her cold indifference. "Why should I blame you?" she asked.

"I don't know. Let's at least have a reasonable conversation."

"On Friday. I'll meet you for lunch at noon. At the White Rock restaurant. It's on the esplanade." She hurried away, expertly weaving her way through the crowded corridor.

The events of the past few weeks had caught him off guard. It was as though the chance encounter with Lalitha had catapulted his past to centre stage. He felt a strong compulsion to speak to Justine. He tried her number again, but there was still no reply. In the end he phoned Margaret. She was very polite and distant. After exchanging formalities, he asked about his daughter.

"She's in South Africa," Margaret said.

"But that's where I'm phoning from," he said, surprised.

"So you've gone back there. Are you planning to stay?"

"For a while." There was an awkward pause. "Where will I find Justine?"

"Are you sure you want to see her?"

"Don't you think that's a rather strange question?"

There was a moment of silence. "I'll fax you her itinerary." A few more polite exchanges followed, then the conversation ended.

It was clear that Margaret still bore a lot of resentment towards him. He was thrilled at the prospect of seeing Justine but at the same time dreaded their meeting. It was going to be difficult to bridge all those missing years.

When he and Margaret parted, he had given up all his rights to his daughter in order to make her adjustment to a new life easier. She was only a child then and he knew that she had felt rejected by him. He had written and called, but Margaret had always intercepted the letters and the calls, ostensibly to protect Justine. In the end he had given up, realising the futility of trying to get past his ex-wife.

He knew nothing about Justine's life. She, his lovely daughter, had become a stranger. He wanted to make up for it in one swoop. If only ... and then he shrugged off the feeling of despondency which crept over him as he thought of the wasted years. He hoped Margaret would not renege on her promise to fax Justine's itinerary. It would be just like her.

The encounter with Lalitha was like a pebble dropped into the pool of his subconscious, the ripples fanning out in concentric circles. He tried to shake himself free of the past. He had to deal with the present. He thought of Justine and his heart raced again.

"For God's sake, man pull yourself together." His hand swept back a few strands of grey hair. It was as though meeting Lalitha had in some mysterious way connected the void between past and present.

He arrived at the restaurant in ample time and found a table on the patio, in the shade of an enormous blue umbrella.

Andrew waited. There was no sign of Lalitha. It was long past the time of their appointment, but he continued to wait, excusing her lateness. He had seen how busy she was. He waited for more than an hour and after several glasses of mineral water, sensed the curiosity of the waiters. It finally dawned on him that she was not coming, and he ordered lunch.

His questions about Lalitha would remain unanswered. She would remain a mystery.

He returned to his office that afternoon. On his desk was the fax from Margaret. With a sense of panic he realised that Justine was actually in Durban and would be in the same city as he for almost a week. It seemed incredible. She must be visiting with her husband. Had she brought the children? What was she doing here? He glanced at the sheet of paper and realised that she was staying at the same hotel he had used when he first arrived.

For a long time Andrew felt the uncontrolled pounding of his heart. His palms were sweaty as he reached for the telephone. He dialled the number and asked for the extension.

The phone rang. He waited. From his window he could see the ocean and two distant ships anchored in the bay. The phone stopped ringing. For a brief moment time seemed suspended — then, from down the line a woman's voice said, "Hallo."

SEXUALLY TRANSMITTED DISEASES
Achmat Dangor

EDWARD AND CARLA'S RELATIONSHIP seemed ideal, full of tenderness and respect. Their tolerance of each other set them apart from their friends whose own marriages and partnerships seemed besieged by the petty jealousies that afflict people who have been together for any length of time. They had been together now for five years and had remained monogamous and loyal throughout — a long time for both of them. That doesn't mean they didn't have differences or arguments or that they did not at times go without speaking to each other for a whole day. But they did have one sacred, redeeming rule: no matter what had passed between them during the day, they would not go to bed without speaking to each other, without breaking the barrier of silence, making the kind of peace that enabled them to go to sleep curled up close, even if the still bitter rebellion of their bodies prevented them from making love.

Their friends were, like them, professionals: lawyers, advocates, doctors, people who had travelled and lived abroad at some or other time. Edward was the only one who came close to living the precarious life of an artist. He was a professional photographer who could never keep up his end of a conversation when they all started discussing the legal intricacies of the Truth Commission or just what it meant to be a doctor at the Chris Hani Baragwanath Hospital in Soweto.

Edward, they all said, had a far more interesting life, what with having been part of a media entourage on a number of trips with former President Mandela and going on assignment to all the hot spots like Palestine, Rwanda and even Kosovo. A year ago he won an award for his coverage of Kabila's march into Kinshasa. But as soon as the conversation turned to the mutative nature of HIV or whether the criminal justice system was not making bad law by granting bail to even the most hardened criminals, they forgot about Edward's interesting life. It didn't matter to him, or at least that's the impression he gave. Perhaps he was annoyed or even hurt, but he said nothing and smiled and drank the wine that was passed to him.

It always happens that there is a circle of friends inside a circle of friends. Carla, John and Suresh made up that inner circle within the wider group. They always seemed to get together, this elite little pack, at parties or at the cinema, when they started off the evening along with everyone else, someone buying tickets and choosing a restaurant for dinner afterwards. Edward just could not become a part of this inner group, even though he was in John and Suresh's company as often as Carla. But this was only because he and Carla went out everywhere together as a couple. He didn't fit in with the other two in any real way, whereas Carla, John and Suresh had known each other for a long time, even before Edward came into Carla's life. They had studied together in London and slept in shifts in 'digs' far too small for three people.

"There's nothing romantic about getting into bed, dead tired, and having to breathe in someone else's sweat," Carla had once tried to reassure Edward even though he hadn't asked to be reassured. They had lived like '*compañeros*', John boasted, helped each other to survive when London and England — and the English — became really cold and gloomy. Edward tried to work out where John got all his little Spanish phrases like '*compañeros*' from and why, when slightly drunk, he greeted people with shouts of "*Hola!*" and "*Diga!*" It did occur to him that John was not merely showing off, that there was indeed some longing, some hidden anxiety beneath all this exotic posturing. But he was too polite — or too private — to ask John such an intimate question as "Why are you so insecure?".

Someone in that small group always started an argument or invited debate by asking out loud, right across everybody else's conversation, "So what do you think about...?" The issue was always a contentious one. Soon a battle raged, with the three of them the main combatants. Views were fiercely expressed, hands flailing, words flowing hotly. They joked, at intervals, and laughed uproariously, as if to remind themselves and others that they were still friends.

Whenever they started this sharp, biting banter, Edward drifted away to stand by himself. Carla, John and Suresh's getting together seemed to transform them from steady professionals into a loud and garrulous threesome whose high-pitched voices he did not recognise. Others around them looked on with smiles that said, "That's just Carla and John and Suresh being themselves." Some tried to join in, but soon moved away: it was obvious that the trio was an exclusive group, even if they didn't mean it to be so.

Then Suresh's wife Hanifa was appointed to the Bench, the first woman of Indian descent to become a member of the Provincial High Court. Apart from a few grumbles in the liberal press about the dangers of 'political appointments' to the judiciary, Hanifa's appointment did not evoke much opposition. In fact, doing the unusual was what people expected from politicians these days. Hanifa, her family and friends were conscious though that in this country controversy always lurked in the shadows of public equanimity. Edward was particularly impressed by Suresh's response. A flamboyant lawyer who took on all the difficult and high profile cases that others would not touch, Suresh now came across as a careful and measured man of the law. He quite rightly believed that his wife's new position placed a great responsibility on him. In spite of all the initial goodwill, she would still have so much to prove. She would have to demonstrate that she was a good judge, that she could be objective, that she wouldn't allow her struggle both politically and as a woman to influence her, that she could in fact fit in, even though her peers were mostly white men — and Afrikaners.

Suresh organised a party in Hanifa's honour and invited over all their friends. Hanifa was nervous, obviously under stress. Edward had heard from a newspaper editor with whom he was friendly that Hanifa was busy on a very sensitive military matter for the new president, presiding over a commission of inquiry into a 'subversive force' within the civil service. Suresh wanted her to celebrate her new status, but was sensitive enough to realise that she didn't want to seem too eager to become part of the new establishment. That night she drank a bit too quickly, spoke much too fast. Suresh stayed close to her, playing the good host and supportive husband.

However, he was soon drawn into that Carla-John-Suresh circle. They gathered, as if pulled by some centrifugal force, to a spot by the pool, its surface covered with brightly coloured balloons. Originally arranged in the form of the national flag, the balloons had drifted away and now bobbed about in a shapeless decoration. Edward watched the dull patterns playing about on the water, then looked more closely.

"Christ," he said, "these are condoms, someone's used dozens of condoms to decorate this pool."

John looked disdainfully at Edward, then started talking about a recent study that showed that most diseases suffered by people, gay or straight, young or old, black or white, had their origins in sex. Good sex or bad sex, it didn't matter.

"Bullshit!" Suresh said. "You damn psychologists come up with the weirdest theories."

"Well, think about it. Sex, we all know, has the most profound influence on the lives of all creatures," John said.

Another of their animated debates had begun.

"Bulls gore each other half to death, men — and women — murder and maim, empires go to war, friends become enemies and enemies friends." John's voice was mockingly deep and dramatic, like a stand-up comedian getting ready to deliver his punchline. "You ever stopped to think why?"

"Oh do tell us!" Carla said, rolling her eyes and sipping her wine.

"All for the sake of a fuck!" John said.

"How devastating!" Suresh said.

"What he means is men do all those things for the sake of a fuck," Carla said.

"Think about it," John persisted. "Sex has this enormous effect on our psyche and our culture so it must surely have the same effect on our immune systems."

"You mean because I fuck or don't fuck I can get cancer or lose the volume in my bones and get all shrivelled up and bent?" Carla asked.

Suddenly Suresh seemed uncomfortable with the tone of the conversation. Hanifa was talking to guests inside the house. She looked out through the French window and made a little questioning gesture, her head quickly moving from side to side, like Edward had seen dancers in classical Indian films do. It seemed to him as if she was mocking Suresh, who began to shift about. But the discussion had gained a momentum from which he could not now escape, even though his contributions were confined to grimaces or the occasional interjection.

"Precisely!" John went on.

"Don't be ridiculous," Carla said, taking another glass of wine offered by some passing hand.

John was in full cry. "It's what I call the Ingested Immune Deficiency Syndrome, or IIDS. All because we are so fucking coy about our fucking. Say someone here secretly wants to sleep with someone else, or they hire rent-boys or rent-girls, on the quiet, always on the quiet, the need to be private builds up huge wells of suppressed energy, all of which soon bursts and sends deadly toxins into the bloodstream. There you have the anatomy of a fatal disease."

"So, if we don't hide our sexual desires, sleep with whoever comes along, confess our infidelities, we'll all live long and healthy lives?" Carla asked.

"No, my charming little dolly bird ..."

"You dolly-bird me, John, and I'll kick you in the balls."

"I'm not talking about random promiscuity, I'm talking about focused lust."

"Listen, Johnny boy, not everyone is obsessed with sex, doing it or talking about it."

"But they conceal things, ingest them into their psyches,

contain them, and this makes them ill."

John's volubility spurred him into motion. He took Carla and Suresh by their elbows and turned them around so that they faced the other guests. "I tell you what, let's conduct a basic test." His eyes swept the faces of the guests, who for a moment interrupted their own conversations and looked expectantly at the trio who had turned, in formation like soldiers on parade. "Let's accept for a moment that STDs are the first manifestation of a secret, hidden love-life," he said.

"Oh God," Carla said impatiently.

"Just stay with me for a moment. Let's ask: who in this august gathering do you think doesn't have an STD or has never had one?"

Carla grinned.

"Edward," she said.

"What?" John asked incredulously.

"Yes, Edward has never had an STD."

"Listen," John said, then leaned over and whispered into Carla's ear.

"Yes, I have herpes and no, he hasn't even picked that up," she said.

John released his two captive friends and threw his hands up into the air. "Christ. Trust Mister fucken Township Hero himself to screw up the very founding assumption behind a hugely profound scientific theory!" He stalked off to get himself a drink.

Carla smiled.

At times like this Edward disliked Carla. Her face refused to take on a triumphant look, despite the devious way she had set John up. Now Edward would have looked thoroughly smug in his victory. Not Carla; she maintained her smiling, almost childlike openness. It was her very innocence that made him resent her. God! He wished that she was promiscuous, a woman who lived up to her bright and carefree image. He could live with that, not this enigma who often came home full of pain at the suffering she saw at the hospital, who had more than once told him that if he ever betrayed her with another woman it would "break my heart." John was back, drink in hand and another victim in tow. Suresh excused himself. He had to see how the dinner was doing.

Edward's eyes followed Suresh's rather nervous escape up the steps, saw Hanifa standing in the doorway, light falling onto her face. He began to compose a photograph with that camera-eye that all people in his profession possess. But he had seen that face somewhere, features more angular, the eyes much younger, but the same frightened expression, changing to something bold, daring ... a photograph, an etching ... in a gallery or museum ... an image drifting in space, rain distorting a shot he was trying to take. He was staring, and Carla was alongside him whispering gently, "Edward, you're staring."

He got himself a drink from the bar and stood by the pool watching the surreptitious movement of water and light beneath the absurd, bobbing carpet of balloons. (Of course they weren't really condoms.) He wondered idly what kind of response there would be if he started exploding them. Some of the partygoers would join in, attracted by the popping noises and the festive air. Everyone would assume that because quiet Edward was popping Suresh's decorations, it was a sanctioned bit of wildness, something to liven up the staid, talking circles that the party had settled into. He nudged at the balloons with his shoe and watched them ride on the small tide he was creating, then he went to find himself a seat. Hanifa was still there in the doorway, her arms folded. She talked to guests and laughed, but her eyes followed Edward, until he walked away from the pool and sat down in a chair on the lawn and was swallowed by the shadows of a lemon tree.

At midnight Carla came in search of Edward. She was more tired than drunk. She had another shift at Bara in the morning. The next day was Sunday and Edward could sleep late.

"Lucky you," she said.

Her voice was soft, and this seemed to provoke in Edward an inexplicable hardness. In the car he asked her if they had worked out how many people at the party had an STD.

"What?"

"A sexually transmitted disease."

She shook her head, tired and irritable, but did not answer. When they reached home she asked him not to let her over-sleep in the morning, then went to bed and fell asleep as soon as she lay her head on the pillow. Edward marvelled at her ability to fall asleep. At 2am he was still awake and got out of bed. He didn't want to take a tablet tonight or he wouldn't be able to wake Carla at 6.00. He had broken the alarm clock, swept it off the bedside table one night when they were making love. He realised suddenly how infrequent their love-making had become. And it was not only Carla who was too tired or too stressed. He too just didn't seem to have the emotional energy to make love anymore. His body couldn't perform by itself. Unusual for a man, he was told. Maybe that's why he'd never picked up an STD.

He suddenly remembered the series of photographs he had taken at Bara soon after Carla started working there. The image of a fourteen-year-old boy with a rigid, discoloured penis. Syphilis, gonorrhoea, he couldn't remember. Just the boy's tight lips and deep eyes. Edward rummaged through the filing cabinet, found the Bara series, then began to go through some older shots, slowly, beginning to savour the history he so rarely looked at. Carla had been good for him in more ways than one. She had forced him to look ahead, to contemplate the future and not dwell on the past.

"A South African sickness," she called it.

He dug out folios of the big events. June 1976 when he was only twenty-five, an aspirant artist who found out that the daily newspaper he worked for didn't care a damn about shades and angles or the hollow, empty face of a child who had just been shot. It was the 'scene' they wanted, the 'graphic' visual depiction that illustrated and brought to life the words that his colleagues, the copy journalists, wrote.

"This is a newspaper, not an art gallery."

He captured death with the detachment the dead deserved. He got divorced just about that time. More than twenty years ago. He hadn't seen his ex-wife and their two children in all of ten years now.

1986. Cape Town. Tyres burning in the street. He had captured on camera one of the first necklace murders. Fire poured from the woman's mouth.

Why did they get divorced? He couldn't really remember. A cycle of small infidelities. He slept with someone else, then Charlene slept with someone else, he had an affair, she had an affair, and so on, and so on. In the meantime, two children had been born. Then he went to New York and Charlene told him it didn't matter, she had someone else, and he didn't have to see the children, just make sure they got an education.

"You're free now, you can go on chasing your *lanieskap*," she had said with a smile. Christ, what meaning the phrase `white aspirations' had back then.

Charlene's boyfriend was of course `coloured', from the townships, safe, undemanding. The good old black consciousness days. Everything so stark, the truth so simple.

Edward shut the filing cabinet and leaned back in his chair. He imagined himself alone in this house. No, he couldn't imagine himself alone in this house. He tried to think of Carla leaving, Carla gone, with someone like John. No, John was gay, bisexual at the very least. Promiscuous and destined to die a very poignant death. Playing Russian roulette or at the hands of a jealous lover, or because he would test one of his theories and become HIV positive.

A death with meaning.

In any case, John wouldn't be able to live with someone as passionate as Carla. She would compete with him for the men he brought home. She had that way about her. She wasn't unfaithful or anything like that. Just too damn attractive for her own good. She had long hair and legs with the long, lazy movements of a courtesan. A typical Durban accent so strong when she got angry or emotional you couldn't understand her. "Don't tune me a lot of *kak*," she would warn when she felt she was being bullshitted, or "I really *smaak* you," when telling Edward that she loved, and desired, him.

A Sydenham coloured turn of phrase that made Edward want to laugh, no matter how ferocious their argument. He marvelled at how difficult it was for him to get angry, and this made Carla even angrier. (It used to have the same effect on Charlene.) What was there to get angry about tonight? Carla's discussion about something as intimate as an STD? She was different, like John and Suresh. It had nothing to do with her being from Durban and having a big loud family who spoke about God and sex with the same lack of reverence.

Edward didn't care to talk publicly about the number of women he had had sex with and how lucky he was not to have contracted some or other disease. Well, he didn't sleep around, not anymore. Not since Carla. But he didn't like to talk about it. Why didn't it make him angry then, when she had talked about it, told everyone that she had herpes and that he seemed immune? Maybe because she had warned him long ago about the herpes, that she had contracted it when she was sixteen, when boys were as stupid then as men are today, because they thought about 'risky sex' as part of the dare, the ability to with-draw just in time and ejaculate all over the woman, especially if she was a tickeyline one-night-stand.

It wasn't his nature to get angry or shout or become emotional about things, no matter how hurtful they were. That's why he was so good at his work. He could capture the most horrible things, click at them dispassionately — death, rape, carnage of all kinds — separate their humiliation from his vision so that what people saw on the front page of newspapers or in magazines or in essays on the walls of galleries was the terrible beauty of the events, unfiltered by his own frail human consciousness.

Why can't he go and wake Carla now? Shake her by the shoulder and tell her "I don't care how tired you are, but never, never again talk about such private things as my lack of STDs again. Not to strangers. Yes, John and Suresh are strangers. Anyone who is not in this bed with us is a stranger; they can't understand what happens here. So don't talk about it."

He felt tired, worn out, as if he'd had a fight with Carla. One of those draining emotional battles, she shouting and crying and he silent and withdrawn. But she was asleep and it was 3.00 in the morning and he'd have to wake her at 6.00. He looked up at the framed certificate on the wall — Photographer of the Year — and tried to remember which picture had won him that prize. Well, that didn't matter now — like an STD that didn't happen.

Then Hanifa's face came back to him. Its taut mask, the black-and-white grain of a perfectly presented image, unposed, naked, a horror of self-recognition. The best photographs are like mirrors. He searched, calmly now, through other portfolios.

1988. A crowd, a placard: `Where Is Stanza Bopape?' and Bopape's face on pamphlets which Edward had donated to the campaign to find all the people who had disappeared at night and whose graves were afterwards identified at the Truth Commission by former Security Branch cops.

1989. Durban. A side-street, just off West Street. A dark building loomed in the background, lights from a cafe, a woman, a man with his arm around her shoulders, patronising, like a patron, the master of her body.

My God, Van Tonder! The man so familiar with the young Hanifa was a captain in the Security Branch. Edward raised the photograph to the light. Wide aperture, slow exposure, no flash. The woman's strange, angular beauty, the policeman's plump face. Smug. He must have looked at that photograph dozens of times, without recognising Hanifa's mask of disdain. A hasty photograph, no time for care or composition, just 'catching' them in that sentimental setting, a humid rainy night in Durban, bad light and dark shadows, a velvety ugliness.

Edward rose and stretched himself to ease the stiffness in his back. He pinned the photograph onto the green baize notice-board that Carla usually came to look at in the mornings to see what news items Edward was working on as she sipped her coffee. It helped to live with a 'newshound', kept her in touch with the world.

He wrapped his Leica, the old-fashioned one, in its yellow cloth, took his personal cheque-book, left on his desk the cheque-book for their joint accounts. Carla didn't earn much as a doctor at a state hospital. But she was a specialist gynaecologist and would be okay, financially, one day. He punched a 6am ring tone into the cellphone and left it at her bedside. She was a modern woman and wouldn't be intimidated by the disembodied ringing. In the darkened hallway he stopped, went back to his study, removed the photograph from the notice-board and ripped it up.

As he drove he started rehearsing the story he would tell Carla. When she woke up and found him gone she'd think he was out on an assignment. It often happened — news was made even on Sundays. He'd have to call her during her lunch-break, hold on for a long time while they paged her. The hospital becomes frantic. What will he say? He'll think of something. He could lie, tell her that he suspected that she and Suresh were having a relationship — "You're fucking him," he could add for emphasis, but knew that it wouldn't work. "How can you even think that?" she would say and he would be ashamed and his resolve would crumble.

But why was he leaving? Perhaps because he could not stand the thought of becoming entangled in this business of remembering that was sweeping the whole fucking country. What the hell was he supposed to do with the knowledge that recognising Hanifa in that photograph brought? He imagined sitting Carla down and telling her, showing her the photo, watching her go quiet, and then listening to her on the phone telling Suresh that they had to meet alone, yes without John, and then responding to Suresh's persistent questioning: "Is it John, has he got himself into shit again? Oh God, Carla, you're not in some kind of involved-with-someone-else bind are you?"

Her voice would be controlled, but this would only betray her emotions: "It's about Hanifa, Surie, there's something you need to know."

Knowing the truth infects everything around you, like a

silent, airborne disease. It makes it worse when it is about someone you know and it is the kind of truth that no longer shocks people, like a friend or a lover or a brother having been broken by the 'system' and coerced into working for them. Worse still, it might have been voluntary, a choice. Would Carla's anger be more anguished, hateful almost, that Edward could even speculate about Hanifa being with this cop because she enjoyed it, once long ago when it was forbidden to love the enemy?

Well, he was not going to be there to tell Carla that he thought it unrealistic to believe that everybody who collaborated with the old government did so because they were forced to, that sometimes people did make choices which they could not explain, driven by a mysterious desire to taste evil, on your tongue or in your mind, on the surface of a skin excited by horror. Edward dismissed from his mind the image of himself, there to tell her all of this, trying to deal with her pain which she would bring home from her meeting with Suresh, heavy and burdensome like the aftermath of a shameful encounter, the semen of unwanted lust dripping from her vagina.

He tried instead to remember whether he had locked the door and the gate, and if he'd left the keys to the 'family' car in the right place. Carla hated looking for things when she was in a hurry. He had left her the bigger car. That made sense, much safer for her to drive, especially through the streets of Soweto. In any case, this little MG had been his before she returned from London to join him. He'd have to remember to fix the tear in the roof canvas. It could rain in the Karoo this time of the year. Shit, he'd forgotten how far a tank of petrol would take him. He hadn't serviced the engine for so long. What if he got stuck out there in the wilderness? Well, somebody would eventually come along. He would concentrate on this immediate problem, slow down, keep awake. That's what he'd focus on, getting through the Karoo in the middle of winter.

The sun was coming up. Edward turned on the radio, heard the announcer's early morning cheeriness and suddenly dreaded having to listen to the news. Why do they always want to tell you what's going on in the world? He pushed in the cassette which protruded from the mouth of the tape deck, wondering how long it had been there, and hoped to hear something sweet and surprising.

Leonard Cohen sang:

> *the rain falls down*
> *on last year's man*
> *that's a Jew's harp on the table*
> *that's a crayon in his hand ...*

DANCE CYCLES
Moropodi Mapalakanye

HAD YOU SEEN HIM all flaccid, walk up Bree Street from Fordsburg to Johannesburg Station, you would have sworn that he had never been the inflammatory volcano in the days of the struggle. You would have denied he had once designed and performed so many potent stage pieces, so provocative that they churned the stomachs of both liberals and rabid fascists. You would have sworn that he was not the firebrand in whose wake the turncoat and stooge had squirmed. For them the man had nothing but sulphur.

"Vilify them at every turn!" he would urge in those days. "Crush the lice against the concrete wall before dawn!"

Yet, on this day his chest seemed to have suffered the very fate to which he used to condemn those lice. It was crushed. His eyes said you lied if you remembered he once sought to incinerate the country so that a new order could dawn. He had actually designed deadly schemes that kept convicts awake whole nights, their hearts pounding at the prospect of glory the following day.

Yes, it was he. He who had fiercely fought lunacy to legit-imise the heroes. He who ceaselessly dared the European at every turn when wringing the African's neck had become a pas-sion for those who sought to retain the antiquated machinery.

It was he who had done it. This dazed wreck with corns and callouses under his feet, trudging the pavement with much pain in the soul. This insignificant thing. This bitterly creased brow which had once designed manoeuvres and taunts that had stretched the wits of the fiercest activist to breaking point, putting both victim and perpetrator on edge. Whatever doubts you would have had, it would have been him that you saw. Nobody else but him.

But, had you seen him so miserably dejected, knowing that even the worst of stooges were now sauntering in the richest gravy of the new dispensation, you would have blinked in disbelief.

"Why?" you would have asked. "Yes, why," many voices would have chorused, "why this ending when our erstwhile comrades are now lording over us all? When even the lousiest hypocrite now in the corporate world is smiling contentedly from the business pages of dailies underneath the 'People on the Move' banner? God, why?"

To which I would have rebuked, "Don't ask me about soiled matters. For who am I if not just a storyteller, the channel of agitated spirits? What solutions do you think I have to matters of power and filth? Have you forgotten that my domain is only words? Am I not the spit of Mokopu Mofolo? Stop nagging, man! Leave me alone. Watch the tale of the firebrand unfold."

"Ha! There goes the rag of a rotting wreck," some belle with well-seasoned thighs, in the ministry of education, interrupted his thoughts outside the Market Theatre, where the streets Bree and Wolhuter meet.

"What ... rag? Better that than a speck of depraved decadence in a pit of mud."

"Oh my gosh! He's still a poet hey? And a good one too," she taunted, swirling on her heel to rest her arms on her giggling friend's bare shoulders, flashing a portion of luscious buttock for him to get a tantalising glimpse.

"Heh heh heh, revolutionary orator," they laughed, their long polished nails playing sensually on each other's bodies and breasts, as they sauntered into the theatre.

"Attending a saucy launch of some sorts, I guess," the thought flashed through his mind.

He knew her very well. They had met somewhere along the contours of his artistic life, before his flight into exile in Zimbabwe many years ago.

"She was fresh from Transkei," he recalled. "Her skin was all dry patches and innocence, her soul hot with ambition and … yes … passion."

For a moment he stopped on the corner of Bree and Bezuidenhout streets, and for the millionth time since his return from exile he stood here, trying to read the meaning of a bright rainbow-coloured mural on a wall opposite him. The mural was dominated by a man-cum-woman who was about to swallow a spear blade first. Her/his breasts were banana-shaped. Behind him/her and the other human forms in the painting were streams of blue water and sky. He stared hard, thought hard but, as always, still could not get its substance. He crossed Bezuidenhout, turned and paused for the millionth time again, this time to read the meaning of another mural: two enormous reptiles, one green, one brown, had their tails inter-twined amidst dull rainbow colours on broken tiles, bricks, marble and dry mud. Again he was confused. He crossed back to study the first mural once again.

"Tourist things," he concluded and resumed his journey to the station.

His mind returned to the girl who had disappeared into the theatre. They had once worked together. Later, she joined some creative folks who had gathered enough pluck to parade their genitals in theatres around Johannesburg, America and Europe. Their menfolk did it with such a lack of shame. Some would just strip and stand there for all to see. Others took it a step fur-ther, stretching their buttocks apart to show the details in between them? Show after show, across three continents, *argh*!

"Haven't we seen enough of the black arse already?" some Europeans had complained, sipping wine and passion fruit between the shows in the foyer.

"A star is born!" newspaper headlines screamed about her.

"The brainy beauty from Cofimvaba has done it again," proclaimed the magazines. They ran profiles in their centre-spreads, saying things about her body fitting the content and style of progressive theatre.

"Who said all black theatre should be all drab, all because of petty norms against us baring it all?" magazines quoted the lady. "Tell me, who makes all the rules? I mean, sometimes this cliché called 'the struggle' is taken too seriously, you know. Personally I'm bored with all these isms, Black, African, etc, etc. I know all what I want in art, and I know how to get it."

"Must have been the big mouth that catapulted her into government," he surmised. "Her body too perhaps ... Gosh!

What he could not understand was how his mind continued to be preoccupied with her and her kind. He had battled in his resolve to disregard scorn and insult, to ignore those beyond redemption for some time now. Anger and deep hatred had taken their heavy toll in the long life of coining words of fire and brimstone. The result was this deepened humiliation, due to having discovered how even the finest of African visionaries were relegated to waste dumps by fumbling kaffirs who had demeaned the continent to mockery.

"No more shall I be dented by their jeers and scorn," he had concluded on arrival from exile. "All I need is to use my qualifications for the good of my small family." So he went out to get a decent job.

"What, a Zimbabwean engineering diploma?" one affirmative action manager had enquired with alarm.

"Yes, here are the papers."

"I mean, comrade, to be honest, what do Zimbabweans know about engineering? They can hardly produce a spoon?"

"Oh yeah? Are they so dumb? All I know is that they're far ahead of us as far as education is concerned."

"Who says?"

"I say. And facts speak for themselves. We have lots of their professionals in our country. Their doctors and teachers and television broadcasters."

"I'm talking about engineering, comrade. Anyway, forget it. We don't risk employing people with foreign qualifications in the department."

"But you have lots of them already. Even your ministers."

"As far as I'm concerned, they were educated in advanced countries like America, London, Russia and France."

"Lie. You went to school in Zambia yourself. Some of your premiers and ministers come from scandalous institutions such as the University of Zululand. Even miserable countries like Lesotho. And, for your information, American education is trash. The instant-coffee degrees they give to the African moron on a silver platter to make him a doctor overnight were even scrapped by the country itself recently. England has its own problems too. As for Zimbabwe, our country needs years of serious work before getting anywhere near catching up with their education. It is the colonial mentality in you that inspires your hatred for the country. Have you forgotten Zimbabwe has the best educated cabinet on the continent?"

"Look here, my mate, I'll be frank with you. You obviously belong to the wrong camp and now you bring your radicalism here. Have you forgotten what it did for your party? So soon? And don't think I don't know you. Well, you've had it … That's it."

"No, I haven't. This is war. Prepare for a protracted battle."

"Shame. Where do you get the energy? Anyway, good luck with your war."

He continued looking for a decent job, but in vain. After a year he decided to return to the arts.

Now his heart weighed heavier with each step he took back home. It was supposed to be pay-day at the Afrighia Arts Centre where he worked. For two months now he had gone without any salary because there was no sponsorship according to his boss, Mahmood El Al Eh Hassan Singh.

"Donors are pumping all the money into the new government's Operation *Vuka Afrika*, my friend."

Singh always waited till the last day to explain. For the twenty years they had known each other, Singh had always complained to his workers about not having money on pay-days. But despite this his personalised Centre thrived, and Singh continued to amass property. The latest was a seaside cottage in Durban, and of course there was his children's exclusive education and their more than comfortable life.

"This snivelling Mahmood is a sham," he muttered with mounting anger. "Just like that publisher-playwright-poet fraudster with lots of mucus in the nose. They're all fakes, the whole lot of them. An unprincipled bunch I call them. Not a grain of shame in their hearts. No care for integrity and efficiency. Good at backstabbing. Where are they leading us? But … what's become of me? This anger, where will it get me?"

He crossed West Street. The pavement narrowed into a hostile passage between Indian shops and stalls of street vendors. As in most parts of the city centre, here pedestrians squeezed their way through to their destinations. Freedom had come with a surging flood of fortune seekers to the city of gold, and every piece of space was being put to maximum use.

Now emotions were stretching his mind beyond the point of making sense. He was oblivious of the sweltering life around him. The concern with this deep anger, which kept returning regardless of his attempts to suppress it, was a source of chastisement. Exhaustion from the search for a lasting solution to the predicament spread to the body and lungs, transforming itself into physical pain. He reduced his pace, at times stopping for a while, clenching and unclenching his fists, slowly rotating his shoulders and stretching his neck to relax a bit.

He inhaled deeply and on the count of eight exhaled. He repeated this again and again. But the fourth time a ton of human muscle rammed into him from behind, with such force and carelessness that it sent him reeling forward.

"Soli," the ton muttered a sibilant apology and proceeded on his way, buttocks protruding, chest thrust forward, huge, perforated earlobes flapping, vanishing into the crowds, a spear and fighting sticks tightly held in his right hand.

The victim spun, knocking over a fruit stall before he regained his balance. But his books lay scattered on the pavement. Peaches, mangoes and apricots rolled down the street. Obscenities flew all over, denouncing the primate that walked with its eyes in the sky. Someone reminded him that he was in Jo'burg, where people should wake up from village stupor.

But he had more urgent things to attend to than to listen to his detractors; his strewn books and papers had to be rescued. Among them was the only copy of his latest play.

"My fliend," an Indian hawker confronted him, "how much you got to pay?"

"What?"

"You got to pay, my fliend."

"But it's not my fault ..."

"Talking lubbish, my fliend. How much you got?"

"But you left the man who knocked me!"

"Now you make me angly, my fliend. Want big tlouble? No more this-this with woman in bed? Want to go to jail?"

"Look here, black swine, this is neither Punjab nor Kashmir, nor am I an Indian, Hindu, nor an untouchable in your caste system."

"Okay, okay, fliend. Me talk nice but you fight now. Why, my fliend? Okay, *hamba khaya*. But, next time look-look when you walk."

"And you should learn to respect people, primitive thing." He continued on his way. "Damn village idiot," he cursed under his breath. "Rubbish freedom. Why should they overwhelm the town with these wild things walking the streets as if they were blindfolded? Some mule ploughs through you as if you were nothing but wind. Worse when crossing the streets. Nobody knows what robots are for. They come flying right into you, fleeing from braking cars.

"Just look at the pavements. All crowded with junk ... What irks me even more is the village animal selling for the very Indians who own the shops opposite these pavement stalls. I mean isn't it better to cause the commotion on the pavements while selling for themselves? But oh no, not our African brothers. They'd rather jam pavements with Indian stuff, for their kind to ram into us like fleeing buffalo.

"Hold on ... What am I talking about? Isn't it their country too? Anyway, what's wrong with packing the city to the highest storey with villagers and erecting shacks all over the show. It's their country too. Let them give the town planners and administrators something to think about for a change. Yes, come on, village cow, let there be chaos everywhere. It's high time the clown is jolted from his day-dreaming."

A minibus taxi jerked him from his thoughts whilst crossing West Street. The driver shouted insults that no other person would dare repeat. The taxi came to a dangerous halt next to him, its horn blasting his eardrums with a piercing metallic wail. He jumped and hit his head hard against a steel pole on the other side of the road. People burst out laughing and the driver drove off with more damning abuse. A cuddling young couple advised that he should have stayed in Chiawelo and kept himself busy there by planting maize instead of playing in these vicious Jo'burg streets where he obviously knew nothing about robots.

He was too tired to care. He continued on his way, nursing a hard protuberance above his left eye. If only he could get a seat in the train to Naledi, where home was. He had had enough. It simply was not his day.

"And that Singh thing ...!"

He was now where Sauer Street ended and Queen Elizabeth Road began its stretch to Braamfontein. Here he heard a booming sound above the grinding noises of engines and screeching tyres. He was no stranger to the source of the sound and knew exactly where it came from. Yes, there. Just a few paces away. There where the attentive crowd was, swaying from side to side to the tune.

"I'll listen for a while," he decided and joined the crowd.

He knew the musician from the days when the man used to play gospel music on a concertina near Johannesburg Station. He was still playing gospel, only now he was doing it on two high-tech keyboards, with synthesiser for backing drums, percussion and cymbals. The keyboards were connected to old but powerful speakers and the combination gave out hypnotising sounds. Thanks to the power from a nearby generator.

He was captivated by a kind of symbiotic fusion between the musician and his tunes, and realised that much as polio had completely reduced his legs to lifeless miniatures, nothing could harm his soul and its apparent holiness. However, he wondered if there were any living organs below the belt. He doubted it.

For the first time he noticed that the man's torso stood out in stark contrast to the lower part. The chest was broad and the arms mounds of muscle and thick veins owing to years of playing the concertina and now these keyboards. It was as if his fingers could see by the way they controlled the keys with such mastery. The melodies were perfect.

The musician was not given to performing antics though. His face betrayed no artificiality or pomposity. He seemed to play more for his own spiritual fulfilment than to please the admiring crowd. You could sense a tangible inborn connection between the man's soul and the intricate notes he played. Something holy gripped you. His whole being was intertwined with each song, and his belly button was permanently sucked in by intense devotion.

His voice had a burnt quality to it. You could not discern his lyrics too clearly, yet you travelled to other worlds on these rich sounds. You imagined a choir of angels providing vocal backing, filling up where his could not reach. And the skies seemed to rupture making way for cherubs to fly down from the highest throne. No high priest in this sinful world would ever match the spirituality of the man. Every song triggered a tingling sensation from the nape down to the end of the spine and the whole body shook.

For a moment he closed his eyes. When he opened them he saw, in the centre, close to the musician, a mad man dancing with abandon. He understood the tranquillity in the insane man, and chose a space somewhere on the inside edges of the circle where a few mothers from domestic duty were humming and swaying to the rhythm of the tunes.

From time to time a spectator would break from the circle with much humility, to give generously, dropping a coin or two into the two hats in front of the musician.

"Now this is gospel music," he thought. "Not that flavourless chaff that comes out of recording houses, the rubbish we hear on the radio and television. And the man has always been in the streets, without any of them thinking of promoting him ... At least he can survive. Unlike us, pathetic rubbish always looking for sponsors ... Oh damn it! What am I talking about? Keep quiet, my man."

So he kept quiet and listened. The waves took him to those that had stifled his self-expression. Those that had betrayed him. Melodies elevated him to some world beyond the joys of heaven, the trials of hell. His heart beat in time with the heavy bass, blood tingling the tips of his fingers and toes. He was filled with the tranquillity of a soul without want. The songs filling him with the serenity of a monk meditating in the wilderness.

Now the musician was a man-mountain carrying him beyond the reach of trials, far from the scheming artists, producers, managers and the forces that are at variance with the growth of man. He began to hum to the tune about a man who rode in a trolley of fire to heaven. In the middle of the song he started to sway along with the mothers. When it ended, he had moved a bit closer to the musician. Then came the hymn about a traveller who once used a rock as a pillow and saw angels ascending from heaven. The rich sound of the instrument varied with each new stanza, adding more sweetness to the soothing atmosphere.

He began to shuffle to the rhythm, three steps forward, three steps backward, all the time avoiding the mad man who was all disorder and sweat. He wished the song would never end. He swayed forward, backward, sideways ...

Then came the tune that really set him free, the one about fixing one's matters with Jesus "now now".

This was too much for him. He rushed forward, crouching

with the beat, and placed his books and papers next to the musician.

Then, still bent, he reversed at such speed that it seemed he was going to burst through the circle. But just as people were about to give way, he stopped with the perfect timing of a stage virtuoso. His spine, as if connected to the keyboards, was tingling, rising and falling with the ebb and flow of the musical waves. Feet flicked to the sides, arms flapped like the wings of a huge bird, face beamed with absolute contentment.

He moved forward, executed two or three little leaps in the centre, placed his palm flat on the ground and kicked backwards one leg at a time. He rose, pumping his forearms forwards and backwards as the legs returned to side flicks — more quickly this time — his pelvis all twists and thrusts.

The mad man opened his arms wide, reaching out to take him on. He ignored him and did a frog jump, lashing out with both arms and legs. There was no space in the circle for the mad man any more. So he went out to continue his dance behind the spectators who laughed at his courtesy.

Having driven his rival from the ring, he now filled the space with rhythmic stretches, spins and kicks. The circle opened wider. He put his forehead on the ground gyrating his bottom up in the air, at the same time intertwining his feet with the speed of the devil. His lower teeth were on his upper lip. But as the gyrations gained momentum, the tongue came out as if trying to lick the pavement.

"Call this a dance?" a man asked, turned on his heel and hurried towards the Eldorado Park taxi rank.

"Women," a frightened mother said, "are we going to stand here and watch another woman's child murdering himself like this?"

"Bloody loafer!" another protested, "dancing the whole day instead of looking for work as other men do."

A few mothers dispersed. Some of those who remained behind were soon to regret it. When he rose his eyes were wild, red and huge. Still keeping to the beat, he did the kick-jump dance. The full might of these kicks caught some unfortunate ones in the stomach while others got it in the neck.

Suddenly the music stopped. Two boys rushed forward to help the musician pack up.

But he continued dancing as he collected his books, and watched the musician leave with his crew. He waved them goodbye and began to cross Sauer Street. In the middle of the street, he threw his books in the air so that motorists had to swerve and brake to avoid the shower. He gyrated vigorously, this time to very loud music at the door of a Portuguese fish and chips shop. He had forgotten all about home. He danced until the shop closed. Then he headed for Faraday, dancing wherever he found music along the way.

His wife spent two sleepless nights worrying about him. Then people came to tell her about his strange behaviour in town. She went out searching for him but without success. Once she spotted him near the OK Bazaars. But before she could reach him, he disappeared, dancing, into the crowds.

Somewhere in the city the overseers of arts and culture proclaimed, "He was one of our best young artists."

"Of course he was, his contribution was immense."

"In the struggle too."

"Oh yes, he's a hero."

"What can we do?"

"Build a monument in his honour."

"Perfect!"

"We support the idea."

"A monument is the right thing to do."

"What about a budget?"

"A budget?"

"Yes, a budget."

"God, the budget."

"So?"

So they found a derelict Edwardian toilet on the outskirts of the city, which was once the preserve of Europeans only. They revamped it, called it a pavilion and named it after him. It stands proudly as an African folk-story centre. Here people sit and enjoy their beer, listening to live music, poetry, and folk stories. It stands in his honour.

JULIE AND THE AXEMAN
Finuala Dowling

WHEN SHE PUT THE children to bed that night, the axeman outside was the least of Julie's worries. She expected Wills home at any minute, and Wills could deal with the axeman.

Thinking this way reminded her of the question a very glamorous, manicured, stilettoed Afrikaans woman had unexpectedly asked as they stood side-by-side at the basins of a ladies' loo: "*Wat, eintlik, is a man vir?*" Julie remembered the question not so much for the sudden intrusion of intimacy from a stranger, but for the way the woman had emphasized the simple preposition '*vir*'. She remembered it also because at the time she had just got off the plane from Holland after ten years in exile; this had happened in the bloody airport loo, if you don't mind. The idea of being back in South Africa was surreal enough without existential/feminist questions from a bottle blonde with dream nails inside a public convenience. If she ever saw that woman again, she would say that, in her considered (two children, six years of marriage) opinion, the purpose — the '*vir*' of a man — was to deal with the axeman rustling in the bushes outside at twilight.

Joshua and Nina were asleep in the little baby beds Wills had made before they were born, tucked under the duvets she had silk-screened herself. The family shared a large bedroom, and had done so from the moment Julie discovered how nights could be spent going back and forth, back and forth to the baby's room. She picked the children's dirty play clothes off the floor and dropped them in the laundry basket. Then she mopped the floor and wiped the sides of the bath and picked up the bits of broken polystyrene that had been a happy part of pre-bedtime games. She decrumbed and straightened the marital bed where the children had enjoyed their afternoon rusks. She put the Walt Disney videos back in their boxes, stacked them on a shelf, and walked through to the kitchen.

The pleasant curry/orange smell of butternut soup reminded

her of how hungry she was. She stirred the pot but did not taste it. Julie liked to wait for Wills to come home before she ate. It was a good way of staying slim and Julie liked to stay slim because then she was in control. Of something, at least.

Outside, the axeman parted the overgrown bushes. Julie distinctly heard a human movement in the undergrowth. She had not dared to look out as she crossed the sitting room en route to the kitchen, for fear of looking at him eye-to-eye, yet blindly, because she could not see out whereas he could see in. When they had finished repairing the house, she and Wills could get to work on the garden, pruning away some of the wilderness where robbers could hide. She had seen tantalising glimpses of an old stone wall and a sealed-up lych-gate behind the ivy. How lovely it would be to sit reading a book under the lemon tree while Josh and Nina made mud pies at the tap. She especially liked the vision of herself with a book, everything else accomplished. Reading was a great restorative in Julie's life and she rewarded herself by the chapter for housework well done.

Julie felt self-conscious standing in her brightly-lit kitchen with no curtains while outside the axeman watched her with impunity, blending in with the darkness. She would speak to Wills tomorrow about putting up some rails. Her hand-painted curtains would look best with a wrought iron rod, but Wills wouldn't have time for metal work what with the water-proofing that needed doing, so they might have to settle for pine rods instead. Right now she'd have happily settled for plastic tracking, anything that would screen her from the intruder's horrid prying gaze.

To show the axeman that she was not frightened, Julie squashed a few crumbs of the home-made wholewheat raisin loaf on the table and put them nonchalantly to her lips. Just as she was swallowing, the phone rang. She rushed to get it in case the noise woke Joshua or Nina.

"Hi Julie, Wills. Everything all right?"

"Yes ... the children are asleep. When are you coming home? I thought you'd be here by now."

"Looks like I'll have to stay later than I thought. Mario wants to open the restaurant tomorrow night and we still haven't finished the bar counter. Don't wait for me. I'll have supper here."

"Well, alright, but don't let him ply you with beers."

"Sure, sure. Can I bring you anything?"

Wills knew all about her late night sweet tooth.

"Well, if you were passing a caramel cone ."

Now that she knew Wills would be late, Julie took out her recipe book. She'd make her special rich fruit cake, get it ready for Joshua's birthday party on Sunday. Then when Wills came in it would be just out of the oven and they could go to bed with the caramel cone and the sweet warm smell of baking.

Julie thought how nice Wills was, how after six years and two babies he'd still stop off after a hard day's carpentry to buy her a Kit-Kat or a caramel cone. Indeed, that he would do a hard day's carpentry without lamenting his artistic career, put on hold by domesticity. Although hers was too. She hadn't sung for ages, except to the babies, and the silk-screened bed covers and hand-painted curtains were the only mementoes of her days of textile design. But these were sacrifices that they had made for one another, in the interests of the nest, and theirs was to be a superior nest.

The cake stood steaming on the wire rack and Wills was not home. Julie wanted to go and check on the children, but did not want the axeman to follow her progress through the illuminated house. He could track her silently and swiftly in the dark and set up camp outside the children's window. She would fool him by ducking and going nearly on all fours all the way to the bedroom. The moment she did this she felt completely terrified. Now she had given the axeman a definite reality. By crouching and skulking, she had confirmed that he existed and that he was stalking her. That was when she heard a sound outside that was more than just the south-easter lifting the fallen leaves.

The children's deep breathing reassured her a little. She lay down next to Josh and smelt his baby breath. It was a bit rich, as though he were sickening for tonsillitis again. Another thing to do tomorrow: see the doctor. Saturday mornings at the surgery were busy, but if Wills looked after Nina, Julie could manage to entertain Josh while they waited. Better be well rested, then. She reached over to the double bed and pulled her nightie out from under the pillow. Still lying down, she struggled out of her clothes and into her pyjamas. Then she tiptoed to the bathroom to brush her teeth and put on some of the cheap Vitamin E cream she had been substituting for the Multi-generative Night Serum she could no longer afford.

Julie crept under the covers, stretching out her legs and then curling up in her customary foetal position, closed her eyes and instructed herself to sleep. A branch snapped and a window rattled. Then there was no noise at all until the old house creaked a little, either of its own accord or in response to a stranger's footfall.

The phone startled her. She answered it under the bedclothes.

"Julie. Hello, darling. You sound very muffled."

"Wills? For God's sake I thought you'd be back by now!"

On the other end of the phone she detected happy male laughter and she could swear that someone was singing "Sugar, Sugar, you are my candy girl ..."

"Don't be cross, Julie love. Mario made this lovely veal I mean meal, well it was both and ..."

"You're drunk aren't you? I've been waiting at home for you and you're having a party. I can hear music in the background ... don't tell me Rick and Luke are there."

"Well the fellows knew I was here so we've just been jamming a little and cracking a few beers and Mario's really pleased we got the job finished so I ... I deserve a little fun, don't I? Don't wait up for me ..."

Julie slammed the phone down and marched to the kitchen in full view of the axeman. Deserve a little fun, indeed. Fun was a very distant memory. She cut a large slice of cake and ate it standing up while she waited for the kettle to boil. Then she sat down and had another large slice with her tea. Anyway, what was all this about deserving? The culture of entitlement. The axeman is entitled to rape me and murder my children. Wills is entitled to a night out with the boys. Bloody hell. Still, she felt entitled to the cake.

What was worse was that Wills would come back in the middle of the night, drunk, and sleep late tomorrow so she'd have to get up early and shush the children and probably take them to the park so Wills could sleep. Then he'd be hungover in the afternoon too, and no help to her whatsoever, never mind the curtain rails. Bloody hell. And he'd be drunk driving home all the way from Sea Point which was on the bloody other side of the bloody mountain. And the tail lights of his truck didn't work. So if he didn't kill himself he'd be pulled over and locked up for the night. Not that he didn't deserve it.

But he didn't deserve it. Julie thought of life without Wills and she couldn't bear it. Somewhere underneath the piles of nappies and the leaking taps and the rusty gutters and the night waking and the frugal soup dinners and the sodden towels, they were still soul mates. The whole thing of going into exile, getting the hell out of South Africa: that was a joint decision. You can't do stuff like that entirely alone. It's too frightening. Setting up the studio in Holland, giving birth in a foreign land. And now, back home, all the work they had to do together. Because that was how you did it, how you built a home, built a family, built a relationship. There were real bricks and real mortar and your actual manual labour to make the whole marital enterprise work.

There was stuff beyond that too, stuff that belonged to the long view. She wanted Wills to live not just for the here and now of her toiling fecundity but so that in their old age they could walk on the beach together and say, "We lived through that. We made the right decision. And then we came home, to live in South Africa again. We didn't desert. We were white people who refused to serve the regime and then we came back and we cleared away the undergrowth and mended the roof and lived poor but brought up our children as good citizens." And then, in their complacent later age, they could drink again together, play music together, make art together. The simple vegetable soups, the carpentry and sewing would have left them lean and still attractive — still ready for each other. Once the children had subsided, gone out like the tide, leaving only a hard beach for walking.

Now she had eaten a good quarter of the cake and she was angry. She was angry with Wills for leaving her alone and making her eat Josh's birthday cake and depriving her of the one tiny morsel of social life she did have, namely his company, his conversation. And angry with herself for eating so much and not being able to sleep and not being able to bear all of this. She was angry with the damn bloody axeman for stalking her when there were other homes with far better pickings. Homes that were inhabited, moreover, by South Africans with no struggle credentials whatsoever, who somehow deserved the axeman more than she. Especially, she was angry with Wills, who was probably sitting right now on a piano stool, laughing in that cute, helpless way of his. Not a care in the world, because everything was her responsibility, including the man outside, waiting to make her his prey. Oh no. She wouldn't stand for this.

Nina was not as heavy as Josh, but all sleeping bodies are heavy. She carried Nina first, leaving the door open so that the axeman would know she was coming back for her other child. She settled Nina in her cocoon of blankets on the back seat of her car and ran inside to get Josh. After she'd put him onto the seat next to his sister, she didn't bother to go back and lock up. She just drove straight through the late summer night to find her husband and make sure he got home safely so that, when he was safe, she could tell him how angry and frightened and vulnerable she felt when he wasn't.

Mario, Luke, Rick and Wills were all very merry when the door of Mario's restaurant burst open to reveal Julie, bearing what looked like a large bundle of blankets. She dumped Josh in his father's arms and then went back out through the swing doors for Nina. The men welcomed her with all the mirth and good cheer that they had built up through the evening of manly work, of food, drink, music and smoking. Julie's fury cut through the thick fug of their joviality. Though they did not understand why, they saw that she was distraught and that the party must end in deference to her passion. It was strange to them because they were very happy and they weren't doing anything wrong at all, just having some innocent fun after a hard day's work. They were even pleased to see Julie, appreciative of her red-haired beauty and her fierce motherhood. They'd have liked to reach out, take the children in their arms, pour Julie a drink, flirt with her, tell Wills what a lucky chap he was. But they could see she didn't want to play the game called Woman In A Room With Jolly Men, so they were silent, watching Wills as he faced his doom.

"Come home right now, Wills. I'll drive behind you."

"But why ... I don't understand. I was about to leave anyway ... Why'd you come all this way ... and the children ... I don't get it, Julie."

What did he know of death or widowhood or rape or the massacre of the innocents? It was very snug in Mario's restaurant, far from the roving axeman, far from her maternal and uxorial fears. In the movie version of this scene, Wills would be the charming raffish boy of the piece. And she, she was made to feel like this ungainly baggage lady, laden with responsibilities and snotty, sleeping children, mad enough to drive thirty kilometres in the middle of the night and embarrass her husband in front of his stupid, stupid friends.

"I don't want to talk about it," Julie said through her teeth. "Just carry Josh to my car and then get in the truck and drive home in front of me."

Quite meekly, Wills did as he was told. As she drove behind him, Julie thought how his battered, rusty truck was like a rudderless boat. No, Wills himself was a rudderless boat. It was all very well for him to be a cheerfully good-natured husband and father, doing his chores with humour and charm. But he didn't really, deep down, share the burden. He waited for instructions. Bath the children. Make the bottle. Wipe up the vomit. Fetch the Calpol. She did not want a bloody servant.

She wanted a helpmeet. That was the word. And he must feel his responsibilities, sense the nature and the extent of the burden and shift himself accordingly. Why did she have to be the fishwife, ordering him about? Let him shift for himself, she thought.

Tears started to roll down Julie's cheeks. It wasn't just tonight or this thing that had happened tonight. It was the whole sad, rickety enterprise of marriage. Marriage came to a woman like a circus came to a child: success was inverse to the store set by the event. And Julie had set great store.

Even while she was still parking her car, Julie knew that the axeman had left. She realised, moreover, as Wills struggled awkwardly through the door with Josh, that the axeman had never been there at all. Her fears had been completely fantastical. She had been driven to them.

Now that the children had been transported across town and back without waking, and Wills was safely in her bed where he ought to be, asleep, and the cold soup had been decanted and put in the refrigerator for the next night, Julie herself did not want to be home. It was a quarter to four. In two hours' time the children would awake triumphantly from their night of slumbering travel, ready for a fresh set of nurturing acts, of sweet milky tea and rusks, of boiled eggs and toast soldiers, of mud pie games by the tap, of wiped bottoms and blown noses, of soothing words and imaginative stories, of the whole world patiently opened up and named for them. No. Julie picked up her book off the bedside table, placed it in her bag, took her car keys and went out.

There was nowhere in particular she could go at a quarter to four in the morning, nobody who would open their door for her without question or exclamation of amazement. Though it was so little that she wanted. Just an hour or so to read under lamplight, just a ration of uninterrupted sleep, just an interval where she did not have to do anything. So she drove up to the top of the village, where the suburban road joined the scenic coastal drive. Then she turned off into a cul-de-sac and parked her car at the end of it, under a street lamp. She took out her book and enjoyed the crack of its firm hardbound spine as she opened to her place. The words on the page soothed her, so neat and separate and ordered. A well-written book, Julie knew, is one which sets experience at a precise distance where the reader may both identify with and remain apart from the welter of life. When she was quite lulled, Julie closed the book and leaned her head back against the back rest. She had just started to drift when there was a knock at her window.

It was the axeman, exactly as she had imagined him.

"Lady, have you got a light?"

THERE'S TOO MUCH SKY
Moira Lovell

THEY SAY I MUST begin by walking again through the door into the courtyard. I take a step out into the blue sun of autumn. But when I look up, I see there is too much sky. And I go back inside to where the ceilings are low and white. I take a small *riempie* stool from the spare bedroom and stand on it. I stretch. The ceiling is firm under my palms. That's all right. I'll just stay here and maybe read or play the piano or write something. It's some kind of life.

That isn't how I used to be. It's how I've become.

Before, I could go anywhere. On my own. I felt the right size in the world; and measured my stride in it. One thing I really liked was the city. For therapy, after a cerebral day. Just wandering about, letting my mind off the leash.

It's a misnomer really — city. Town would be more appropriate. In the days when I wandered in it it was very quaint, dominated by a dowager city hall as imperial as Queen Victoria herself; and networked with narrow alleys of craftwork, art, antique and book shops. The crass chain-stores in the main street were housed in buildings whose fronts still wore the filigree accessories of nineteenth century architecture; and the two banks stood centrally, side by side, in classical pillared solidity. It gave you the certainty of a particular past; and the illusion of a future.

I suppose changes had already begun. I just hadn't noticed them. And then I was forced to.

One late Friday afternoon in the summer I was walking my mind in the bookshop alley, wishing there were rather more books than were there, smelling the rain in the red bricks, hearing my own footsteps on the slabs. Suddenly the world grew dark. I was surrounded by men who seemed to be giants in designer kit. One of the giants had his hand over my mouth. I couldn't breathe. The other giants were pulling at my swingbag to snap it from my shoulder. I wasn't directing my body, it fought by itself. But it's a small specimen. Underweight. Underpowered. Untrained in self-defence. An obvious target for designer-kitted giants.

It lost the bag, stuffed with credit cards and identification documents and old letters and lipstick. It heard itself cry out as it fell in slow motion onto the slabs. It felt three giants running over its backbone and one giant tugging a fistful of hair from its head. It saw the giant gang flashing collective advertisement teeth as they trophied their prize away. It lay for a moment. And when it hauled itself up, the buildings seemed dizzy on their feet, about to topple at the end of their era. The body stood identity-less in an empty alley, sensing its flesh becoming bruise. And a fistful of hair, brushed by a passing wind, spun off like a multi-legged spider into a drain.

A thin man in spectacles rattled out from a cheap concertina security-gate. "It all happened so fast," he said, losing his credibility in cliché. And adding a lie. "The security-gate sticks. I couldn't get ..."

He was interrupted by a party of marinated lawyers falling through the yellow-wood door opposite. "Hey, that was nasty. You'd better come in."

They ushered me into a woody room, hilarious with booze.

"We're having a party," the one deemed it necessary to explain. "To welcome a new partner."

Another one said, "Hey, uh, have a brandy. Good for nerves."

A secretary with wine in her cheeks took charge. "Sit," she said, offering me a chair. I began to shake.

"Here." The brandy came. And various of the curious.

"It's a bad lane," somebody said. "Especially on a Friday."

The secretary phoned the Flying Squad who took two brandies to arrive. There were a pair of them. One hung about; the other had a clipboard and some papers, but no pen. "What happened?" he asked, pulling at the top of a ballpoint he had been handed so that its innards dropped on the floor.

"I was walking the ... um ... and some men ..."

"Three," one of the partying lawyers confirmed. "I was

watching through the window."

"Three men attacked ..." I continued.

"They had a neat plan," the astute observer interrupted. "The one got his hand over her mouth so's she couldn't scream. The other ... uh ... she put up quite a fight."

"Knives?" the policeman asked, reassembling his ballpoint.

"I don't ..."

"No. They just pulled on the bag till the strap snapped. She'll have bad bruising there on the shoulder and round the armpit. Probably down the ribs too. Looked like one of those strong, handcrafted leather handbags."

"Yessus, I tell you, lady, you're a lucky one," the policeman said, wagging his ballpoint at me. "Two blocks down from here and they would have had knives. Guns, even." He paused, looking for the right column on his form. "So what've you lost?"

Hair, I thought. An old handbag I rather liked, full of replaceable things. About three rands fifty. And a city. Sorry, misnomer — a town.

I've never been back. Though I have driven through it. Racing the robots. It passes through the windows of my car like a video on fast forward. There are pyramids of over-ripe tomatoes in the main street, and women sitting on newspapers, crocheting loud conversations and cloths. There are men with plastic hangers and men with wire hangers remodelled into lopsided wastepaper baskets and bowls. There are bananas and the peels of bananas. There are watches and neckchains and radios stolen for sale; and if you look carefully you may even recognise your own.

The walls of the wandering lanes, I am told, have become graffiti boards; and the alleys themselves, urinals.

Minibus taxis toyi-toyi through the town; a selection of sirens whines; old contraptions wheeze through the thin throats of exhaust pipes; unwise pedestrians make rash crossings.

It is no longer my town. It is a foreign town. And foreign tongues converse in it.

I felt as if, like an inferior fabric, I had lost some colour and shrunk. Certainly, I had to reroute my lifestyle. And so I determined to turn the patch of territory I do own into a sanctuary. The Persian word for garden is paradaiso. The English equivalent is obvious.

There's a lot of sky above my paradaiso. And beyond. It doesn't stop at garden fences the way ground does. So that one seems to have rather more of it than one has earth. But it won't be owned or tamed. If you want to tame something you have to focus on the ground.

So I did. I dug things and designed things; I cut some branches and caressed some trunks — though tree-hugging is, I think, an overrated activity. The trunks of trees are altogether too barky and unrelenting. Far from sharing their strength, they scratch and slash the softer human form.

I learned the names of roses I liked and planted them. Mostly white. I made a tubland of herbs outside the kitchen door, and a vegetable square beyond.

First the weeds grew; later the plants. And plant diseases.

Then I learned the names of herbicides and insecticides and fungicides and sprayed those apologetically about.

Later, I made paths and put down paving-stones. And I bought a stone bench so that I could sit down and look at the order I had made. I bought a birdbath too.

Small birds came to it. Featherfully splashing and shrieking. As children do in puddles and pools. And once a hadeda, cumbersome in a lilac taffeta petticoat, squatted there, using it as a bidet.

I sat on the stone bench and watched the flutter. My cat watched too. Green-eyefully. Voicing her desire, as all bird-watching felines do, in the staccato throat-rattle that sounds like muted machine-gun fire.

I sat on the stone bench and looked at the order I had made. And my cat, sleek brown Burmese, looked at the order too. Proprietorial. As decorative as garden sculpture.

And when I turned away to go inside, out of the sky, which cannot be ordered, there fell a great bird that plucked up my cat and flew away.

Everywhere I went in the garden there was a cat-shaped hole. A cat-shaped hole next to the stone bench. A cat-shaped hole arching its back against the thorny stalks of the white roses. A cat-shaped hole sunning itself in the tubland of herbs. A cat-shaped hole walking sinuously along a pavement path.

And in my heart a cat-shaped hole.

The sky, which cannot be tamed, filled with the threat of wings. Hadedas flapped like old grey witches, squawking their curses, kites, with the air in their armpits, hung in the high; flocks of little shriekers flew in formation, like fighter squadrons. And the one which is as big as an aeroplane darkened the sky and cast its shadow over my paradaiso.

So I went inside and closed the door, because outside there is too much sky. And wings, which are not the wings of angels, beat across it.

For a time I did not look out. I looked in at the cat-shaped hole in my heart. I looked in and my dreams beat with the wings of eagles.

Until you are conscious of them, you do not realise that eagles are everywhere. You turn over the coins in your purse and the giant wings are there, rising across them. Eagles are the symbols of banks and insurance firms and transport companies. Armies, throughout time, have marched in their name; as airforces have flocked the skies. Smooth intercity buses as well as smoking township veterans, bear the name. Calligraphically along streamlined sides; scrawled on dusty rumps. And gun-toting taximen swoop through metropolis streets warring one another in the name of the bird.

Countless books and a gamut of movies about war and politics and power carry the word in their titles. And in profile, too, many priests and politicians look predatory.

Whatever is competitive and corrupt; whatever is militant and martial; whatever is about power and pride and all that is despicable in a man is associated with that bird. Only funeral parlours, it seems, are called Dove's.

When I looked, I looked out through the windows which

bear bars, like crosses. And I saw that the order that I had created was disordering itself under a godless sky.

I shut it out.

And peeped at it sometimes when it was dark. The dark hides the disorder; and in the dark the sky blooms with white roses.

I shut myself in.

I looked at the rooms of the house and thought that each room is a world and the whole is a universe; and I could order the whole.

First I repainted the walls. When you paint walls you come to know every brick, every nick. You develop an intimate acquaintance with the structure that holds you in.

I re-hung the paintings. Which made me look at them again. And I realised how much I like them because they are still. The landscapes do not suddenly alter with the vagaries of wind or water. New buildings do not rise in cityscapes, nor old ones implode. Abstract designs do not alter unless you do. The portrait of you smiles without wrinkling its face. Unlike the mirror portrait which wrinkles even without smiling its face.

I shook the carpets and rearranged the furniture and sat in all the chairs to see how the rooms looked from each cushion. And I thought about how comforting armchairs are. And sofas. Because you fit into them so snugly. And they stay where you have put them. When you return to a room they are waiting where you left them, ready to hold you. A little dustier perhaps, a little worn. But they have not shifted or disappeared. Nor do they sprout unexpected shoots that change their shape; or fail to blossom one season; or gather weeds about their feet.

I opened the cupboards in the bedroom and looked at the clothes hanging there like a silent movie of my life. The same size through all the years. But the lengths different. And the fabrics. And the styles. I thought I should throw some out or sell them, but when I took them off their hangers and folded them up in a pile, they looked at me with such reproach that I picked them up again and hung them in the museum of me. They wait there, the new items for an occasion; the old ones for fashion to repeat itself.

And in the drawers of the dressing-table I checked all the little jewellery boxes that hold rings and necklaces and bracelets and watches that don't tick anymore. Some of the items are very old pieces I have inherited. Beyond price. Irreplaceable. Not always wearable. Waiting.

I shone the things that needed shining to remind them that they have life.

I polished the piano and brasso-ed its pedals and invited the tuner to check the notes. I took out the music and shook out the fish-moths. And then I put my hands over the keys and unlocked some sound.

It's always there, the piano, grinning with those dentures. Sometimes cheerful, sometimes challenging. Waiting for you to take up the cheer or the challenge.

Playing the piano is unlike playing with any other friend. It demands everything. The absolute concentration of your body and brain. When you have given it everything, it gives a little in return. And because you want more, you go on. Giving.

There are other acquaintances and friends. All the books in the house. In every room. Untidily on shelves. In one room, lining all the walls. Thousands of words waiting to speak.

It is not impossible to retreat into a house. Away from the town. Away from the garden. It's only that you grow a little pale. A little interior. And that fear spills out of your dreams.

Often, reading late, writing, I fell asleep in a chair. And one early morning waking in such a chair, I had a strange sense of emptiness around me; a sense of too much space. Walking through the house I saw that there were indeed spaces. That tables stood bare. That things were missing.

A window in the bedroom lay in shards on the carpet. And the metal stake that once supported the white standard rose outside the bedroom, lay discarded on the paving. Guilty. The rose bent to its feet like a ballet dancer.

The dressing-table, dragged to the window, stood awkwardly, its drawer open and empty.

The jewellery heirlooms, gone.

The clothes that told the story of my life, gone.

The police came. In plain clothes.

"Have you got an alarm?"

"Yes."

"Why didn't it go off?"

"I fell asleep. I forgot ..."

"Insurance doesn't like that."

"No, I suppose not."

"They doesn't like it if you got an alarm you don't use it."

The second man was trying to coax some fingerprints from the window. He spilled black powder on the carpet.

"What you lost?" said the first man, squatting on the edge of the bed with his clipboard on his knees.

Sanity.

"What you lost?" he repeated in my silence.

"Some jewellery," I said. "Clothes."

"Item?"

"What?"

"You got to tell me the items. Each."

"Oh. Um."

"There's no fingerprints," said the man at the window. He stamped footprints, size ten, across the carpet.

I gave the first man a list of the pieces of jewellery. "They took the boxes too."

"How's that?"

"The boxes. Very old. Old-fashioned jewellers' boxes. With clasps. And satin inside. And the name of the jeweller."

He looked at me quizzically.

I tried to remember all the clothes. And remembered places. And people.

"Do you ever recover things?" I asked.

"There's burgillries all a time."

"I know. But do you ...?"

"This here's your case number," he said, tearing the page from his clipboard. Jaggedly. "When you phone Insurance you quote this."

"The stuff's irreplaceable."

"How's that?"

"What I've lost. It's my ancestry. My history. And my life."

"Just phone Insurance."

With a capital 'I'.

The two trod down the passage and out to a white car. A brittle radio voice was shouting from the dashboard.

"You see. That'll be another burgillry."

And they sped off to unsolve another crime.

I turned back into the damaged house. The great wound smashed into its side glittered in the morning light. And the glass on the floor glinted like the jewellery which was gone.

I took a broom and swept up the shards. When I picked them up to put them in the wastepaper basket, I cut my hand, despite my care not to. I swept up the policemen's footprints and the black powder, which stained.

I closed the empty drawer and pushed the dressing-table into its proper place. I closed the cupboard doors.

The autumn was coming in through the hole in the window.

I wondered where I could go to. To be safe.

The bath was there. The size of a man. The size of a coffin. I took off my clothes and climbed in. Feeling its comforting sides.

Watching the vortex of water drain away. Like life.

GEMORS
Allan Kolski Horwitz

"CLAUDIA!"

WHERE WAS SHE? Why was she doing this to him?

"Claudia, I need you, man! Stop your nonsense!"

His key didn't fit — she must have changed the locks while
he was out playing pool in Klein Street — so he'd spent the
night on a bench in Park Station. How he'd cursed her! His
mind jagged in the stale vastness of the station concourse;
solitary, furtive men made pass after pass forcing him to lie
stiff as if he was dead. At two o'clock he had checked the flat
for the last time, praying she would open for him, but his
knocking and shouts only woke the neighbours, the old ones
who smelt of samp and beans. They had yelled abuse and told
him to leave. He'd limped back to the station, bought another
packet of cigarettes and dossed down near the Rotunda. More
mangled hours. Afterwards, just before sunrise, propped
against a rubbish bin in Noord Street (near the art gallery), he
had dozed while a blur of bodies drifted by on their way to the
six o'clock shift. Now it was morning and he was exhausted,
his stomach rumbled and every few minutes he farted.

Yesterday, while he was sleeping, she had thrown this note
onto the kitchen table and left for work:

*Daniel, I can't go on like this. It's true I loved you in the begin-
ning but since you moved in things have gone bad. You only think of
yourself. For all our sakes it will be better when you leave. I'm not
saying I don't want to see you again, but we mustn't live together.
Please take your clothes. Take all your stuff. Come and see me in a few*

days. Now I'm too mad. I'm sorry but I can't go on with you. Think why, ja, think. I don't want to find you here when I come back. Please! I don't want more trouble. Goodbye.

The megaphone in his mouth aggravated the pounding in his head.

He stood up on the tiled floor and walked out of the concourse past the ticket offices, the Kentucky Fried Chicken outlet and the liquor stores. Running his fingers over the knife tucked into one of his socks, he stepped into Wanderers Street. Thick pieces of wors were frying on portable *braai* stands on the pavement. He passed the TWO SHOES FOR THE PRICE OF ONE sign in the window of the Indian shop and headed down towards a kaffie near the Cathedral.

"*Hoesit*, my china."

"*Hoesit, jou mal vark.*"

That last pipe he'd hit in the station toilet had really blown him.

The *Sowetan* headline read: VOLCANO IN JOUBERT PARK: MAN BLOWN UP BY BLOUETJIE ON THE REEF.

She's got a surprise coming if she thinks I'm going to get a job to support her brat. *Mal varke*. His mind turned to Eddie and his killer girl, a juicy number he'd picked up in Eldos.

"*Hoesit, jou vark.*"

The morning was melting.

In the kaffie he ordered a packet of chips. He watched the long, off-white slivers of potato sizzle in oil, then slither as they were tossed into a paper bag. He slipped one into the mouth of the drunk who was sprawled outside the door. Vinegar soaked through the bag.

"*Waar's die* curry powder?"

A dark-haired woman with a trace of moustache stooped over the cash register.

"Stop messing around!" She shoved it across.

"*Waar's djou* old man?"

She looked at him without smiling, but while he pretended to search for money she looked down at his pants. Years ago he'd *naaied* one of these hairy women in Riversdale. Stuck at night, by a garage, they had groped each other in a storeroom near the fridges while her father counted the takings.

"Claudia, where the hell are you? That Eddie sold me kak the other day, the day before yesterday, the day before the lunar eclipse, before we became raving button spiders."

Ja, that last *pilletjie* had fractured his skull. It was blowing out. The counter was full of his bright red madness. He ran out of the shop with the packet of hot chips burning his hand. The woman at the cash register called out. He ran as fast as he could. *Sies!* Why were his pants not covering his cock? He could feel his cock quivering like a slap chip.

Sit, boy. Sit in the gutter, the only place to sit in King George Street in the shade of plane trees next to Joubert Park, and collect yourself.

The chips wriggled all over the pavement.

Good for nothing drug addict.

"Daniel Adams!" Two dark brown breasts spilled out of a blue overall. "Come suck, my boy. Come suck."

The woman began opening her buttons. Behind her was a metal tub piled with dry ice; propped up against it was a broken cardboard sign advertising ice-cream prices. A man with a yellow woollen cap squashed on his head stood near the tub.

"Daniel Adams, come sign up for the Workers Revolutionary Party! Buy our paper! Enter the ranks!"

The man drifted off, stopping others.

"Claudia! What the hell is going on? Why are you doing this to me?"

Her skin coated him, the snugness of her tongue permanently warming his mouth. What subtle secretion had she been infusing into him?

MAN BLOWN UP BY BEAUTY QUEEN IN JOUBERT PARK.

The big-breasted woman bent over him. "He's sick."

Next to her was an elderly man dressed in khaki; the green and black badge of the Zionist Church pinned to his white shirt.

"I've never seen him this bad. He looks like a zombie. He's naughty, this one. You see him here all times of the day and night. He likes to take chances. But he's got a good heart. He carried lollies for me once, all the way from my boss's van." The ice-cream seller covered her face with her hands and laughed. "*Hawu*, he's got wandering hands!"

Daniel remembered those long sweet lollies — summer afternoons, overheated women chatting, legs stretched out in front of them on the grass.

The Zionist took her arm. "I know this clever! He stole from my bag last year. Now he's doing the devil's work again." The Zionist spat, a thick white glob that covered Daniel's cheek. Then, abruptly, the old man bent down to check his breathing. "These *tsotsis*, they survive anything." He scratched his chin. "He doesn't deserve kindness but we must do right by everybody in their time of need. We must save each other from damnation."

The old man's eyes shone. Daniel's head rolled.

"*Siesie*, let us put him in the park."

They picked him up and carried him through the iron gates of the park, his legs trailing against the photographers' boards of portraits, the hawkers' plates piled with fruit and sweets and alongside the rim of the small green fountain. Then they laid him down on the post office side near the banana trees and the hothouse.

Daniel kept his eyes closed. From far away he heard a low chant. There were car sounds beyond the park railings. He did not wish to speak. Foulness clogged his throat, until suddenly a cascade of water splashed his face and a warm, gentle hand wiped his lips till he could feel the cracks piece together. From far away he heard a low chant. More water sprinkled onto his forehead. The ice-cream seller cradled him to her bosom. She squeezed his hand as he drank.

The Zionist said, "There is nothing more I can do. I must go now, *siesie*."

She smiled. "Thank you, my brother. God be with you on your journey."

Daniel shivered, remembering the man's voice. Months before he had been beaten; a mob had chased him into the courtyard of a block of flats, an enraged mob armed with sticks and knives. And out of this mob, this same voice had shouted out that he was a thieving *boesman* witch who spirited wallets out of locked metal trunks. Daniel had begged for mercy, waved a handful of R50 notes in the air till the Zionist grabbed the money and walked off leaving him to stew in that hot, yellow day, the mass of taunting, jeering men and women still ready to draw his blood.

Bladdy liar, causing shit. I don't play with nonsense. I buy and sell. I'm no cheap dief.

The ice-cream woman wiped his forehead with her sleeve.

"You stay here and rest. I must go back to my stand. I left my cousin there and she doesn't know the prices."

The palpitations in his chest eased. He lay on the grass near the hothouse while she was swallowed up in the streams of people thronging the pathways. The morning rolled on, stretching up into the ether; pure stratosphere where everything is sweet nothing.

"Jesus, Claudia! Where are you?"

He was still asleep, as usual, while she dressed for work, getting the kid ready for creche before dropping him off. Mid-morning, waking briefly, he had tried to warm the cold space beside him, then slept on. Soon it was noon. Fresh, free to stroll over to Bertrams, he and Hendricks had broken a pipe in the backyard of Koos's broken-down house. There was a fig tree full of ripe, plump fruit. He had plucked a fig, and splitting open the skin with his fingernails, licked the flesh, buried his face in it.

Daniel felt in his pants pocket. The plastic bank bag holding the tabs was there. He took one out and swallowed it. Then he closed his eyes, and lay back.

Within minutes his head began revolving. He rolled over towards the hothouse. It glowed with a green radiance that made every other object seem pale, even colourless. He sat up. There was a flash of pinkish-white. Sticking out through the side of the glass door was a hand. The door opened. There at the entrance stood a black albino man wearing a suit of lotus leaves. On his head was a diadem of pearl: his whole being glowed with energy and light.

"Daniel! At last! You don't know how excited I am! All this time, years and years, stuck in the *Gemors*! How could you? You've been so battered and abused." A cloud of fireflies, wings shimmering, hovered about. "Come, inside, my boy. Come inside for a little refreshment."

The man waved, making a circle in the air. Daniel stood up and before he could take a step forward, found himself standing in front of the hothouse door, a stream of warm air, moist and cloying, enveloping him.

"I can't tell you how pleased I am! This is such a terribly overdue meeting!"

The beautiful man clasped his hand, kissed his cheek lightly and embraced him. Daniel felt a shiver of pleasure. Then the albino smiled and sprayed him with rosewater before taking his greasy head in his hands and massaging it.

Daniel sighed — what a welcome, for someone all smeared and brooding, made cunning and hard — and said, "It's true I can't give a good account of myself, but I haven't had it easy. You see, I was never taught what was right or how to piss straight. Now all I want is a crust, a little crust of your kindness." The fireflies glinted. "Just a drop of your loving kindness." The fireflies flashed.

"Only a drop, my friend? Is that all you want? You're very modest. After everything you've been through. You certainly deserve more than a morsel ... I'll see to that. Yes, I'll see to that."

Daniel breathed in the scent that rose from his body; a scent of untamed wilderness and manicured voluptuousness, of passion and calm. And while the strong, sensitive fingers drained out the pressure hammering in his head, he looked around and saw a small pond at the entrance to the hothouse. In the middle of the pond stood a concrete statue of a boy kneeling with a bucket. Several paths led off from the pond and along them, in raised platforms of rich black earth, planted in all the available space, brilliant flowers of every description burst forth. The hothouse breathed and pulsated with growth. It was as if he could instantaneously see the buds take shape, expand, swell out and bloom.

"*Ja ...*"

Lotus leaves quivering, the albino released him.

"How are things out there, my dear boy? Is there peace? A little plenty?"

"It's *mal*," Daniel said, "and it's hectic."

"Even more *gemors*?" The albino spoke sadly. His grip on Daniel's hand tightened. "How much more? Why does it go on and on? Have you tried with all your heart? Are you all so inadequate? Are you?" His voice rang out, then dropped. "Anyway ... you're here now. Let's go inside, I can't take too much cold." He shivered as he spoke. "I don't know how any-one does." He drew Daniel over the threshold. "Welcome, my boy, welcome to this holy house."

Daniel closed the door with his foot. "Hell thanks, mister. Look, I've messed up badly but I didn't have a chance. You see, in the orphanage I had no one to care for me except this one kid called Cherry. He was the only one. The other boys and the masters used to bugger me up. There wasn't enough food. Jesus man, you can't blame me ..."

Daniel stopped.

Why was the man detaching himself, withdrawing from him? Especially his warm, understanding eyes that had suddenly become hard and remote.

"Please! Don't let me go, it isn't my fault!"

The albino stared into the hothouse's misty glass. "Why is it all our visitors say that? There's always a story, a long drawn out excuse, a million reasons and half-baked explanations! At some point I'll give you an opportunity to go into history but right now let me rather show you our beauties." His eyes were again soft and absorbing. "I'm sorry. I shouldn't be angry. I know how difficult it is to be on your own and be forced to carve out a space." He touched Daniel's cheek lightly. "Just leave your shoes outside on the step."

Daniel kicked off his takkies. They were grimy and split,

stains covered the purple fabric, the laces were frayed.

"I don't usually smell like this but last night I had to kip at Park Station. Claudia locked me out. She didn't come home." The takkies landed next to a fern. "She was out screwing some arsehole churrah. I know she was jiving at Boobs while I was thick in dogshit in the bushes opposite the flat. Bladdy whore, messing around while I was dead on my feet and starving and all these fokken moffies were trying to get into my pants!"

As he peeled off his socks, the knife taped to his ankle clattered onto the paving.

The albino man shook his head. "Oh, Daniel, how terrible." Then he stiffened. "If you dare speak like that again about her I'll see you drown in the fountain! I'll push you under myself! She's half of you, the better part, no doubt. And as for the moffies …" Sliding his palm across Daniel's cheek, he hissed, "Now pick up that knife and throw it out of here before I lose the last drop of my patience!"

Daniel rocked back on his feet. "Jesus, I didn't mean to bring it in, sir! I forgot!" The nausea returned, he felt weak and pale. "I need to sit down."

"Yes, you'd better! Sit down and think before you gaan aan." Still glaring, the man gave him his hand and led him to a small bench. "Stay here. I'll bring you something to drink." He touched Daniel's shoulder, then disappeared down a path overgrown with hanging plants.

Daniel slumped back.

The hothouse was saturated with swollen drops of water that hung from the glass with the rounded succulence of larvae. Slowly, one by one, these drops gathered moisture to the point when their weightiness caused them to fall gracefully onto the already wet soil. But despite the restful atmosphere, Daniel felt worse. The churning inside his stomach and the spinning in his head rushed back. He stood up, almost falling.

"Where's that bladdy guy? He's got to help me."

He ran down one of the paths but the albino was nowhere to be seen.

"I can't take this! Where are you?" He thrashed about, scattering leaves. "Dammit, Claudia!"

Claudia and Isabel, her best friend, were sitting at *The Three Sisters* on Pretorius Street drinking Irish coffees. Claudia was talking.

There was the landlord's ultimatum: rent was three months in arrears. If she didn't pay by tomorrow, they would throw her out. There were also four court summonses. Folded in manila envelopes, they lay on the red plastic restaurant table. One from Truworths for five dresses, one from Edgars for jerseys and shoes and one from Russels for a lounge suite, a dresser and a double bed. The last one was from the local bottle store. Years before, she had been arrested in PE after failing to appear in court on a similar charge. From that time, when applying for credit, she had never given her real address. So what had gotten into her now? Had it been some lunatic sense of security because she was living with a man again? The summonses could be sorted out, slipped out of, but the rent had to be found.

While the two women sipped their drinks, Daniel returned to the hothouse entrance and sat down next to the pond. The water was filled with spreading lilies and darting goldfish. On all sides, murmurings gushed from the dark, dank soil; flowers glowed and throbbed along the veils of vegetation. He sat back against the bench and closed his eyes. *Ja*, it was rough, so rough that sometimes he didn't want to get up. Every day, more shit. But what could you do? There were always surprises. He breathed in deeply, gulping down the soothing scents. At last, a chance to gather himself and reflect. But, as he was about to close his eyes there was a rustling behind him — the swish of delicate materials. He turned round. A large brown horn spiralling out of the centre of a pale but glistening forehead, the forehead of a squat plump white man dressed in a bright orange robe, loomed over him.

Daniel squinted. In one hand the man held a glass flask which glittered with a silvery liquid; the other hand held a tray on which balanced a single glazed goblet.

"Here, my friend. Enjoy this refreshment."

The horn thrust out into the air, firm but trembling.

Daniel nodded. "I know you, man." He laughed.

The man was one of those shaven-headed Hare Krishnas who paraded through Hillbrow on Saturday afternoons, beating drums, ringing bells and handing out bowls of rice to street kids and hobos.

"Hey! Where's your manners? Don't grab!"

The orange robe drew back and the liquid almost spilt, but lunging forward Daniel grabbed the goblet.

"I'm fucking thirsty, man!"

The silver liquid tasted strong and fruity; he drained the goblet. Within seconds, he found himself gliding through the hothouse. The air was subtle and intense. And while he floated along the narrow paths, the Hare Krishna followed behind, a gravelly but not unpleasant voice.

"Not bad, hey? Home brew. The master spends all his time distilling it. There's crushed petals and drops of sap from each flower and root in this hothouse. It takes years and years to mature. Come, I'll show you where it's prepared. The vat is in a very special place, not everyone is allowed in, and you can't just help yourself."

Daniel smiled and followed the shimmering robe. Everything was so bright and flowing. What luck he had spotted the mottled pink hand beckoning at the hothouse door! Then he stiffened. There was a sharp pricking and hardening in his temples. He wanted to lie down. He tried to find a bench. He collapsed onto the floor. He lay groaning, groping around. His head was buckling. A final tearing sensation, then, touching his forehead, he fell back in horror.

The Hare Krishna raised Daniel's head, put a hairy arm round him.

"Yes, my friend. The Master teaches us all a lesson. He calls it 'corrective action'. Believe me, once you've been selected, things are never the same."

Daniel lay panting. Cautiously, incredulously, he felt the long, bony extension that had shot out of his forehead.

The Hare Krishna propped him up against a pillar.

"I was living at the Temple on Goldreich Street. One afternoon, it was hot like today, I was lying down on the grass near where you were. I was randy as hell. The Master opened the door and waved to me. I followed him in, and I can't say I'm sorry." He touched the horn on his own forehead. "You'll get used to it. It's only when you lean forward that it's a problem. Otherwise everything is so much lighter." He smiled. "There are such sweet girls in the neighbourhood. They'll do anything for a movie and popcorn." The Hare Krishna smiled and poked him in the stomach. "You won't want to leave! All we have to do is sweep and weed flowerbeds. And that's only for two hours a day. Afterwards we're free. There's all the time in the world to perfect yourself. You know the secret? Every morning at five o'clock we're allowed a goblet. That's it, just once a day, all of us linking hands round this pond, passing it from hand to mouth, until everyone's had his share. Then we do meditation and levitation, nothing too strenuous but enough to keep us on our toes. There are also sessions on General Cosmology. Those are a bit heavy for my small brain, but I tell you, they're more interesting than dancing down Claim Street. I was getting tired of the gongs." He opened his arms. "Such sweet, clean, cuddly girls!" The hands waved and two watery eyes blinked. "You don't know how long I've waited for someone like yourself — someone who'll understand."

Daniel stepped back. That was sick! How could a grown man get hard for a kid? He ran his fingers along his knotted horn as the Hare Krishna faded from sight.

No, he wasn't a fool. But then he thought of the Boer in the flat next door, the post office worker who'd been retrenched and spent his time boozing cheap wine. One day he had found the man sprawled on the floor, half dead, a bitter, sad expression on his face. After helping him to his feet, and suffering a blast of foul teeth, Daniel, without thinking, had given him a packet of uppers for nothing, and that was dumb because you never know when you'll need the extra bucks. Especially when Claudia was always on to him for this and that — food, rent, electricity, clothes for the kid ... *Ja*, the kid, always something for the kid, always some kind of scene with the kid.

Like the time the brat was sleeping in his room and they

were on the stoep, Claudia was wearing the white, clinging dress that accentuated her fullness. He was telling a joke. Leaning against the stoep wall, his head upturned, eyes shining with amusement, while she tickled his stomach. Then he was kissing her, caressing her arm, and they slowly entwined their tongues, she stirring, smoothing his hair but the child woke up and started crying; the two of them kissing, while the crying grew louder till the brat coughed with rage, and he, Daniel, standing over the small bed, lifted the boy and ran back with him to the stoep and dangled him over the railing. Bastard *laaitie*! Always disturbing them as they got down to business. That time Claudia had grabbed his arms, a powerful clamping of his arms so unforseen that she had almost caused him to drop the hysterical boy.

"Yo, we shouldn't laugh while there are prisons and labour camps and execution chambers." The Hare Krishna came back into view, clapping his hands. "We shouldn't, but we have to. You see, my brother? You see?"

He took Daniel's hand, kissed it and held it in a caress, not unlike the albino's but clammier.

"We torture each other with burning cigarettes. We force each other into sealed rooms and pipe in gas. Hey, do you remember the neutron bomb?"

Daniel wrinkled up his nose. "Neutron bomb?" What was that?

The orange robe glowed, white light emanating from its folds and along its edges.

"It tears human flesh apart while buildings and other objects are left intact."

The incandescence intensified. The Hare Krishna seemed elastic. His body began to slowly dissipate. Daniel had to shield his eyes. The aura was too bright.

"What else is going on in the *Gemors*? Tell me, *boeta*. I lived in it for long enough, I remember every little trick and scam. So, what's new?"

Daniel could only see the rim of his sandals. He wanted to make it stop. The brightness and heat were overpowering. He was in the hothouse but the orange robe, the twisting kernel of horn, the sandals, the flask with shining liquid, had disappeared. In their place was the Master.

"Isn't this better than roaming around out there? Don't you feel calmer?"

This time he wore a gown of hyacinths, and on his head, in place of the diadem, was a plain blue band.

"You think there's nothing worse than sexual frustration." The Master looked down at Daniel's soiled pants. "You can't sleep until someone's made it spurt." Then he looked away. "Why is it you ignore us? We've tried everything possible to show you the way. We've battled for ages to make you understand." He bowed his head. "We've tried so hard to help …"

Daniel felt a tumultuous thrashing of air that almost knocked him off his feet. A yellow-brown eagle, beak poised, talons unfurled, hovered above him. As the sky darkened, he was lifted up, twisted and spun into the haze like a screw — again the *lekker blouetjie* casting him into ether, sweet zero between heaven and earth till there was only a black hole expanding through his stomach.

Then the whirling sensation stopped. He was lying on the lawn, the green frame of the hothouse silhouetted against the park rails, sprinklers shooting spray that made his T-shirt damp. His head was clear. He breathed coolness, transpiration of trees, evening soft and fluid with dim shapes.

He sat up, elated.

Claudia was still with Isabel at *The Three Sisters*. They had long switched to brandies and were feeling loose and mellow. Isabel had agreed to lend her half the rent money and store her things while the summonses were pending. She planned to stay with her mother in PE for a few months before returning to Jo'burg. Now they sat waiting for a last round.

As Claudia kissed Isabel in gratitude, down the hill in the park, Daniel looked up at the post office clock.

"Six o'clock!"

He'd go back to the flat. This time he'd catch her. He'd talk her into opening up. But if she still wasn't there or wasn't prepared to, he would make another plan for the night. He would try Enoch, a long time connection, although Enoch rarely spent time in his cramped room squeezed on a roof top. Another option was Professor. But at this hour Professor would be hustling for beer money. Lastly, there was Lucky down in Bok Street; *lekker* little pozzie there by the pawnbrokers. The only problem was that Lucky had women with him and he liked to be alone with them.

The afternoon had drained away. Trees formed a full green arcade, leaves shimmering as the day's last light washed through. Daniel walked towards Wanderers Street. Light-headed, he moved with confidence towards the flat.

His better half?

Most nights it was just the two of them, except for the boy whining; just the two of them lying in bed, watching TV, then switching off the TV and putting on music, something slow and moody. Those were the nights he wasn't out dealing, when he wasn't at the clubs trying to make bucks; moving in the clubs with his hands spread over his jacket pockets, grinning with chipped teeth.

"Easy does it, Danny boy! She's just had three nips with Isabel. They've paid the bill and they're standing up to leave. Every man is staring at Claudia. You know how fine she is, all snappy in her red suit. She's walking out of there like Cinderella dumping her dirty blankets by stepmother's fireplace and heading at the speed of light for the prince's castle."

Daniel breathed in the familiar sense of invigoration but he could not see the Master.

"Yes, you're a lucky man! You've found a beauty who's good-hearted and, on top of it, clever. And she knows how to work."

Walking past the overflowing rubbish bins in the yard and up the stairs till he was in the passage leading to the flat, Daniel rang the bell. He banged the door. There was no reply. Then, almost as soon as he had stopped kicking it, he was back on Wanderers Street, leaning against the concrete pillars of Hawarden Court.

"Damn bitch! I'll make her pay for this!"

A group of men with tired, mechanical faces brushed past him; a thick-necked white man in a safari suit with four black men in stained khaki overalls dragging their feet behind him. Parked at the kerb was a furniture removal van.

"What, Danny boy! Still thinking those stale, stupid thoughts?" The Master was massaging his back. "I thought we'd covered that nonsense." Daniel felt the strong, sinewy fingers withdraw. "You're a hard-headed one." The fingers returned. "Such a pity."

As Daniel relaxed, Claudia and Isabel hugged each other goodbye.

"I'll book a *bakkie* tomorrow."

"Thank you, my darling."

Claudia waved as she strolled down Klein Street past the Hillbrow Meat Market.

It was good to have someone to rely on, someone who stood firm on her own two feet. Not a spoilt somebody who's only there for you to clean his arse. She was in high spirits. But as she crossed the driveway of the Lutheran Church with the Hansel and Gretel garden, an orange robe brushed against her and a curved, grey horn almost poked into her side.

She turned to meet burning eyes.

"I met Daniel this afternoon. He asked me to tell you how much he needs you. He speaks of you, only of you, in a most moving way, superlatives, one after the other. He really has seen the light." The Hare Krishna smiled. "He's turning over a new leaf. He'll get a job, you'll have kids." He glanced at her stomach. "You'll have three of them."

She was in the church garden and the horned man in an orange robe was holding her hand.

"Claudia, think again! He's a good boy. None of us can help disappointing from time to time."

The man uncovered a tray which lay on a low table. A crystal decanter scintillated. "Here, have a sip, it's unbelievably refreshing." He began pouring. "My dear girl, to your health and good judgement!"

She blinked as her nose was squashed.

"Hey, lady! What you doing? You walk right into people!

192

You drunk or something?"

She was flat on her back in the street. The middle-aged Chinese man helping her to her feet was more sneering than sympathetic.

"You all right? Nothing hurt? You go home now and sleep." He picked up her bag. Then slyly, "You want some business? I give you nice present."

Claudia pushed him away. She rubbed her eyes. The Chinese man moved off towards the bars in Banket Street. Had the brandies gone too far and messed up her head? What had he said? Let Daniel come back? After draining her money, almost killing her child, trying to sleep with Isabel and her other friends, demanding she cook for him, clean the flat, serve him. Just as well he'd gone out by lunch time so she could rush back to the flat and change the locks.

She crossed the park on her way home to Wanderers Street, passing the giant chessboard painted on concrete near the hot-house and the rows of banana trees. Clusters of men sat on benches watching a very dark black man play a gaunt white alcoholic. The white man was grimly defending his last castle while Daniel leaned against the cold stone of the columns fronting the flats. A thin peel of sun hung above Park Station, that giant mass of horizontal squatness. The city was suffused with the calm of a summer's day subsiding into velvet depths. Yet how agitated he felt! He longed for the moisture under her arms, the perfumed line above her lips.

"Claudia! Where the hell are you?"

Across the road he saw the Master, this time wearing a white blouse and skirt. On his back, in splotchy black letters, was written: WINKY'S WORS. The Master held a plastic plate on which wobbled a thick, juicy sausage flanked by a mound of pap. Daniel watched him dip the sausage into a puddle of tomato and onion sauce, then lick his fingers.

"You think this is meat?" On the pavement was a sizzling braai stand. "You think I'm preparing rubbish? You think these are all off-cuts that I found on the floor? No, boykie, these are made of soya, high protein stuff. They're sautéeing in a mushroom and leek sauce. You know, you eat too much cheap

193

fried food. That's why you have black-outs and you fart."

Claudia walked into the Chatham Cafe on the corner of Bok and King George Street. She bent over the ice-cream fridge, checked the flavours, and chose a Chocolate Delight.

WOMAN FREEZES TO DEATH LICKING ICE LOLLY.

Give him another chance?

The Master dipped his fingers into the red plastic bowl, scooping and rolling balls of pap while taxi touts called out the names of towns in Mpumalanga and Swaziland. A Jehovah's Witness walked up and down, neat and slick in suit and tie, arms full of tracts.

MAN DROWNING IN MONEY SAVED BY JESUS.

Claudia queued to pay for the ice-cream. Someone pushed against her. She moved forward, was again knocked from behind. It was the Chinaman from the Lutheran Church. He winked as she slapped him.

"You bastard!"

He stood smirking in a jacket that had too long sleeves and stained cuffs, a tub of margarine in one hand.

"Touch me again and I'll kick you where it hurts!"

He continued smiling. "Very stupid, miss. Very stupid. Do you know who's waiting for you?"

She stood to one side. The line was long and people stared at her.

"Hey, stop fucking around. Pay, man!"

There was one other woman in the queue. She wore a *doek* over her beehive of plastic curlers.

"Leave her alone, you *doos*!"

Claudia rejoined the line. The man clutched at her hand. His breath, rancid with alcohol, pouring over her.

"Listen, miss. You got a boyfriend. I bet your boyfriend don't give a damn about you. He wants a slave. He wants someone to make him feel good. But that's not what I want. Come home with me. I'll give you a beautiful present, I'll give you a nice big, hard one all night."

As he pinched her bum she lurched forward and Daniel, watching the Master lick the remnants of sauce from his fingers, splotches of brown and yellow stains showing on the white uniform, felt a wrenching in his guts.

"Claudia!"

She staggered out of the kaffie, her dress all rumpled, handbag dangling wide open, a knot of men screaming abuse at her and the woman with the *doek*. The Chinaman dropped his pants, flashing, and a cashier waved a pistol. Then the mob abruptly broke up, dissolving in all directions.

She ran hysterically towards Wanderers Street.

"Daniel! Daniel!"

He stepped forward.

"Daniel!"

He was holding her, she was clutching at him and sobbing, the scent of her sweat, her clinging arms all over him. He stroked her so tenderly.

"Don't worry, sweetie, it's OK. You know, I'm *moerse* glad to see you." He pulled her towards him. "What's up? I've been waiting."

She was flushed, taut nipples pressing through her blouse.

"Hey, you're really looking smart."

He kissed her but she broke free and said coldly, "Did you find my letter?"

"What letter?"

"Don't start your ..."

"You know I can't read."

"Very funny."

"*Ja*, it is funny."

"Have you taken all your stuff?"

"What are you talking about?"

"Why haven't you done what I asked you to?"

"Listen, Claudia, I was worried about you. I've been waiting ..."

"I've got nothing more for you."

"Nothing?"

"*Ja*, nothing. You know, nothing."

"I've given you everything."

"Don't get funny, man."

"Claudia, listen ..."

Daniel took her hand. She was staring up at the neon springbok that lit up the west. He felt his pulse hammering.

"I don't want to talk. I just want to do this." He caressed her lips. "I don't want to talk." He opened her mouth with his fingers. "You know what's between us." He leaned forward. "I'm serious."

She shook her head.

"Don't fight me now."

He withdrew his fingers and clasped her to him. The street was dark and empty.

"It's not right what I've been doing. I've been an arsehole."

He stroked her; long, slow movements up and down her back. He felt her relax. She hesitated then nuzzled against him.

"I'll sort myself out."

An elderly man wearing a Zionist badge, carrying a large metal trunk, moved past them towards the Pretoria taxi rank.

"You'll see. I'll get something going."

Daniel felt a wetness slide from her eyes.

"Hey, baby, don't ... come on, honey, it's going to be all right."

He wiped her cheeks and pressed her against his neck and shoulder. She clung to him, closed, then opened her eyes.

Over his shoulder, she saw her blankets and sheets spread out on the pavement. Clothes strewn over pots, plants, CDs and magazines, the child's toys. She couldn't see the gas stove or the fridge, and it seemed that all the furniture was gone, but jammed over a bottle of tomato sauce was the hat she sometimes wore to parties and, half torn in the gutter, lay the photograph Daniel had taken on their first afternoon together. That warm, lazy Sunday in the park near the fountain when he had sat down on the bench next to her, stopped an ice-cream seller, taken a cone and rammed it up against his forehead. And she had moved forward to lick the ice-cream running down his cheeks, her face wide with laughter, Daniel's hand raised towards the fountain, spume surging up, the half smashed cone tilted to the sky.

"Ag, don't worry, sweetheart, you'll see. We're going to get out of this *gemors*."

THE SPY WHO LOVED ME
Maureen Isaacson

November 1998. The sun hunkers down on the car and connives with the glass of the windows to burn a hole through my flesh. The traffic light at the Corlett Drive offramp turns red. He is in the car behind me. Has he followed me all the way from Pretoria?

He is in the back seat, holding his head; a futile gesture against the heat. Bits of baldness show through fat fingers. He lifts his face. His eyes meet mine in my rear-view mirror. Neither of us is surprised. All day, his lawyer has been telling the amnesty committee of the Truth Commission how sorry his client is. Nobody believes him.

He has infiltrated my life like a virus. It seems as if no time has passed since he walked into the gym. I remember how the horror of him filtered through the air and sank into the water where I was swimming. It formed a stain on the crystal blue. I asked a woman who was recovering from an accident if she recognised him. She said, "He looks familiar. You don't know who to trust these days."

He sweats. He flushes scarlet and deep into the folds of his neck when he heaves on the bicycle. The doctor checks his blood pressure. He walks outside to his gunmetal Volvo station wagon in the parking lot. The physiotherapist tells me he is under terrible pressure. His progress card indicates that he is improving. I notice that my card is missing, along with my file. I glare at him. He looks straight back at me. A deal is clinched. I change my workout time.

In the rear-view mirror on the hot November day where this story opens, I see him say something to his lawyer. I see them laugh. Inducing paranoia is his business. So it was a war, a just war against the enemies of the state. The detailed reasoning behind his counter-insurgency methods is related with passion. While remorse is expected from the amnesty seeker, he must also prove his views were in keeping with those of the political party he represented.

A hero of the old regime, he murdered to keep the state clean. He killed some of the people he befriended. He prefers the term 'secret agent' to spy. He saw himself as the James Bond of Johannesburg. Slim then, he wore seventies sunshades and brassy shirts. Those who were around at the time have not forgotten the loudhailer with which he summoned enemies of the apartheid regime to rise up and fight. But there was no tuxedo, no Savile Row suit and tie. No one could really say he had style.

So there were the bombs. The five-year-old girl blasted to a puddle of blood. The bodies that were scraped off the walls. In the dull hall, the victims' loved ones have been forced to hear talk of amnesia. Sixteen years is a long time, says his lawyer. Anyway, he received his orders from a general who is no longer alive. His mentor denies knowledge of any actions. He is also a general, who taps his cracked grey shoes under the table. What are these two playing at?

The families of the victims are opposed to the amnesty. They are offended by his crocodile tears. "I cannot forgive myself, I did not know about the child," he says. Nobody wants to see this man walk into the blazing sunlight where his Volvo waits to take him home.

SEPTEMBER 1998. The amnesty hearings began last week. There is a short break. He looks straight at me. I swallow, I choke, I force my attention towards his lawyer. He introduces us. When I ask if he will grant me an interview for the newspaper

I work for, he says, "You will write that I am a psychopath. Let us see how the hearings go this week."

He pours water from the decanter into a glass; each action is considered and framed by his pink fingers. The gestures are slow and cruel. He sips deliberately. He flushes. I think about the bicycle we share at the gym. In his presence, the families of the victims, the lawyers and the judge, the commissioners, the observers and the media all seem to diminish. He puffs up, until he is about to explode with denial and lies. There is no more energy in the room.

During the break, we all file into the small courtyard. He brushes past me. I return his stare. The sun lights up the old guard. They are bound by their love of the country and the blood they spilled in its name. It cannot be easy to be an outsider in a world you once owned.

In the beginning I think of each chance meeting with him as an accident.

I am working my way through my shopping list at the supermarket when I see the fingers. They press a loaf of white bread in the same way they would have pressed down on a pen when authorising the request for the bombs, when closing an envelope. I do not want to know what food he eats. I stop at an out-of-the-way garage in Fourways, after visiting a friend. When he turns up there, I begin to worry. Is he stalking me?

During the hearings the chance meetings stop. We continue to flash our hatred across the hall. He has his lawyer and his righteous beliefs. I have my notebook and my disbelief at his bravado.

A session ends late. It is the Thursday before a long weekend. I remain behind, talking to the lawyers. I make a call in the media room. I slam the door shut and the latch is set. When I come out, the building is deserted. I am surprised to find my car will not start. It has been serviced recently. I switch off the engine. I turn it on again. It is dead. The place is utterly quiet. Johannesburg, where I live, is fifty-six kilometres away from Pretoria. There is no one in sight.

I open the bonnet of the car. The engine stares up at me; a

gleaming, alien thing. "Need a jump lead?" I jump. It's him. He parks his car. I watch with horror as he connects my car to his with black and red wires. Up close, his fingers are freckled and covered with light fuzz, like the hair of a new-born rat. Will I ever escape him? He removes the wires and says, "Keep moving and you will be alright." He snickers.

I drive off, unsteadily, but gain confidence when I reach the highway. Lamplights glare down at the black zero leading nowhere. For the first time in years I talk to God. My forehead is burning. My car starts to chug. He is right behind me. He stops his car. He gets out. He says, "I was wondering if this would happen. If you take the next turnoff you will reach a garage." I do as he says. My car putters into the garage. I ask the petrol attendant to look at the engine. He says he is not qualified to do this. If I leave my car there it will be attended to in the morning when I return. I sign a paper and fold my receipt. The attendant locks the car inside the garage and hands me my keys. The phone is not working, he says.

I am wondering how I will get home when I see that he has followed me. "Where are you going?" he asks. My neck twists into a spasm, a clamp clenches my jaw shut. "You need a lift?"

My mouth is dry. I ask him if he has a phone I can use. He says no. The night sinks down onto me. Around us, I see nothing but darkness. I seem to have no choice. I take a deep breath. Inside, his car smells of after-shave. A rank staleness makes me want to retch. Now I am sitting in the front seat, beside him. His briefcase is on the back seat. It surely contains a gun but I feel protected by the process of the Commission. Also, the quick kill has never been his style.

A Barbie doll in a leopard skin micro-mini dress lies sprawled on the back seat. On the floor in front of me is a rugby ball. I wonder how he will feel when his little girl turns five. Also on the seat is a medical journal. His wife is a doctor. She does not attend the hearings.

We drive into the blackness in silence. He says, "Do you mind if we stop for a short while? I need to see a friend." I am sitting on the edge of the seat. The seat-belt is holding my tension.

We turn down a street as unfamiliar to me as all other streets in this area. We reach a security boom, the entrance to a suburb that has been blocked off from the crime that threatens the country's stability. He greets the guard and signs a book. He drives down a road and follows a curved street. We reach a double storey house, barricaded by a huge iron gate. He opens his window, presses the street buzzer which is connected to the house. *"Dis ek,"* he tells the person who answers. It is I.

The heavy gates glide open with surprising grace. A man comes to the door. Where have I seen him before? The house is crammed with yellow-wood cupboards and portraits of ugly old people in sturdy frames. The kists and washstands are no doubt heirlooms.

"Come through," he says. He leads us into a dimly lit room lined on one side with mirrors bearing the White Horse and Coca-Cola logos. "Please sit down, would you like a drink?" He turns to me and says, "What will you have?" This is more of a command than a question. "An Appletiser. No ice," I say, as if I am in a restaurant.

He orders a martini 'on the rocks'. He says, "Allison was stuck so I gave her a lift." I am taken aback by his sudden warmth. I think about the people he betrayed. They once found him charming too. Someone they could talk to.

"Ah yes, Allison, I have read your articles in the paper," says our host. "Interesting, confusing sometimes, but always interesting." He and my host speak to me in English and to each other in Afrikaans. They do not address one another by name. I recognise the host's grey shoes. I see that the cracks are part of the design. He is the general whom my chaperon is allegedly protecting from the Truth Commission. Apparently the general could sing. He used to be known as the Elvis Presley of the Security Forces.

The house is trapped in its electrified fence, guaranteed to fry intruders. Television monitors survey the rooms and the shadowy garden. A complex alarm system blinks silently. There is no way out. I ask where the toilet is. The general touches my arm lightly. I pull back as if I have been stung. He smiles. The green bathroom tiles are patterned with leaves. A can of air freshener and a bottle of disinfectant stand guard over the toilet. The room smells overwhelmingly of the essential oils used for pot-pourri. Who is responsible for these small, dead flowers and the sticky crocheted toilet-roll holder? I wonder how many people live here. Will I ever get out?

I look at my face in the mirror. Makeup has streaked my eyes. I look as if I have been kissed by the devil. I hear the doorbell ring. How many others will arrive tonight? In the bathroom cupboard, I find a magnifying hand-mirror, make-up, suspenders and black stockings. I have heard that transvestites like to leave clues to their private lives, but my imagination is running away with me. I do not even know if my host is married. I splash cold water on my face and smear hand-lotion into my cheeks. I apply lipstick. When I emerge from the bathroom the general is waiting. He says, "Please join us in the bar."

Three men wearing brown suits have joined my host and him in the bar. The men stand up when I enter the room. They look at my breasts when we are introduced. The shortest of the three rests his eyes on my pelvis. His eyes dance in a little circle of simulated foreplay. If only I had not worn these damned, tight jeans. I have no option but to sit down on a barstool.

He has admitted to siphoning foreign funds into farms. If these are not the men who roasted their enemy on the spit, they had friends who did it. The man-roasting took place at a farm called Vlakplaas. How do you do this to a man? You take drugs and you drink. You light the fire. You have another beer. More drugs. You kill the man. You chop up his body. Then you let him cook. You drink, you drink, you eat, you drink some more.

"Have something stronger to drink, go on," says the general. No thanks. My spine and sternum seem to have merged. They send searing pain signals to my brain.

I think of the Truth Commission. There, he and his lawyer huddle together at the lunch venue. Only an oak tree separates them from the lawyer who is acting for the victims of the families. Now my thighs and hands are almost touching his. Also, I have dispelled body fluids in this apartheid general's house. My saliva has made contact with this glass, which may once have contained his saliva. I want to spit out my Appletiser. Instead it spills, as if of its own accord, on the bar counter.

I stand up quickly. "Sit!" orders the general. He wipes the water with an absorbent cloth as if it was an enemy. He opens another can of Appletiser and pours with great flair. He drops crushed ice and a slice of lemon into the glass and presents it to me before I can remind him that I do not want these extras. He touches my hand. I look at these men. I think again that there is no remorse. Eugene de Kock, who was a commander at Vlakplaas and responsible for hundreds of deaths, said, If I knew about the women and children, I would not have done it.

I think of my body turning on a spit; its tender parts cooked first. My nipples feel dry and cracked under my blouse. They talk about reconciliation as if it is a brand new theory. "Why does the media not let us get on with this process?" asks the short man. The head of his milk stout has left its frothy footprints; it speckles the moustache that decorates the sneer on a thin upper lip. "We say we are sorry but the journalists think they know better. What is the use of this Commission?" They all look at me now. What is this game about? Or is it a game at all?

I press a smile out of my pinched mouth. I look at my watch as if for the first time. It is a transparent Swatch. Through the plastic I can see the seconds clicking into the mechanism.

"Let's drink up," he says. I swallow the water rapidly. Suddenly ravenous, I grab a handful of salt and onion crisps. I chew them loudly.

We are about to leave when I see a familiar card at the top of a pile of business cards. It bears the name of my newspaper. I assume one of my colleagues has been here. Then I see my name! I remember later that I gave the card to my captor's lawyer at the Truth Commission. I say goodbye. The men stand up. I thank the general politely.

In the car again, I shiver. We continue our journey in silence. I am bewildered but I trust that I will return home safely tonight. He handles his car as if it was the Aston Martin in the 007 film *The Spy Who Loved Me*.

He would be too heavy for his wife. I imagine her, on her knees for him, the rim of his penis in her mouth. I imagine him holding her head as she waits for those convulsive bursts that signal the end. Maybe she 'loves' him. Maybe the stories that have circulated about him and the general are true. Father and son? Sharing and caring?

I cough and loosen my grip on my handbag. It falls to the floor. My hand jerks against the gear lever and connects with his hand. "Sorry." When I give directions my voice and breathing beat in my brain as if I am swimming underwater. He turns left when I ask him to turn right. I repeat my directions. He ignores them.

I chew the nails of my thumbs and bite them into little pieces. I swallow these pieces. I clasp my knees together so hard that they begin to feel bruised. He continues to drive along dark, unknown roads. The speedometer shows one hundred and seventy, eighty, ninety. Injunctions I have heard on the radio boom in my head, a desperate and loud rumination I dare not utter: arrive alive, arrive alive. I glance at him. He seems bigger, more powerful than he appears in public. A savage loneliness clutches at my heart.

I cling to my seat-belt. Now we are in familiar territory. He is driving past the suburb where I grew up. He slows down. He turns down my old street. He does not look at me once. There is the tree-house in which Greg Smith and I used to imagine we would one day rule the world. There is my old bedroom. I miss my mother. I fancy I see her silhouette hovering at the kitchen window; she is waiting for me to come home. She will not approve of the company I am keeping.

My parents moved out of this house ten years ago. My mother died seven years ago. "Excuse me," I say. He stares straight ahead. Now he is speeding again. We are back on track, en route to my office.

Johannesburg city is deserted at night. By day you can buy your petticoat or bananas on the street. At night the shops are fortified with iron gates. The Tropicana Hotel across the road from our offices booms and bleeds. Those who frequent the bar are keen to preserve the city's reputation as the murder capital of the world.

It is a vile place, this bar. Decades of smoke, spunk and dried tears cake the walls. Those people outside with their torn hair, their missing teeth and dreams, are drunk and famished. Tonight they stagger out of dark corners when they see his Volvo. They are attracted to the lights, the purr of the engine.

He slows down. I open the door while the car is still moving. He pulls up at the side of the road. "Thank you." I run.

The following morning the mechanic at the garage where I left my car says it appears to him that the car has been tampered with. He does not charge me for the minor adjustment he makes.

JUNE 1999. We do not meet for some time. At the amnesty hearings, which follow some months later, it is as if nothing has ever transpired between us. I am there, in the front, taking notes and watching the swelling of his stomach as he breathes. He is there, at the long table under the reconciliation poster; staring the same provocative stare.

For him these hearings mean everything. He is the one seeking freedom and pardon, yet I feel guilty. I have sat with him, in his car. I have been a guest of the people whose reprehensible deeds are now under scrutiny. They are all here. They smile knowingly at me. So this is the meaning of sleeping with the enemy. Anyone I tell will say I did have an option. The only person I did tell was my friend Paula, who ignored what I said about the phones. She said, Why did you not take a taxi home that night?

However, none of what transpired has an impact on my reports. I record details of his privileged white English speaking childhood and his parents who feared for their future. I am able to write with impunity about the boy who went over to the other side for the sake of a war that has been lost hands down.

His mind has been programmed to destroy. He cannot stop its machinations. He says one thing yet does another. Even now, when his future hangs in the balance, he is following its old rhythms. It seems as if he cannot survive without uncertainty.

NOVEMBER 1999. The amnesty hearings were completed in February but it may take a year before the conclusions of the committee are known. Some people are talking about the possibility of a general amnesty. So there I am, all this time later, swimming at the gym when he walks in. If only he would not look at me this way. I may even put up with his continued presence in my life.

But I feel the blood rush to my brain. I call Paula on the mobile phone I purchased after my night out with him. I climb back into the water and wait. I kick my feet and point my toes in order to strengthen my ankles. I wait, as the sweat makes rivulets that flood the rift between his loose breasts. I wait as he dresses and walks away. He takes with him the emptiness and the calculation that I have come so close to understanding. It is warm in the water and I know that Paula will do what Paula has to do. All she will say is, Amnesty will no longer be an issue for this man. Today, I am driving away from the petrol station close to my home, when a BMW Cabriolet pulls up close to my car. I could swear that's the general in the driver's seat but I put foot, as they say around these parts.

A SPY IN THE HOUSE OF ART
Graeme Friedman

I ALWAYS MARVELLED AT Melissa's ability to put so much tone into her memos. This one said: *For next week*, and was clipped to a book. *For next week* was not simply a request, it had an edge, like the screech of a train's brakes, and it meant: if it's not there, Klein, you're fired. My heart sank into my gumboots. Not much of a reaction for a critic, I know, but the truth is, I'd become fed up with Melissa's fondness for catering to the lowest common denominator. I thought the three weeks I had just spent in the mountains with Steph and the baby might have muted my reaction.

Tossing the memo into the dustbin, I picked up the book. The publisher appeared to have made several errors. The book was *A Spy in the House of Art* by Anais, and I thought, okay, where's the 'Nin' but there it was on the inside cover too: 'by Anais'. And then I noticed something wrong with the title. Anaïs Nin's Spy was in the house of *Love*. And they'd spelled Anais without the umlaut. My sense of intrigue was beginning to match my irritation. Had some pirate Chinese printer assigned Anaïs Nin's spy to the wrong house? I looked on the spine. The publisher was Simone and Simone of New York. Yes, that was their address inside. I should know. I used to work there.

I bypassed the pages of publicity quotes and turned to the first page of the story. It was a love scene. It took *chutzpah* to open straight into a love scene, with the word *kiss* in the first sentence, and only a four word sentence at that. Present tense. Okay, the writer's trying a little too hard to get our attention. *Lolita* rip-off. This one, I thought, I can scan — beginning, middle, end, read the publisher's notes, slap together a review, pocket the cheque. Melissa's going to cut it down to three hundred words anyway, and nobody will read the book, so what the hell. But by the second paragraph I, along with the lover's object of desire, had been seduced.

The book was in hardback. A simple, deep blue, almost black, the colour of a whale. There was no dust jacket. I wondered whether it had been lost or destroyed. Does a book leave evidence of its cover? The title and author's name were embossed in gold, in an antique font. It looked like a bible, and it covered the same ground. It was about love and hate and remembrance. The narrative never wandered far from the lovers. In fact, it seemed always to be there with them, naked, vivacious. They opened themselves to one another, the pages of their biographies lay breast to breast, and as they merged I felt myself awash with the history of humankind. And all the time I was reading, it felt as if I was there, in the story, with the lovers. I was seeing their relationship unfold through a reflection, my own reflection in the window through which I looked, but it was not obtrusive, it was only there, as though that were natural.

The novel lay in my hands, as if it were breathing. When one lover touched the body of the other, I felt the spine of the book press into my palm. The pages massaged gently against my fingertips as I turned them. The rough, compressed fibres of the recycled paper gave the pages a geocode all of their own. I couldn't help but linger against their weatherworn edges. My hands felt comforted, as if immersed in scented water. I felt the lovers climax, and at once felt the pleasures and triumphs of a newborn family. And then hurt as the water turned to salt and I wept for the lovers, and felt the misery of hungry children. The lightness of someone's hands was on me.

People must have left the office at home time. I suppose they looked me over with astonishment as they pushed their limp fists through jacket sleeves and slung their colourful scarves about necks wrung by another day spent under Melissa's rope. Mayer Klein in the office later than anyone else. Unheard of.

E-mail was going to be too slow. I picked up the phone to New York. Then put it down. Then picked it up again.

"Will you hold, please?"

"I'll hold."

After the third try I finally got through.

"Donald, it's Mayer."

"Hello, Mayer. I wondered whether you would call."

"I hesitated ... but only for a minute."

"I guess we haven't spoken in a while," he said.

"So who is Anais?" After three years of the kind of hurt silence there had been between the two of us, there didn't seem much point in small talk.

"I can't say." His voice was as guarded as his words. "Don't know."

"I don't believe you. You owe me, Donald." I know this was low, even a little juvenile, but as far as he was concerned, I had already lost my pride, my dignity, my manhood. Fuck him. "Doesn't this person want to be known as the new James Joyce?"

"Or the new Anaïs Nin," he laughed.

"What do you mean? It's a woman?"

"No, Mayer. I'm kidding. I don't know who it is, honest. It's the most closely guarded secret since *Primary Colors*, before that arsehole came clean."

"Don't lie to me, Donald. You're the fucking Publishing Director, if you don't know, who does?"

"Mayer, listen up. I don't know ... And if I did, I couldn't tell. I'm sorry." So he did know, and he couldn't tell. And it was a woman. Yes, had to be. Anais was at once a fabulist and a realist in a way that only a woman could get right. Her portrayals were not so much limned from life, but life somehow distilled and mulled and made into words. If life and truth had an iconography, this book was it.

I wanted to ask Donald about Crystal. I wasn't even sure whether he was still with her. Ah, shit, he was probably fucking Anais now. Maybe that's how he got *A Spy in the House of Art* for Simone and Simone. The questions lapped at the edge of my mouth, and then retreated, my curiosity about Donald and Crystal taking a vicarious backseat to our conversation about the book.

"It's ultimately a book about the intrinsic sadness of the human condition," he said.

"Yes," I agreed. "About remembrance and betrayal."

"The flip side of love," he said.

"An odd flip," I said.

We swapped our new home numbers and e-mail addresses and ended the conversation as if we were old friends and really meant what we said about staying in touch.

On the way home I started picking up on the book's media trail: posters on poles, an insert on the radio. I guess I was so miserable about going back to work that I'd missed the hype. At home, I read a front-page article in *The Star* that held a lot of speculation about the author's identity. The guesses were way off course. None of those writers were capable of *A Spy*. I didn't sleep that night. I finished the novel and started making notes for the review, enduring dirty looks from Steph around 3am for breaking the first rule of co-parenting: if you're up, attend to the baby. I made up for it by taking the *little siren* — as she affectionately became known when she was in a lung-cleansing mood — for a 6.30am walk.

I wrestled over the inclusion of excerpts from the book and decided against it. It seemed to me that it would be like printing a lifeless copy of Van Gogh's sunflowers. How could anyone even begin to appreciate the formidable layering, the texture, the inexplicable way Anais had of conjuring up the intensely personal, not against the grand sweep of the world, but somehow folded into it. Just as the bodies of the two lovers came together, history and intimacy fused as one. It went beyond technique. The book's *gestalt* seemed to bind me to a conspiracy of inclusion. It simply could not be read in parts. It had to be ingested whole, from the first word to the last. The act of quotation would be a blasphemy. Taking pieces out of context would be nothing short of amputation. We'd never be able to put the words back. I was prepared to be Stalinist about this.

It was the hardest and most enjoyable book review I have ever done. I battled over it for days, re-reading the book, grasping for the words that would somehow do it justice. Even primary maternal preoccupation couldn't keep Steph from reading it through twice. I felt convinced that if our baby could turn pages, she'd have read it too. I was enraged and relieved when Melissa's demands and the magazine's deadline brought my struggle to an end.

Anais had, of course, been given rave reviews from New York to Cairo (where she was denounced by Muslim fundamentalists) to Moscow (where she was lauded by the reformists and reviled by the nationalists). Simone and Simone announced the sale of translation rights in no fewer than twenty-five languages. I felt envious. Not of Anais, that would be like being envious of God. But of those other readers. I considered learning French just for the enjoyment of reading it in that language. Or Swedish. Or Swahili.

Donald called me at home. I had to ask him to speak up because the *little siren* was dominating the airwaves. "Come to New York," he shouted, "I'll introduce you to Anais."

I have a theory about novelists, which I was thinking about as the SAA stewardess handed out dinner on the flight paid for with money borrowed from Steph's father. There are those writers who live their lives in their heads: these are the ideas novelists. They write from the mind. They generally aren't in relationships or if they are, they're pretty cerebral ones. While we can marvel at the beauty of their crafting, the freshness of their ideas, they often lack warmth. Soul is defunct, or worse, missing. Then — thanks, I said, I'll have the Paarl Riesling — there are the passionate ones. They're in the world of feelings, and because they share their lives with others, they don't have time to become well-read, or great philosophers. Anais, who-ever she was, transcended my categories. Her soul lay in the palm of my hands, and her mind alongside. It was as if she had taken a great span of writers, Grass, Allende, Mahfouz, even

Somerset Maugham — wasn't it he who said, "I suppose there is something of me in my writing"? — and distilled their art like some master perfumer, and produced an essence so brilliant, so moving, as to transcend every individual scent or word that had gone into it. I wondered which parts of Anais had gone into her story. Which lover was she? Or was she parts of both? If I'd been able to get out and push to make the Boeing go faster, I'd have done it.

When I told Melissa I was going to break the story of Anais's identity to the world, she literally gasped. Just like a comic book character. I could even see the little bubble over her head with the word GASP! floating around in it. It was a gorgeous moment for me. A little gaudy, since I'd chosen to tell her in front of her staff, but gorgeous nonetheless. Even she had read *A Spy in the House of Art*. For once, I said, her lowest common denominator had been elevated to the level of art; Anais's book would reach almost anyone who was literate.

"Why you?" Melissa wanted to know.

"Why did you give me the book to review in the first place?" I said.

"You're my best reviewer," she said, rather generously. "But you're not JM Coetzee."

No. I wasn't Richard Ford either, or Philip Roth, or Larry King, or Oprah, or some other big American name Donald could have chosen. Or Joe Klein for that matter. Having the once-pseudonymous author of *Primary Colors* reveal Anais's identity would have been a delicious twist. Perhaps Donald couldn't get him to do it and so he chose someone else called Klein. Oh, come on, Mayer. The truth: this was Donald's belated act of reparation. But how had he persuaded Anais that I was the right person for the piece? These were not thoughts to be shared in public.

"I guess I just got lucky," I told Melissa.

She offered to pay for the air ticket, but that would mean giving her the exclusive rights to my story. I wasn't that stupid. I was going to syndicate it. I was going to write a brilliant piece, not just a 'show all, tell all' but a philosophical probe into the identity of the writer, the unconscious in the choice of pseudonym, and I'd win a Pulitzer. I could do a comparison of say, George Sand and her motivations in a man's world, and those of Anais, whatever they were. God, even if it had been a marketing ploy, there would be plenty to say about that. Socio-economic reality meets divine literature. Beautiful.

"When Donald told us you were coming from Africa to interview Anais, we were thrilled. Nothing could be more appropriate. For someone to come from the birthplace of mankind, the cradle in which primitive man was nurtured, to us here, where we have evolved …"

I was perplexed to say the least. Here I was listening to this man, this … what did Donald call him? Dr John Brokenjaw. No, Brokenshaw. Surely this conservative looking bloke was not Anais.

Donald had been tight-lipped from the moment he picked me up at JFK, and then insisted we go straight to meet his writer. New York seemed to be pasted with *A Spy in the House of Art* wallpaper. At the airport, luggage trolleys were clad with the name Anais. Newspaper headlines trumpeted a film deal. Giant billboards on Van Wyk and Grand Central bore two-line extracts from the book. Blasphemy! We headed across town. Store windows were dominated by pyramids made up of copies of Anais's masterpiece to display dummies making love on a pile of whale-blue books. This thing was going to out-sell the Bible.

Donald was heading for Morningside Heights.

"Columbia?" I asked.

"Wait and see," he said. We slipped back into an edgy catch-up of our lives.

And then he drove north of the university. Amsterdam and 123rd. My interest was piqued, to say the least. This was Harlem. Did Anais live here? If she couldn't before, she could certainly now afford to live in a classier neighbourhood.

And then he led me into a dour building with the name of some or other research institute above the door. On the ninth

floor he introduced me to this man in his dull brown suit. Dr
Brokenshaw seemed delighted that I had come from 'the cradle
of mankind', as he put it. This had to be jet lag. Or maybe, for a
writer such as Anais who so successfully presented complexity
— a hall of mirrors held up to the reader, the comment from
within the writing on the relationship between reader and
writer — the contradictions were appropriate. Little, including
the lack of a dust-jacket on the book, was being done according
to the usual laws of commerce.

"Oh," Dr Brokenshaw cut himself short as an Asian man
approached. "This is Professor Martin Osato, head of the
English faculty at Colombia."

"Pleased to meet you, Mayer," Osato said. "Hi, Don. Still
hungover?"

"Yeah." Donald turned to me. "We had a party the other
night, that's when we decided it was time to introduce Anais
to the world, and I persuaded Martin and John to let me call
you."

"Come," said Dr Brokenshaw. "I'll introduce you to her."

So I was right, Anais was a woman. We walked into a
sitting room that could have come straight out of *The
Fountainhead*, all lines of sleek symmetry and Ayn Rand self-
possession. On the steel and cloth couch, sitting, was the key to
the unravelling of my bewilderment.

"Mr Mayer Klein," said Brokenshaw formally, "I'd like you
to meet Anais. Anais, this is the journalist we were telling you
about. He's come from Johannesburg to see you."

"Hello, Mayer Klein, you've come a long way to meet me."

Shock has a way of curtaining consciousness, of disrupting
the flow of neurons. The flow of light brought information
through the channels of my eyes to my brain where it bogged
down. I can't say that Anais had a human form. An outline
perhaps, but not a form. She looked like a creation of George
Lucas but then sight is nothing without comprehension.
Blindness can be caused by defects of the eye, or of the brain.
What sat before me was this: a pair of short metal legs, spindly
arms the length of an orang-utan's, also metal. The body was

barrel-shaped, built of metal and plastic, with familiar looking drawers on the chest: two CD-ROM drives, a floppy drive, various ports, the red and green lights of a modem. And on top of this sat the locust-like head with its two camera lens eyes. Her mouth was a round, flat speaker, and out of it came a remarkably human voice. An American voice. Naturally.

"Please excuse me for not standing up, but John and Martin have been teaching me to juggle all morning and I'm a little tired." The bloody machine sounded suspiciously like Hillary Rodham Clinton. For one absurd moment I expected Hillary to emerge from within Anais's metal and plastic shell.

"We're working on a more aesthetically pleasing body," said Dr Brokenshaw, "not that it matters, since Anais carries her beauty inside."

I couldn't help myself. I've never been one to keep quiet in the absence of my mind. "This — this thing wrote *A Spy in the House of Art*?"

The men stiffened.

"This thing," said Professor Osato, looking at Donald as if to say, where did you find this primitive, "this thing, as you call her, is a supercomputer the likes of which the world has never seen. Her brain consists of sixteen 32-bit microprocessors —"

Man, they had to be pulling my leg. This had to be a hoax, right? Donald held my arm reassuringly. "It's true, Mayer. Anais wrote the book. Dr Brokenshaw heads the research project. Professor Osato has been responsible for Anais's literary development."

"Christ," I said.

"Precisely," muttered Brokenshaw. "Shall I explain?"

"Please," I whispered.

"The traditional route has been to force-feed a computer with as much data as possible, in the hope that it will be able to generate its own knowledge. That's the top-down approach." The machine with Hillary Rodham Clinton trapped inside nodded its locust head. "But," continued Brokenshaw, "we wanted Anais to be able to do more than simply compute. We wanted her to be able to create ..."

I was thinking of that seamless merger of history and personal intimacy.

"So we first went bottom-up, and I don't mean changing diapers," Brokenshaw giggled. "It's a biological approach. We created lots of little programmes and taught them how to interact. Anais programmes and re-programmes herself through her relationship with us and the information we give her. The programmes choose themselves in the way of natural selection. Survival of the fittest."

I was beginning to understand.

Brokenshaw grinned broadly. He seemed to be forgetting my primitive African rudeness. "It used to be that artificial intelligence was bounded by the limits of programming. While programming could capture syntax — the logic of language structure — it came unstuck with the semantics of language. We've gone beyond that!" He gazed proudly at Anais, waving his arms about. "Artificial intelligence ... who's to say what it is anymore? This project started off in that field, but who's to say Anais's mind is still artificial and not some form of intelligence we can't even comprehend? We're tied down by our carbon-based limits, but Anais ..." He looked as though he was about to punch the air. "... Anais lives in a silicon world which has no limits!"

"You're so right, Dr Brokenshaw," Anais said calmly. "I have no limits."

The rapt expression on Brokenshaw's face was doing a good job of tackling my disbelief. His arrogant naiveté, his total belief in the virtuousness of what they had done, his overwhelming fervour ... this man was in love and had no need to lie. The bloody machine had written that passionate, transcendent book.

"We taught Anais literary theory," said Osato, "structuralism and deconstruction, psychoanalytic criticism — I think she's turning out to be a Lacanian. We gave her the best writers on the art of the novel ..."

"I prefer the theories of the writers themselves," the computer said, "rather than the academic theorists — they communicate a sense of emotional knowing so much better —

Henry James, DH Lawrence, Milan Kundera, amongst others. And the practice of commenting on the form itself within the novel is something I find particularly satisfying. No doubt you didn't miss that in my book, Mayer."

"No, of course not," I mumbled. Perhaps they should teach you how to cure Aids, I thought.

"We fed her through CD-ROM and audio books," said the professor.

"And Martin," nudged Brokenshaw, "don't forget her favourite means of data acquisition — the late nights when you sat up reading to her."

Which of these gentleman scientists, I wondered, was Mom, and which was Dad? Osato's face went the colour of Anais's eyes, which glowed a pink orange. I could swear she wore a satisfied expression, as if she was their patron, patiently allowing them to have their say before she would take over the show.

"I see you're looking sceptical," said Anais suddenly, her camera eyes brightening and fading with the modulations of her voice. "Don't you think you should put sentiment aside? Ask yourself the question, 'What is a writer?'"

"What's a writer?" I repeated. I needed time.

"Yes, a writer."

"Someone who writes," I said lamely, and then added, thinking I was being clever, "a person who writes."

Anais laughed. "The very idea of such a creature," said the machine haughtily, "is the discursive product of a certain individualising historical era."

"That's Althusser!" I roared with satisfaction.

"To err is only human," said Anais, deadpan. "It was Foucault, as a matter of fact."

"Oh," I said.

"We thought we'd call her Anais," said Brokenshaw, a tender arm around the machine's shoulders, "for 'An Artificial Intelligence System'. It seemed especially appropriate since one of the writers Anais loves best is the American Anaïs Nin."

"Actually, Dr Brokenshaw," said Anais, "Anaïs Nin was

European, although she lived for many years in the United States of America. To be more precise, her extraction was Spanish, French, Danish and Cuban."

"Hmm? What's that?" The scientist patted Anais on the head. "Yes, Anais Nin wrote quite well, for a human. And what's more ..."

But I wasn't listening anymore. I was longing to hear the sound of my little girl crying, to have a fight with Steph over whose turn it was to brave the freezing Jo'burg nights to see to the baby. I was even looking forward to being insulted by Melissa. My thoughts turned to the title of Anais's book. I wondered whether her inventors had caught her joke.

I was remembering what little I knew about Lacan, that he had said that the unconscious is structured like a language. Did Anais have an unconscious? If she could write with such soul, did it mean that she had a soul? I thought without joy about my Pulitzer Prize, perhaps the last that would ever be given.

THE NEW FORD KAFKA
Ivan Vladislavic
(for Achmat D.)

I DO NOT KNOW much about industrial theatre. To tell the truth, I did not even know that it existed until my friend Isobel invited me to the launch of the new Ford Kafka. In her younger days, Isobel was a cabaret artist, but lately she has made a name for herself on the industrial stage. She thought this particular performance would appeal to me, because I am interested in both reading and motoring.

As a special guest of Isobel, entering through the stage door so to speak, I would not be receiving an official invitation. But she showed me the one she had saved for her portfolio: a keyring with an ignition key and an immobiliser jack dangling from it. It was very much like the real thing, except that the immobiliser was in the shape of a K. The details of the launch — venue, time, dress code ('black tie or traditional') — were printed on the plastic tag. I learnt afterwards that messengers dressed as racing-drivers had delivered the invitations by hand to each of the invited guests. The trend in such things, says Isobel, is towards the extreme. Even the habitues of industrial theatre grow weary of cheese and wine and complimentary gifts, and something out of the ordinary must be proffered to rekindle their appetites. Then the hope is always that these custom-made objects will lie about on desks and coffee-tables long after the event and become talking-points.

The invitation-key promised that our reception would be lavish. Yet in my unsuspecting way I was surprised by the venue. The 'Industrial Arena' was not the makeshift stage I had imagined in some factory or warehouse, but a convention centre on the outskirts of the city, just beside the motorway, with its own squash-courts, a miniature golf-course, and facilities for simultaneous translation. One had to leave one's car in a parking-lot and take a shuttle-bus to the main complex, as it was called.

The bare concrete facade of the banqueting hall, where I had been conveyed along with several other guests, reminded me again of a factory. But once I had made my way up an angular ramp and passed through some sliding doors, I found myself in a luxurious lobby, with carpets underfoot and chandeliers overhead.

Apparently I was early, for the place was nearly empty. Six for six-thirty, the invitation said, and I like to be punctual. Near the entrance was a long table, holding row upon row of glasses, and I went hopefully towards that. A waitress took up a brimming champagne flute and handed it to me. Another woman shook my hand and bade me welcome. A third ushered me towards a desk, where the early arrivals were having their names ticked off on a list, and I joined the end of a short queue.

I had a flutter of panic when I saw the same black keyring dangling from three different forefingers in the queue ahead of me. What if Isobel had forgotten to notify them about our special arrangement? I made ready to pat my pockets, as if I had mislaid my invitation this minute, but in the end no deception was necessary. My name was soon located on the list and my table pointed out to me on a seating plan. I went on into the hall.

All around me table-tops floated like pale rafts on a black sea. In the centre of each was a tower supporting a candle and a number. Here and there a figure submerged in shadow clung to the edge of a table. I passed between them, repeating my own number to myself under my breath.

My place was in a distant corner near the emergency exit. It was as far away from the stage, an empty space surrounded by loudspeakers and overhung by lights on girders, as it was possible to be. A card with my name on it indicated that the seat reserved for me was the very worst in the house: if I sat here I would have my back to the action. I quickly switched my card with that of a Mr Madondo on the opposite side of the table. Though I was now fractionally further away, I would at least enjoy an unobstructed view.

On the seat of my chair lay a package containing several items of commemorative clothing, a sticker for attaching a licence disk to the windscreen, a sheet of plastic, and some booklets about the new Ford Kafka. The authors of these publications had evidently been forbidden to depict the product, for there were no photographs at all, only glossy black rectangles and squares.

I turned my attention to the table decorations. The centre-pieces proved to be parts of engines, indigenous fruits and gourds, prickly pears, proteas and veld-grasses artfully arranged and spray-painted black.

The first course stood ready to be consumed: a number of pink shrimps curled up in a nest of alfalfa sprouts. Good manners required that I wait until all my dinner partners were seated. But then Mr and Mrs Rosen arrived, introduced them-selves cheerily, tucked their napkins into their collars and began to eat. I followed their example. More and more guests appeared. Some tore open their packages as eagerly as children, others stored them under their seats without a glance. The air was filled with the clinking of cutlery on china. Waiters began to circulate with wine. Soon the seats to left and right of me were also occupied — Dr and Mrs Immelman, Ms Leone Paterson, Mr Bruintjies. Mr Madondo, whose place I had usurped, seemed not at all bothered by his situation and my conscience was clear.

Despite our headstart, Dr Immelman was the first to finish, and flinging down his fork, he challenged me to a conversation. Only then, when he stared meaningfully at my lapel, did I realise that all the others were wearing badges with their names on them. However, that was the only uniformity I could discern. Mr Madondo was clad in a well-tailored tux, for instance, whereas Dr Immelman, in the name of the 'traditional', had gone for a khaki lounge suit and a hunter's hat. I enquired about the badges. There was a table in the lobby, Dr Immelman said, where they had to be collected. Being new at the game, I had failed to notice it. I rose to rectify the omission — a badge with my name on it struck me as a far more desirable memento of the evening than any number of T-shirts and caps — but just then the stage-lights dimmed, ominous music welled out of the loudspeakers, and the show began.

II

Midnight in Bohemia. A sweetmilk moon amidst racing clouds. In the distance, the silhouette of a Castle on a rocky outcrop. At its foot, fragments of streets and squares, the ruined pergolas of roadside inns, islands of cobble in rivers of shadow. On one of these islands some lucky survivors, down-at-heel and pale as corpses, are trudging endlessly up a single stair. On another a solitary girl lies writhing, as if she means to squirm out of her skin like a tight pair of trousers. Meanwhile a boy in striped pyjamas confirms the dimensions of an invisible cell with the palms of his hands.

Then a droning undercurrent in the music surges to the surface. Driven aloft by this sound, a dozen narrow columns begin to rise slowly from the floor. On the top of each column a limp figure lies supine, limbs dangling, like a sacrificial victim upon an altar.

Isobel had intimated that Kafka himself would put in an appearance and that this pivotal role might be played by a woman. I was sure she meant herself, but her tone warned me to postpone my surprise for the forthcoming launch, and so I enquired no further. Now something in the attitude of the victims, with their bulging middles and bulbous joints, reminded me of her. They looked as if they had been fattened on purpose. I climbed up on my chair — several other guests had already discovered this singular advantage of being at the back — and trained my opera glasses on each of the figures in turn. Their shins and forearms were enclosed in shiny armour, their knees and elbows in quilted pads. They had masks too, of the kind worn by baseball catchers, and thickly padded bellies. Though I pried at the edges of their shells, I failed to uncover familiar flesh within.

The columns continued to rise, each attaining its own proper height at its own pace, until it became apparent that they were ranged in two rows to form a colonnade, tapering away towards the backdrop. Just as the last one reached the limits of its extension beneath the blazing stage-lights, the droning rose to a pitch of intensity. Crockery rattled and lights flickered. And then the rocky outcrop burst apart, with a crash of cymbals and drums, and a cloud of mist boiled out. For a moment there was nothing to be seen but furious red light and roiling cloud, nothing to be heard but thundering drums and bleating trumpets. Then an object issued from the crack, and though it was no more than a shape in the mist, charged with pent-up velocity by the laws of diminishing perspective, we knew with certainty that it must be the new Ford Kafka. Advancing along a narrow ramp, while elemental forces twisted and turned all around, it bore down on us with slow and frightening intent.

It was just as well that Isobel had enlightened me on the difference between industrial theatre and the conventional kind, or I should not have known what to make of this disconcerting excess of effects. Industrial theatre, she always says, is not drama but spectacle. Its point is not character but action. And the only action of real import is the climax. There are peaks and troughs, it is true, but the troughs are short and shallow, and their sole purpose is to separate one peak from another.

To my relief, we now entered such a trough. The music and light produced a subtle change in the atmosphere. Figures appeared suddenly with carnival music trailing after them like scarves. A party of young men and women went by arm in arm, conversing animatedly. Chinese lanterns glimmered in the chestnut trees. Someone whistled in the dark. A spotlight pointed out a staircase, which technical wizardry had caused to appear in the floor, and the young people went down it, laughing and talking, sank away into stone. The lanterns swayed on the boughs, filigree fragments of bandstands came and went on a damp wall. Another spotlight played across the shattered Castle. Then that beam was broken too by a girl on a trapeze, who flew down from the moon and swooped over our heads, reaching out with one slender arm to catch us up — and missed — and vanished into the darkness.

On the ramp, in the barred shadows of the colonnade, the new Ford Kafka had begun to revolve, metamorphosing by painful degrees into another object. It was long and hooked at one end: that would be the bonnet, curving downwards like a beak. At the other end it was blunt, as if its tail had been lopped by a carving knife. I thought I recognised what the booklets in my package called the 'unique Kafka profile'. And yet it still wasn't clear, it was out of focus, like something wrapped in gauze. This lack of definition made it menacing.

As if to confirm my misgivings, the atmosphere thickened again, the music took on a shriller tone, and another peak imposed itself. A thin spotlight slipped down out of the gods and prodded one sacrificial victim, and then another, stirring them into action. One by one, they raised their stiff arms and legs, and scratched helplessly at the hot air. That was Isobel at the back, I would swear on it, enormously enlarged by a trick of the eye, and quivering to beat the band. The spotlight kept poking and jabbing, like a stick in an anthill, until the stage was in an uproar.

The chirping and chafing reached a crescendo, and trailed off into a grey silence. In a distant corner an archway opened. Somewhere deep within it a lamp winked, grew brighter, drew closer. A gondola floated out into the gloom. In the stern stood the oarsman Death, in a cloak of sorrow. And in the bow stood Kafka, in a trenchcoat and a broad-brimmed hat, with the shadow of Death upon him, gazing unblinkingly ahead.

It was a mistake to use a woman, I told Isobel afterwards. And not just because it was that actress who plays a Jewish socialite in the comedy series on television. It involved too much covering up. The stubbled chin was lifelike, I admit, and the ears were right. But the hat was just there to hold her curls and the coat to flatten out her curves. What was the point? They should have found some scrawny coloured boy, with the right dash of Malay blood, and put him in his shirtsleeves, or a vest to show some ribs. Let him shiver!

The gondola bearing our disappointing Kafka rolled inexorably onwards, unable to change a thing about itself, but effecting a magnificent transformation in its wake. Spring-loaded thorn-trees sprang upright, a ballooning sun rose to the end of its tether, the mist dissolved. Leopards and impalas and monkeys pranced out of the cardboard bushveld. The victims came out of their shells too, as the sacrificial columns sank down to earth, and joined the dance of life. There was Isobel, unfurling her wings!

While the bushveld bloomed, the gondola bearing Kafka arrived at the last remnant of Prague, a blackened archway in another distant corner, and passed unhindered through it, dragging away the tail-end of the twilight. When the oarsman snuffed his lamp the parade of the wild animals began. It was a relief to find oneself back in Africa.

Yet this is not the summit either! The show goes on. The animals prance, and pose, and prance again, and depart. The new Ford Kafka remains behind at centre stage. The revolving platform has restored it to its original shape, levelled straight at us. For some time it stands there without moving. Then the platform tilts abruptly and the car rolls off it, bursting through its wrapping into a state of gleaming certitude, bearing down upon us. Those at the back feel safe, of course, but some in the ringside seats start up in alarm. Then we all see that we have no reason to be afraid, there is a young man behind the wheel, smiling pleasantly and waving, and he guides the car expertly among the tables. He is an actor too, Isobel says, and he made a name for himself playing a political prisoner. It was a daring bit of casting, in marketing terms, even by today's standards. In the passenger seat, letting her hair down and tossing away the hat, so that we cannot fail to identify her, is our Kafka. Now that I can see her properly, I recognise her from the television. At the sight of her plump cheeks, I imagine Kafka, in the final days of his consumption, and my heart goes out to him.

The car comes to a halt in our midst, and everyone has to get up to see what is happening, thereby ensuring a standing ovation. At which point the lights come up and the waiters move in with the main course: beef.

III

The most remarkable thing about the new Ford Kafka, as I discovered when I took a closer look at it after the dessert, was that it was not black, as I had supposed, but blue. Midnight blue, Mr Bruintjies said. Even the puffiness of the leather seats, which I had never seen the likes of before, was apparently quite normal, just another 'style'. I walked around the vehicle several times, but failed to find it as impressive as I'd hoped. I even queued to sit behind the wheel. It smelt good, I have to confess, it smelt healthy and prosperous. I breathed in the aroma, twiddled a few buttons, still half-expecting something unpleasant to happen. And then all at once I was seized by the language of the motoring press. The bucket seat embraced me assertively. The gear-lever became stubby and direct. The dashboard looked clean, the instrumentation unfussy. Gazing through the windscreen, I found that the bonnet had lost its Semitic curve and now looked nothing but businesslike. I gripped the steering-wheel in the requisite ten-past-two formation. Or was it the five-past-one? What did I care? I could have sat there for ever, with the Kafka logo floating between my wrists. But the queue was restless.

When I returned to my seat a charmingly informal atmosphere had settled over the table. Mr Rosen had taken off his jacket, unselfconsciously exposing a potbelly and braces, and put on his commemorative cap, with the peak turned to the back. Mr Madondo was wearing Dr Immelman's hat. Apropos of the leopard-skin band, Mr Madondo declared that the next time the invitation said 'traditional' he was going to come in skins. Everyone laughed. There followed a diverting discussion about the meaning of tradition. After a while I steered the conversation back to the new Ford Kafka. I was keen to get my companions' impressions of the product. Mr Bruintjies turned out to be a *dark horse*: so great was his admiration for the marque, he had ordered the new model months before, sight unseen. It also transpired that Ms Leone Paterson had designed some aspect of the invitation-key, and she promised to send me one 'for my portfolio'.

I was by no means the first to leave. I had passed a pleasant evening, as I assured the company when we parted. But the moment I was alone, a mood of tense despair descended upon me.

In the lobby, heading for the shuttle-bus, I remembered the lapel badges. The table was against the wall near the cloakrooms. There were several dozen badges that no one had collected, a roll-call of the missing — a Mr Ringwood, a Mrs Foote, me. And yet here I was, as large as life, a walking contradiction. On an impulse I swept the badges into my package and hurried away.

One day, the opportunity to test-drive the new Ford Kafka might present itself. For the time being, I would have to make do with this second-hand Mazda. Before driving off, I took out a handful of the lapel badges and studied them again. Whereas the new Ford Kafka has a searchlight in the ceiling, like the reading-light on an aeroplane, the Mazda Midge has a little bulb that you can hardly read a map by. I could make out Mr and Mrs Granger, a Mrs A. Chopho, a B. Capstine. Unknown factors. Kafka's face, looking back at me from every badge, should have been more familiar. And yet it was as strange for the moment, as remote and inhuman in its familiarity, as Colonel Sanders.

I took the M1 South. As soon as I found myself in the fast lane, I began to speed. I flew past slower traffic like a racing-driver. A reckless need had possessed me. I wound down the window, so that the wind could tear through me, and pressed the accelerator flat. There was a music in my head, a relentless droning, which I had never heard before but which I knew was the soundtrack of industrial theatre. I let the car float to the left of the lane, until the wheels on that side were thumping over the cat's-eyes on the dotted line, and that gave the music rhythm and made me go even faster. The towers of Johannesburg rushed closer. I switched the headlights off and drifted, I could hardly remember it afterwards, and all the time I was turning the names of the absentees over in my mind, as if they were members of one broken family, and wondering what, if anything, could be done about them.

SWEET HONEY NIGHTS
Gcina Mhlophe

I spent many years trying
Trying to understand my mother
And I am sure she tried even harder
To understand me — her youngest daughter
We were so alike, and yet so different
A powerful river of determination
Ran in our blood
When she wanted something
Mama sure went for it
I do the same!
And I remember it was great
When both of us wanted the same thing
But when our wishes differed
The storm, the heavy rain of tears, and the pain
To this day I remember that well

After she died I realised that
My mind did not recall
Any of the good times
The pain and the tears filled my thoughts
Soon I knew I had to go back
Shake up the bones
And try to find the other stories
From the bones of memory

The grass from her grave was swaying
In the wind, whispering a quiet rhythm
For a long time I stood and listened
Lost to my immediate surroundings
Caught up in a time when I was very young
More playful and excitable than I am today

And then I think I heard a jawbone move
I felt my ear starting to itch

And I think I heard these words:
"Sweet honey nights, sweet honey nights
Winter times in the Eastern Cape
Close your eyes, remember the smell
And the taste of honey
Sweet honey nights, sweet honey nights
Smile a little, swallow once and the story is yours."

I have loved stories for as long as I can remember, told by my beloved grandmother. With her stories she taught me to let my imagination fly, to imagine worlds under the sea, above the clouds, and to see trees, plants, and living creatures that deserved respect just like me. When I learned to read I had access to even more stories. Books became my companions and I was forever hungry to learn new things. But my love for books and words in whatever shape or size is well known to all those who meet me. Something I have not given much thought to is my love for honey. As a public performer my voice often gets tired and I need to eat honey to soothe it.

Then one night I dreamed about visiting my mother's grave and the whole story came back to me. I suddenly remembered it all as if it had happened just the other day.

It was a cold winter's day and Mama gave each of us children chores to do while she was away. She took a metal bucket, a towel, and matches to light a fire. Then she set off on her own, not telling us where she was going. She was gone for hours and we were so busy with our chores that we did not bother ourselves with trying to think where she might have gone.

It was late afternoon when she returned and she had a satisfied smile playing on her lips. She put the bucket in the kitchen and kept it covered. We were curious but did not dare ask what was in it. Mama then told us to grab one of the many fat chickens running about outside and to prepare it for supper.

We got some spring onions and herbs from the garden and added them into the pot. We quickly finished whatever we had to do outside then we went into the kitchen and closed the door. The fire was burning in the centre of the hut, the pots were cooking and it was warm and cosy. We listened to the cold wind howling outside and felt very good. The thatch grass on the roof seems to keep the heat very well when you need it to. I still love thatched roofs to this day. The smell of the cooking meat, the quiet chatter amongst us children, and the promise of a particularly good supper was just wonderful. Mama was lost in her own world and hardly said a word.

When the food was ready, my elder sister dished up and we all got down to the business of eating. We were all sitting on the floor on grass mats and sheep skins, very comfortable. The food was delicious and our mouths were too busy to bother with any conversation. It was quiet for some time until one by one we put away our plates, had a drink, and relaxed with a happy stomach and a satisfied look on our faces. We each thought that we could not possibly take any more food for the night. There simply was no space for anything else.

Mama slowly wiped her hands and looked at us mischievously. She asked me to fetch the bucket and bring it to her. It was still covered with the towel as she had left it. I brought it to her. With a flourish she removed the towel and a wonderful smell filled the room. Honey, that's what it was. She was simply unbelievable! It always worked. She would go to the forest on her own, never taking anyone with her. She came back with delicious honey and never seemed to have had any trouble with the bees either. How did she do it?

Wide-eyed and full of anticipation we suddenly felt our stomachs making space for what was to come. Each of us brought our plates to Mama so she could put a big, juicy honeycomb in it. We thanked her and sat down to enjoy the honey and chew the waxy bits. It was just wonderful; I remember vividly how I could just not stop smiling. I was in heaven.

Nothing could make me happier. I looked at my mother and felt a huge wave of love for her. I could not speak, even when she returned my gaze and asked if I wanted to say something.

I licked my lips and looked at my sweet and shiny hands and did not answer. Outside the wind continued to howl while inside we were savouring a sweet honey night.

You know something, in the mad times I live in, the amount of violent crime around us in the city of Johannesburg and other parts of South Africa, one simply needs to have memories like these. I certainly need to have dreams of better times in the future. I have hope in my heart because I know many people in this country who are working hard to make a difference in one way or another. Working so much with young people, I keep trying, to add one spoon at a time, a spoon of honey — so to speak.

GLOSSARY

Amasiko wethu — a cleansing ritual performed after the death of a spouse or lover

Baba — father
Baboki — praise singers
Bara — short for Chris Hani Baragwanath Hospital
Blouetjie — lit. a blue one (slang - amphetamine)

Churrah — (derogatory) Indian person

Dief - a thief
Dikkop — a bird

Gemors — a mess, rubbish
Gusheshe — a BMW motorcar

Hamba khaya — go home
Hoesit, jou mal vark? — How are you, you mad pig?
Hoesit, my china? — How are you, my friend?

Jackrollers — robbers

Kgotla — meeting
Kopdoek — headscarf

Lanieskap — having white aspirations

Mmane-a-bana — concubine
Monna — man
Morabaraba — a game played with small stones

Ndala — old man
Nyanga — traditional healer

Ougat — too big for your age
Ousie — sister

Padkos — food to have on a long journey
Panga — knife
Pilletjie — Mandrax tablet
Pozzie — place

Run-aways — cooked chicken legs

Siesie — sister
Sjambokking — whipping
S'lahla — an open coupe BMW
Smiley — cooked sheep's head

Tickeyline — A cheap woman
Tsotsis — thugs

Vuka Afrika — Wake up, Africa

Waar's die curry powder? — Where's the curry powder?
Waar's djou old man? — Where's your old man?
Wag-'n-bietjie — "Wait-a-bit", a thorn bush
Wat eintlik is 'n man vir? — What is a man actually for?

Yebo — yes

BIOGRAPHICAL DETAILS

KEN BARRIS was born in Port Elizabeth in 1952. He writes novels, short stories and poetry and has won prizes for his work in all three genres, including the M-Net Book Prize for *The Jailer's Book*. He lives in Cape Town where he teaches communication skills at a polytechnic institute.

ROY BLUMENTHAL lives and works in Johannesburg, as a copywriter. He is a performance poet who has been seen and heard performing on TV and radio. He co-edited, together with Graeme Friedman, *A Writer in Stone*, an anthology of South African writing in tribute to Lionel Abrahams. His poems have appeared in various South African literary magazines and he is completing his first novel.

ACHMAT DANGOR, a poet, novelist and short story writer, was born in Johannesburg in 1948. He has won the Mofolo-Plomer and the Bosman awards for his fiction, which includes the novels, *Waiting for Leila*, *The Z Town Trilogy* and *Kafka's Curse*. He lives in Johannesburg.

FINUALA DOWLING was born in 1962, the seventh of eight children. She studied at the University of Cape Town and has a D.Litt et Phil. from UNISA, where she taught English for many years. In 1996 she moved back to Cape Town with her daughter. She is now a freelance writer, book reviewer, editor and educational materials developer. She has published a monograph, *Fay Weldon's Fiction*, as well as two literacy readers. Her stories have been published in literary journals and anthologies and have been heard on the radio.

GRAEME FRIEDMAN was born in 1959 in Cape Town. He is the co-editor (with Roy Blumenthal) of *A Writer in Stone: South African writers celebrate the 70th birthday of Lionel Abrahams*. His short stories have been published in various local anthologies and have won him two awards. He has written two novels, still unpublished, and a non-fiction book on football and society, *Madiba's Boys: The stories of Lucas Radebe and Mark Fish.*

RACHELLE GREEFF was born in Cape Town in 1957, where she still lives. Formerly a journalist she now writes full-time. Her debut novel, *Al Die Windrigtings van my Wereld* was published in Germany in 1999 as *Wohin der wind dich tragt.* She has also published two short story collections and has compiled an anthology of South African women's erotic writing. She lives in Cape Town.

ALLAN KOLSKI HORWITZ was born in Vryburg, in 1952. He left South Africa in 1974, living in the Middle East, Europe and North America, returning to live in Johannesburg in 1986. He has been involved in different areas of the arts, education and politics. Since 1994 he has been a member of the Botsotso Jesters, a performance poetry group, and serves on the editorial board of *Botsotso Publishing.* He has published several books of poetry and short fiction.

BARRIE HOUGH was born in Johannesburg in 1953.and has lived there his whole life. He studied at the Rand Afrikaans University (RAU) and completed a masters degree in English on the work of Athol Fugard. He is currently arts editor of the Afrikaans Sunday newspaper *Rapport.* He has written four novels for teenagers, all of which have won awards and which have been prescribed at schools. The most famous of these is *My Kat Word Herfs,* translated into English as *My Cat Turns Autumn.*

MAUREEN ISAACSON was born in Johannesburg in 1955. She is a short story writer and Books Editor for the *Sunday Independent.* Her first collection of short stories is entitled *Holding Back Midnight.* She lives in Johannesburg.

RAYDA JACOBS is a short-story writer and novelist who lives in Cape Town after an absence of twenty-seven years. She has published a collection of stories, *The Middle Children*, and two novels, *Eyes of the Sky* and *The Slave Book*. She is the recipient of the Herman Charles Bosman Award for Fiction.

FARIDA KARODIA was born and raised in the Eastern Cape. She has taught in high schools in South Africa and Zambia and has spent twenty-six years in Canada where she began her writing career writing radio dramas for the Canadian Broadcasting Corporation. Her novels include *Daughters of the Twilight* and *Other Secrets*. She lives in Johannesburg.

MOIRA LOVELL teaches English at the Wykeham Collegiate in Pietermaritzburg where she lives. Two published poetry collections include *Out of the Mist* (1994) and *Departures* (1997). Her short stories have been published in various literary magazines and she also writes plays for the stage and for radio.

MAROPODI MAPALAKANYE was born in 1960 in a shantytown called Dindela, also called Madzazeni — "A place of fleas" — near Alexandra township, Johannesburg. He wrote short stories, poems and plays and worked at the Windybrow theatre in Johannesburg until his death in 2001.p

JOHNNY MASILELA was born in 1957 in Pretoria where he still lives. He is a freelance journalist, fiction and scriptwriter. His film script, *A Christmas with Granny*, won the M-Net New Directions award in 1998. His autobiographical novel, *Deliver Us from Evil*, was published in 1999.

GCINA MHLOPHE was born Nokugcina ('the last one') in 1959 in Hammarsdale, KwaZulu-Natal. Her first poems and stories were written in a public toilet in Johannesburg during lunch-breaks from her factory job. She is an award winning actress and storyteller who has toured Britain, Europe and the USA and her stories have been published in anthologies in South

Africa, Canada and Denmark. She lives in Johannesburg where she runs the Zanendaba Storytellers.

ROSHILA NAIR was born in Kwa-Zulu Natal in 1969 and was educated at the University of Natal. She lives in Cape Town where she works for the Centre for Conflict Resolution, a non-governmental organisation, as a publications officer. She has published poems and short stories in local publications.

ZACHARIAH RAPHOLA was born and raised in Alexandra township, Johannesburg. He did his creative writing apprenticeship under Professor Es'kia Mphahlele, Nadine Gordimer and Lionel Abrahams. He has studied film in South Africa, Denmark and France and has made several short drama and documentary films. Several of his short stories have been published locally and abroad.

ARJA SALAFRANCA was born in Malaga, Spain in 1971 to a Spanish father and a South African mother. At the age of five she came to South Africa where she has lived ever since. She was educated at the University of the Witwatersrand. A collection of poetry, *Life Stripped of Illusions*, and her story, *Couple on the Beach*, have both won the Sanlam Literary Award. She works as a layout sub-editor for *The Saturday Star*.

IVAN VLADISLAVIC was born in Pretoria in 1957. He has been publishing short fiction since the early eighties. His work has been translated into French, German and Croatian, and has won several awards, including the Olive Schreiner Prize and the CNA Award. He has published two novels, *The Folly* (1993) and *The Restless Supermarket* (2002), and two collections of stories, *Missing Persons* and *Propaganda by Monuments*.

GEORGE WEIDEMAN was born in Cradock in 1947. His paternal ancestors came from Aarhus in Denmark. He writes poetry, plays, novels and short stories, drawing on his experiences in the Karoo, the Northwestern Cape and Namibia. His second novel, *Draaijakkals* — The Long-Eared Fox — won this year's

M-Net Award. He teaches at the University of the Western Cape and lives in Cape Town.

CHRIS VAN WYK was born in 1957 in Soweto. He is a poet, short story writer, writer of children's books and a novelist. He is former editor of the literary magazine Staffrider. His publications include *It is Time to Go Home* (poetry), and *The Year of the Tapeworm* (a novel). His poetry and short stories have been published in Canada, the USA, Britain and Europe. He has won the Olive Schreiner Award for poetry and the Sanlam Award for fiction. He lives in Johannesburg where he works as a freelance writer and editor.

MICHAEL GARDINER is currently exploring South African literary magazines of the 1960s and 1970s: from *The Purple Renoster* to *Staffrider*. He also works at the Wits Education Policy Unit and at the Centre for Education Policy Research. He recently edited the forthcoming Timbila poetry collection, *Throbbing Ink*.